Who Is Maud Dixon?

Who Is Maud Dixon?

ALEXANDRA ANDREWS

TINDER
PRESS

First published by Hachette, USA

First published in Great Britain in 2021 by Tinder Press
An imprint of HEADLINE PUBLISHING GROUP

1

Cataloguing in Publication Data is available from the British Library

Hardback ISBN 978 1 4722 7467 0
Trade paperback ISBN 978 1 4722 7468 7

Offset in 12/16 pt Bembo Std by Jouve (UK), Milton Keynes

Printed and bound in Great Britain by Clays Ltd, Elcograf S.p.A.

Headline's policy is to use papers that are natural, renewable and recyclable
products and made from wood grown in well-managed forests and other
controlled sources. The logging and manufacturing processes are expected
to conform to the environmental regulations of the country of origin.

HEADLINE PUBLISHING GROUP
An Hachette UK Company
Carmelite House
50 Victoria Embankment
London EC4Y 0DZ

www.tinderpress.co.uk
www.headline.co.uk
www.hachette.co.uk

For Chris

We had fed the heart on fantasies,
The heart's grown brutal from the fare.

—W. B. Yeats
"The Stare's Nest by My Window"

PREFACE

Semat, Morocco

"Madame Weel-cock?"

Her left eyelid wrenched open, and warm yellow light flooded into the crack. Her vision was crossed by a blurred figure in white. She shut her eye.

"Madame Weel-cock?"

A shrill beeping sounded from somewhere. She forced both eyes open this time. She was lying in an uncomfortable bed flanked by two dirty curtains.

"Madame Weel-cock?"

She turned her head stiffly. A man in what looked like a military uniform sat in a chair pulled up to the bed, leaning forward onto his thighs and watching her intently. His face had the puffed, plastic curves of a baby doll. He was not smiling.

"Madame Weel-cock," he said for the fourth time.

"Helen?" she asked in a patchy voice.

"Helen." He nodded. "Do you know where you are?"

She looked around. "Hospital?"

"That's right. You had the big night."

"The big night?"

"The very big night."

She let out a small, involuntary laugh. The man frowned, visibly annoyed. Then the curtain on her left swished open. They both turned their heads. A woman in a white headscarf and white jacket stepped through. A nurse? She leaned over the bed and smiled warmly. She said something in a foreign language and smoothed out the thin blanket.

Then she turned to the man at the bedside and said something to him in a sharper tone. He stood up, holding out his palms in appeasement. He smiled coldly and pushed the curtain aside. He was gone.

The young woman in the bed turned to the nurse, but she too was leaving.

"Wait," she called hoarsely. The nurse either didn't hear her or didn't heed her.

She was alone.

Her gaze settled on the ceiling. It was mottled with brown water spots. She tried to push herself up to a sitting position but found herself hindered by a cast on her left wrist. That's when she noticed that she was in pain. Everywhere.

She looked back at the empty chair the man had sat in. He had called her Madame Weel-cock. The information seemed significant, but she couldn't place it within any meaningful context. She shut her eyes again.

A few moments later—or perhaps it had been hours—the curtain opened again. The nurse had returned with a different man.

"Madame Wilcox," he said. "I am glad you are awake." He spoke English with more precision than most native speakers, each syllable demarcated crisply from the next. "I am Dr. Tazi. I was on call when you arrived last night with two fractured ribs, a broken wrist, and hematomas across your face and torso. I was told you had been in a car accident. We often see injuries like these caused by airbags. You are lucky they are not worse."

The nurse, as if waiting for her cue, presented a Dixie cup of water and a white pill the size of a molar.

"Hydrocodone. For the pain," the doctor said. "I will return this afternoon to assess your condition, but I do not foresee any reason to keep you past tomorrow. Until then you should rest, Madame Wilcox." He left, trailing the white-robed nurse behind him like a veil.

Madame Wilcox. She mouthed the name silently. Helen.

Then the light withdrew and sleep descended.

PART I

1.

Two young women climbed a narrow set of stairs toward the sound of laughter and music. Florence Darrow, in front, dragged her hand along the blood-red wall.

"There's something perverse about throwing publishing parties here," she said.

Both women worked as editorial assistants at Forrester Books, and tonight was the office holiday party, held every year on the second floor of a dark bar called The Library, where the theme was literary kitsch.

"It's like having a United Nations summit at EPCOT."

"Totally," agreed Lucy Gund in a small voice. Her dress had hitched up on her tights during the climb, and now it was bunched around her thighs.

They reached the top of the stairs and stepped in to survey the scene. The party had started only half an hour earlier, but already a noisy din rose from the crowd and hung above it like smog. Nearly a hundred people—some who worked with them, many who didn't—clustered in tightly packed groups. Florence hadn't wanted to get there too early, but she wished they had arrived in time to stake out a corner for themselves. The girls scanned the room, looking for familiar and approachable faces. They found none.

"Drink first?" Florence suggested. Lucy nodded.

The two women had started at Forrester at the same time,

nearly two years ago, and Lucy had immediately granted Florence her unconditional loyalty.

On paper, Lucy was just the type of friend Florence had hoped to make in New York. Lucy had grown up in Amherst, where both her parents taught in the college's English department. Her father had written the definitive biography of Nathaniel Hawthorne. Florence had spent her first Thanksgiving with them after moving to the city; she'd been delighted to find that their old, book-filled house lay just down the road from Emily Dickinson's. It was the type of intellectual idyll Florence had always wished she'd grown up in herself. It was everything her mother's cramped apartment in Port Orange was not.

In practice, however, Lucy lacked the confident sophistication that Florence assumed would be the natural inheritance of a childhood like that. She was painstakingly shy, and Florence sometimes suspected that Lucy's mother had told her to find just one friend in New York and she'd be fine. Florence had been the first person Lucy met at Forrester.

They had never really been incorporated into the company's larger social scene, mainly because Lucy hadn't tried and Florence hadn't succeeded. Since Florence had also cut off contact with her old friends from Florida—she thought of her past as a gangrenous limb that needed to be severed for the greater good—Lucy was, for all intents and purposes, her only friend.

They wormed their way through the crowd, past a long table piled with grapes and cheeses, toward an imposing mahogany bar in the back. A bartender in a black satin vest smiled at some point just above their heads. They did not, apparently, meet the qualifications for his undivided attention. Lucy was used to being overlooked—in fact seemed to prefer it—but Florence had had just enough success with men to be disappointed when her charms went unnoticed.

Florence was not unattractive, but without exception the first thing anyone noticed about her was her pallor. She looked like someone who had grown up in a bunker rather than the Florida sunshine. Evidence that she had been born in the wrong place, she often thought with satisfaction. Her fair skin flushed easily, whether with shyness or fervor was never quite clear, as if her creator had been torn between the competing impulses of purity and perversion. Some men found this effect entrancing, but many were put off. She also had dark, nearly black eyes and dirty blond curls that sprang from her head like Medusa's. Despite the hundreds of dollars her mother had spent over the years on gels, sprays, and holding creams, Florence still had not learned how to tame them.

"What'll it be, ladies?" the bartender asked in a practiced tone. The light glinted off the stiffened spikes of his hair. Florence imagined crunching them under her fingers like frost-covered grass.

Lucy pointed to a placard advertising the specialty cocktail. "I'll try the Dewar's Decimal System, I guess."

Florence ordered a red wine.

"I've got Cabernet or Pinot."

"Either," she said in a tone she hoped sounded breezy. She knew nothing about wine.

They each took a sip, then set off to find a group with breachable borders. They spotted some other assistants huddled by the food table and joined the fringes. A junior editor named Amanda Lincoln was arguing showily with a tall, lanky twenty-something in a tan corduroy suit.

"There's literally no way, you fucking misogynist," Amanda said.

Gretchen, a perky assistant whose desk faced Florence's, turned to explain, "Fritz claims he knows for a fact that Maud Dixon is a man."

"No," whispered Lucy, drawing her hand up to her mouth.

Maud Dixon was the pen name of a writer who'd published a spectacularly successful debut novel a couple of years earlier called *Mississippi Foxtrot*. It was about two teenage girls, Maud and Ruby, desperate to escape their tiny hometown of Collyer Springs, Mississippi. They are thwarted at every turn by their age, their gender, their poverty, and the cold indifference of their families. Everything comes to a head when Maud kills a contractor traveling through town on his way to a job in Memphis. He had made the mistake of setting his sights on sixteen-year-old Ruby and refusing to look away.

The murder ultimately releases both girls from the clutches of their hometown. One ends up in prison; the other lands a scholarship to Ole Miss.

Critics had remarked upon the sharp, unsentimental prose and the freshness of the perspective, which caught the attention of the literary crowd, but the book didn't really take off until a famous Hollywood actress chose it for her book club. Whether by prescience or by luck, the novel had appeared at the height of the #MeToo movement and perfectly captured the strain of righteous, brutal anger in the air. Whatever happened the night young Maud Dixon stabbed Frank Dillard—an undeniably menacing, lecherous figure—behind the Driftwood Tavern, you couldn't quite bring yourself to blame her for it.

The book had sold more than three million copies in the U.S. alone, and there was a mini-series in production. Curiously, its author, Maud Dixon, was a cipher. She did no interviews, no book tours, no publicity whatsoever. There wasn't even an acknowledgments page in the book.

The novel's publishing house—one of Forrester's competitors—admitted that "Maud Dixon" was a pen name, and that the author preferred to remain anonymous. Naturally, this set off immediate and rampant speculation about her identity. "Who is Maud Dixon?" was the question asked in countless magazine articles, online forums, and publishing lunches all over town.

The two known Maud Dixons in America had been duly

tracked down and ruled out. One lived in a nursing home in Chicago and couldn't remember the names of her own children. The other was a dental hygienist who'd grown up in a middle-class town on Long Island and by all accounts had never shown any talent for or proclivity toward writing.

Many people assumed the story was autobiographical since the author and the narrator shared a name. A few amateur sleuths had identified crimes that shared certain markers with the one in the book, but none matched closely enough to be a smoking gun. Besides, Mississippi sealed the court records of juvenile offenders when they turned twenty. The town of Collyer Springs didn't even exist. The investigation stalled there.

In general, Florence tended to look down on books that owed their success to the dramatic machinations of plot. Murder, in her eyes, was cheap currency. But when she'd read *Mississippi Foxtrot* she'd been astounded. The murder wasn't a technical ploy to up the stakes; it was the novel's raison d'être. The reader could feel the author's urgency; the murderer's absolute imperative; even the satisfaction of the knife going in.

Florence could still recite the passage:

> The knife slipped in easily, a sharp-edged interloper among the warm, feminine folds of Frank's insides. She raised the knife again. This time, it hit a rib and shuddered violently. Her hand slipped off the handle and slapped the soft pale flesh. His stomach was coated in blood now, the coarse, dark hairs slicked down like a newborn's scalp.

The voice was like nothing Florence had ever read before: sharp and savage, almost violent. Ultimately, she didn't care whether Maud Dixon was a man or a woman. She knew that whoever she was, she was an outsider, like Florence herself.

"Why are you getting so worked up about this?" Fritz asked

Amanda. "Jesus, I'm not saying women can't write. I'm just saying that *this particular writer* is not a woman."

Amanda pinched the bridge of her nose and took a deep breath. "Why am I getting so worked up? Because *this particular writer* was the best-selling novelist of the year *and* she was nominated for the National Book Award. But of course it can only be an 'important' book if a man wrote it; if a woman wrote it, it's just book-club drivel. For god's sake, you can't have all the fucking cookies and then come take our crumbs too."

"Technically," Florence interjected, "James Patterson was the best-selling author that year, even though *Mississippi Foxtrot* was the best-selling *book*." The group turned to look at her in one synchronized motion. "I think," she added, though she was sure, and immediately hated herself for it.

"Well thank you, Florence, there goes another crumb."

"This isn't about whatever absurd scorecard you keep in your back pocket, Amanda," said Fritz. "My friend—who happens to be a woman, by the way—works at Frost/Bollen and swore to me that Maud Dixon is a man. She *could* be a woman, obviously, but she happens not to be, in this case." He shrugged in apology. Frost/Bollen was Maud Dixon's literary agency.

"So who is it then?" Amanda demanded. "What's his name?"

Here Fritz faltered. "I don't know. She just overheard him referred to as a 'he.' "

Amanda threw up her hands. "Oh, this is total bullshit. There's literally no way a man could have written that book. There's not a man on earth who can write women that convincingly. No matter how well he may convince *himself*."

As if to punish herself for her earlier timidity, Florence said: "Henry James? E. M. Forster? William Thackeray?" She'd always felt a special affinity with Becky Sharp.

Amanda turned to face her. "Seriously, Florence? You think *Mississippi Foxtrot* could have been written by a man?"

Florence shrugged. "Maybe. I don't see what difference it would make."

Amanda looked at the ceiling and said in wonder, "She doesn't see what difference it would make." She turned back and asked, "Are you a writer, Florence?"

"No," Florence said quietly. In fact, she wanted nothing more than to be a writer. Didn't they all? Every one of them probably had half a novel tucked away in some drawer. But you don't go around calling yourself a writer until it's out of the drawer.

"Well then it may be hard for you to fully appreciate how important it is for female writers to have female exemplars. Women who have come before them and refused to let their inner lives be explained by men. I don't need one more *man* telling me how women *are*, okay? Can you understand that?"

Florence performed some motion between a shrug and a nod.

"Unhappy the land in need of heroes," Amanda added.

Florence said nothing.

"Brecht?" Amanda prodded, raising her eyebrows.

Florence felt heat rushing to her face, and she turned her body instinctively away from the group to hide it. She downed the rest of her drink in a single gulp and walked back to the bar, where she raised her empty glass in the bartender's direction with a tight smile.

She leaned against the wood and lifted her sore feet out of her heels one by one. She had never liked girls with Amanda's easy confidence. They were the same girls in high school who had taken Florence under their wing for a week and paraded her around like a rescue dog before losing interest in the game. Florence knew that to them she was nothing more than a prop to be used in their performances. And if she didn't cooperate by playing the grateful protégée, they had no use for her. It was such a fatuous routine, too—that was what annoyed Florence the most. Amanda, who had grown up on the Upper West Side, wore her feminism the same way she'd probably once worn her private school uniform—casually, without thinking too much about it, but committedly.

Florence had never been able to reach the pitch of outrage the times seemed to require, and this immunity to communal indignation often left her on the outside of, well, everything. This outrage seemed to be the glue that held everyone else together: couples, friends, the target audience of most media conglomerates. Even the young petition hawkers on the street ignored Florence, as if they could sense her innate solipsism.

She wasn't placid, certainly not, but she reserved her anger for more personal uses. Though what these were she couldn't say precisely. She could be as surprised as anyone by her flights of rage. They were rare, disorienting experiences that left her feeling weak and confused, almost jet-lagged, as if her body had raced ahead without her and she was just catching up.

Once in a creative writing seminar in college, Florence's professor had ripped into one of her stories in front of everyone, calling it dull and derivative. After class, Florence had mounted an increasingly hysterical defense of her work and then moved into a personal attack on him, a second-rate author who'd only ever published a single, overlooked book of short stories. When she finally lost steam, the teacher was staring at her with what could only be described as horror. Florence could barely remember what she'd said.

After the bartender finally took notice of Florence's empty glass, a voice behind her startled her: "I'm with you."

She turned around. It was Simon Reed, Forrester's editorial director, a tall, thin man with floppy hair, delicate features, and a smattering of freckles across his face. He was considered handsome in this milieu, but Florence could only imagine what they would say about him back in Port Orange, where delicate features weren't exactly an asset on a man.

Florence turned to face him. "In what sense?"

"In the sense of who fucking cares who Maud Dixon is." The

words dribbled from his mouth like soup. He was drunk, she realized. "It wouldn't change the words on the page," he went on. "Or rather, for some people it would, but it shouldn't. Ezra Pound was a fascist, but he still wrote some beautiful fucking sentences."

"The ant's a centaur in his dragon world," Florence said.

"Pull down thy vanity, I say pull down," said Simon, nodding. They shared a silent smile of complicity. She caught sight of Amanda watching them, but Amanda's eyes darted away when she saw Florence notice. The bartender set Florence's fresh glass of wine on the counter. When she picked it up, Simon tapped his own glass against it and leaned in close.

"To anonymity," he said quietly.

2.

For the rest of the evening, Florence felt Simon's attention follow her around the room. Being appraised by an older man was not an entirely unfamiliar feeling for her, but back home she had found their leers repellent, as if their gaze implicated her in something she wanted no part of. Tonight she enjoyed Simon's scrutiny. He was in a different class of men from the ones she'd known growing up; instead of crossbows and a tank-top tan he had first editions and a sense of irony. And then, of course, it was no secret that he was married to Ingrid Thorne, the actress. To be appreciated by a man like that made Florence feel like she had earned a spot on a higher plane of existence, as if his attention had called forth, with magnetic force, something in her she hadn't known she possessed.

Two hours later, the crowd began to thin, and Lucy asked Florence if she was ready to leave. They both lived in Astoria and often took the train home together.

"You go ahead," said Florence, "I think I want another drink."

"It's okay, I'll wait."

"No really, go ahead."

"Okay," she said, wavering. "If you're sure."

"I'm sure," Florence said pointedly.

At times she found Lucy's friendship stifling, though if pressed, she would have to admit that the extremity of Lucy's devotion gave her a sense of comfort that far outweighed the claustrophobia, perhaps because Florence's mother had trained her early on to recognize only the most acute forms of emotion. Anything tempered felt cold and false to her.

Lucy left with a limp wave. Florence ordered another glass of wine and drank it slowly, surveying the room. There were only about two dozen people left, and she knew none of them well enough to approach. Simon was entrenched in a conversation in the corner with the head of publicity. He showed no signs of ending it.

Florence felt like a fool. What had she thought was going to happen?

She set down her glass on the bar with more force than she'd intended and went to find her coat in the messy tangle by the door. She yanked it free and left.

Outside, the wind whipped at her bare legs. She turned uptown and started walking quickly toward the subway. She was just rounding the corner onto Eighth Street when she heard someone call her name. She turned around. Simon was jogging after her, his navy overcoat draped neatly over his arm.

"Care for one more drink?" he asked with the casualness of a man who has not just chased a woman down the street.

3.

They went to Tom & Jerry's on Elizabeth Street, where Simon insisted they order Guinness. "I must have drunk *swimming pools* of this stuff when I was at Oxford," he said. "So now it makes me feel young." He spoke with the cadence, if not quite the accent, of an Englishman. Now she understood why.

They found an empty spot in the back and sat facing each other across a sticky table. Florence took a sip of her drink and grimaced.

Simon laughed. "It's an acquired taste."

"You shouldn't have to *try* to like things," Florence insisted. "It's like people who force themselves to finish a book they're not enjoying. Just close it! Go find another story!"

"I hate to tell you this, but you might be in the wrong business. Do you know how many books I don't like that I have to read every week? Sorting the good from the bad is the job."

"Oh, I'm not interested in becoming an editor," Florence said with a wave of her hand.

"Just to be clear," Simon replied with a bemused smile, "you realize that I'm your boss's boss, right? You might want to fake a modicum of enthusiasm for the work we're paying you to do."

Florence smiled back. "Something tells me you're not going to be telling anyone about this encounter, least of all Agatha."

"Christ, I forgot you work for Agatha Hale. No, she would

not be amused by this *encounter*. That woman's moral compass is in dire need of some WD-40."

A guilty laugh erupted from the side of Florence's mouth. To hear someone casually mock a woman who ranked above her on every measure of power—both personal and professional—gave her a giddy feeling of vertigo.

"Alright, settled," said Simon, bringing his palm down lightly on the table. "Tonight will stay between us. Since you insist."

"To anonymity," said Florence, raising her glass.

Under the table, Simon answered by putting his hand on her thigh. Florence did not react. He started moving his fingers upward very, very slowly. They sat looking into each other's eyes without speaking as Simon stroked her with his thumb. No one noticed. Most of the crowd was huddled around a wall-mounted television, watching football.

"Let's go somewhere," Simon said hoarsely. Florence nodded. They left their still-full glasses on the table, and he led her out of the bar by her hand. Outside, she yelped as a cold gust swept past them. Simon took off his scarf and wrapped it around her neck twice, finishing it with a tight knot.

"Better?" he asked.

She nodded.

They half-walked, half-ran, heads bent into the wind, a few blocks north to the Bowery Hotel, where a doorman was sprinkling salt from a large plastic jug onto the sidewalk. A homeless man leaned against the building, rattling coins in a cup. It sounded like a child's cough. Florence tried to make out what he was mumbling. "They say men don't cry; men cry, men cry."

Inside, the desk attendant casually swiped Simon's credit card as if it were two in the afternoon. So this is how it's done, Florence thought. She'd always assumed that getting a hotel room for just a few hours would involve dark glasses and false names, a bed that shook when you added quarters to it. But it seemed that four hundred dollars a night was an effective bulwark against such seediness.

They rode the elevator with another guest, a middle-aged man swaying lightly. Simon smiled at Florence in conspiracy. He reached for her. She smiled back but shook her head.

Their room was dark, lit only by a pair of brass sconces next to the bed. Florence walked across it to look out of the large windows that dominated two of the walls. "Casement windows," she said, running her fingertips across the cold surface. They left four beaded wakes in the condensation.

"Come here," Simon said, and she did.

4.

Florence woke the next morning animated by a sense of anticipation, as if the night were ahead of her rather than behind. She was alone. Simon had left the hotel at 4 a.m. She had watched from the bed as he'd gathered his belongings from around the room. His charcoal-gray suit, which he'd hung up in the armoire. His wallet, phone, and keys from an orderly stack on the bedside table.

While buttoning his shirt, Simon had drawn his hand sharply to his neck and said, "Shit. I've lost a collar stay."

She'd asked him what a collar stay was, and he'd cocked his head with almost paternal bemusement. "You're adorable," he said, without explaining anything.

Florence had expected some awkwardness, but there was none. He chatted amiably as he dressed, then kissed her lightly on the forehead and went home to his wife. Florence didn't think of herself as someone who would sleep with a married man, and she prodded herself to feel some guilt. But, like the awkwardness, it was curiously absent.

She stretched expansively in the large bed. It was Saturday, checkout was at noon, and she had nowhere to be. The room was flooded with bright, yellow sunlight—light that belonged to a different season or a different city. Rome, maybe.

She got up and went into the bathroom. Her makeup was smeared around her eyes, and her curls sprang from her head as if electrified. After showering, she dried off the miniature bottles of shampoo and conditioner to take home with her.

Simon had told her to order breakfast, but when she called downstairs, she was informed that the room bill had already been settled and she'd have to pay by credit card. "Never mind," she said and hung up roughly. She dressed and sat on the bed. There was nothing else for her to do. She didn't even have a book. She walked to the door and put her hand on the knob. Then she quickly stepped back into the bathroom and pocketed the sewing kit.

———

Back in Astoria, Florence shut the apartment door and stood still, listening for her roommates. She hoped they were out. She'd found Brianna and Sarah on Craigslist a few months earlier and knew them hardly better now than she had when she'd moved in.

She opened the fridge and took out a nonfat yogurt marked "BRIANNA!!!" in Sharpie. In her room, she settled onto the bed and pulled her laptop toward her. She Googled "collar stay."

A collar stay is a smooth, rigid strip of metal, horn, baleen, mother of pearl, or plastic that one inserts into a specially made pocket on the underside of a shirt collar to stabilize the collar's point.

Florence thought about tiny pockets on the undersides of shirt collars. She thought about men like Simon who worried about the stability of their collar's point. The men Florence usually slept with—bartenders and low-level office drones she met on Tinder—were all transplants to New York who seemed as lost as she was. The only guy she'd gone on more than two dates with since she'd arrived had asked to borrow fifty dollars on their third and last. She doubted he knew what a collar stay was either.

There was a world beyond her world, Florence knew, that was entirely foreign to her. Every once in a while, someone took this other world in their hands and rattled it, dislodging a small piece that fell at her feet with a plink. She gathered up these fragments like an entomologist gathers rare bugs to pin to a board. They were clues that would one day cohere into something larger, she didn't know yet what. A disguise; an answer; a life.

She looked up Simon's wife next. Ingrid Thorne starred mainly in independent films with the occasional foray onto Broadway. She wasn't the type of actress whose picture appeared in *People* or *In Touch*—most of their readers wouldn't know who she was—but she had been on the cover of *Paper* magazine, as Florence discovered. The grande dame of avant-garde cinema, the interviewer had called her.

Ingrid's background was an unlikely incubator for avant-garde anything. She'd grown up in a small, wealthy town in Connecticut, the child of a successful lawyer and a homemaker. "Connecticult," she called it in the *Paper* interview: "They worship at the twin altars of gin and chintz." She and Simon now lived on the Upper East Side and sent their children to a prestigious private school, but somehow she managed to make those choices seem radical.

Ingrid was no longer young, and she wasn't classically beautiful, but her features had a fascinating complexity to them. She had a face you wanted to look at for a long time, which is precisely what Florence was doing when her phone buzzed beside her. She glanced at the screen and watched the phone shimmy on the quilt for a moment before picking it up.

"Hi, Mom."

"Listen," her mother started in with a confidential air. "Keith told me last night that *hedge funds* is what you want to be in." Keith was the bartender at the P.F. Chang's where her mother worked. For reasons Florence couldn't quite glean, the entire waitstaff credited him with almost supernatural powers of intelligence.

"I don't really have the qualifications for that," Florence said.

"You graduated summa cum laude! I know you think I'm some simple-minded hick, but I do know that *summa* means *best*. I'm not sure what other qualification you could need."

"Mom, I don't think you're a hick, but——"

"Oh, I see, I'm just simple-minded."

"No, that's not what I said. But I'm not good with numbers, you know that."

"I do *not* know that, Florence. I do not know that at all. In fact, now that you mention it, I remember you being very strong with numbers. *Very* strong." Her mother spoke with the cartoonish cadence of a preacher or newscaster, an affectation absorbed perhaps by the hours she spent tuned in to both every week.

Florence said nothing for a moment. "I guess I just don't really *want* to work in finance. I like my job." This wasn't entirely true, but she had learned that it was best to communicate with her mother in stark black-and-white terms. Shades of gray offered her a foothold.

"You like being at someone's beck and call all day long? I've been at someone's beck and call for the past twenty-six years for one reason and one reason only: so that my only child could tell anyone who tried to beck and call *her* where to put it."

Florence sighed. "I'm sorry, Mom."

"Don't apologize to me, honey. God's the one who gave you your gifts. He doesn't like to see you squander them any more than I do."

"Alright, I'm sorry, God."

"Oh, no. Don't get smart with Him, Florence. Not with Him."

Florence said nothing.

After a beat, her mother asked, "Who loves you?"

"You do."

"Who's the best girl in the whole world?"

Florence glanced toward her door as if to ensure that no one would overhear her. "I am," she said quickly.

"That's right." Florence knew her mother was nodding forcefully on the other end. "You're not small fry, baby. Don't act like it. That's disrespecting me, and it's disrespecting your Maker."

"Okay."

"Love you, baby."

"You too."

Florence hung up the phone and closed her eyes. Her mother's bloated and wildly imprecise flattery had the unintended effect of making Florence feel utterly insignificant. All through high school, her mother had kept up the fiction that Florence was the most beautiful and popular girl in her class when in reality she was a lost soul clinging to a small group of friends held together more by mutual desperation than any particular affinity. The only thing she'd really had in common with her closest friend, Whitney, was a 4.0 GPA. "Don't you *see* me?" Florence had wanted to shout.

She sometimes wished her mother were outright cruel; then at least Florence could cut ties without feeling guilty. Instead, they were locked in this endless masquerade: her mother supplying encouragement undercut by disappointment and Florence responding with affection and contrition she didn't feel.

Vera Darrow had been twenty-two when she got pregnant— not young enough to garner stares but certainly not old enough to know what she was getting into, as she'd told Florence often enough. The man responsible, a regular guest at the hotel where she'd been working at the time, had wanted nothing to do with the baby, but Vera had gone ahead with it anyway. It was, she told anyone who would listen, the best decision she'd ever made: Her life began when Florence's did. Though she'd also found God when she was pregnant, so perhaps some credit was due to Him too.

Someone at work had told Vera about a church that had helped out her cousin, another single mother, so Vera had gone with some vague notion that she would leave with a free pack of diapers. Instead she'd left with a community.

Ever since childhood, Vera had been told to quiet down; calm down; simmer down. Here, her enthusiasm had found a purpose. That's what Pastor Doug said. He also assured her that the baby she was carrying wasn't a sin, but rather a precious gift from God.

Florence knew that there were some in the church who thought her mother wasn't quite as devout as she made herself out to be: Vera never hid the fact that she found certain parts of the Bible dubious (like the idea that the meek would inherit anything), and she managed to introduce discord into any committee she joined. But her detractors would have been surprised to learn how strong her faith really was, even if she didn't bother much with the details. Above all, Vera believed with unwavering fervor that God had something special in store for her child.

Growing up, Florence had been told about this divine plan with the regularity of a bedtime story. She accepted it as she used to accept everything from her mother—passively and without question. Skepticism is a risky venture for children of single parents.

Florence had stopped believing in God in high school, but she still assumed that she was destined for greatness. It had been ingrained in her for too long. Giving it up at this point would be like asking her to stop having blond hair or to stop hating mustard.

The problem was that Florence and Vera had vastly different ideas of what greatness looked like. To Vera, it was simply the best version of a life that she could recognize, so that in effect, her expectations were hemmed in by the limits of her own imagination. God would grant Florence a good job and a good marriage. And in turn, maybe Florence would grant her mother a condo.

But the word *great* had stirred up something much wilder and more foreign in her daughter—something out of Vera's control. Florence's horizons, it turned out, could expand in ways that her mother's could not.

It was through books that Florence first felt the edges of her mother's world chafing at her. She'd always been a voracious reader, and it dawned on her that a corporate job in Tampa or Jacksonville was not, in fact, the be-all and end-all. Something lay beyond that point.

Florence had haunted the library, desperate for glimpses of lives unlike her own. She had a penchant for stories about glamorous, doomed women like Anna Karenina and Isabel Archer. Soon, however, her fascination shifted from the women in the stories to the women who wrote them. She devoured the diaries of Sylvia Plath and Virginia Woolf, who were far more glamorous and doomed than any of their characters.

But without a doubt, Florence's Bible was *Slouching Towards Bethlehem*. Admittedly, she spent more time scrolling through photos of Joan Didion in her sunglasses and Corvette Stingray than actually reading her, but the lesson stuck. All she had to do was become a writer, and her alienation would magically transform into evidence of brilliance rather than a source of shame.

When she looked into the future, she saw herself at a beautiful desk next to a window, typing her next great book. She could never quite see the words on the screen, but she knew they were brilliant and would prove once and for all that she *was* special. Everyone would know the name Florence Darrow.

And who'd trade *that* for a condo?

5.

Forrester Books occupied two floors of an office building on Hudson Street in downtown Manhattan. It was not one of New York's biggest publishing houses, but it did have a sort of niche cachet in which its employees took solace. When Florence interviewed there, a senior editor had told her, "We don't do *commercial* fiction," as if it were a euphemism for child pornography. (There was a rumor that that same editor had turned down *Mississippi Foxtrot* when the manuscript came in, but that had never been substantiated.)

On the Monday after the holiday party, Florence walked through the lobby with a heightened sense of alertness. Her familiar routine—swiping her ID card, nodding to the security guard—took on an element of performance. She looked for Simon in the throng waiting for the elevators but didn't see him.

Her desk was on the thirteenth floor, clustered with the printers, file cabinets, and other assistants in the bullpen. The editors' offices lined the perimeter, blockading daylight. As she waited for her computer to wake up, it finally hit her: Nobody was watching. Her life would continue as if Friday night had never happened.

At eleven, Agatha hurried in and struggled violently out of her coat. She was a short, tightly wound woman in her early forties with prematurely graying hair and endless amounts of energy. She was also six months pregnant. Florence stood up to help.

"My god! I hate my doctor, I really do," Agatha declared. "If it weren't too late I'd switch." She threw her tote bag on the floor by her door. It had a pin on it that said, "Be a nice person."

"Oh, no. What did she do this time?"

Florence had quickly learned that what Agatha mostly wanted from an assistant was someone to commiserate with her struggles and validate her beliefs. In fact, Florence was oddly fascinated with Agatha, who seemed to have been built according to the exact specifications of what people back home suspected a New York liberal to be. She lived with her husband, an immigration lawyer, in Park Slope. She marched. She resisted. She called movies *films*.

"I mean, she literally can't wrap her head around the fact that I don't want an epidural!" Agatha stomped into her cramped office and Florence followed, wheeling her desk chair into the doorway.

"You don't want an epidural? Why not?"

Agatha settled down at her desk and regarded her assistant seriously. She often referred to herself as Florence's mentor but less frequently behaved as such. "Florence, pain has been a prerequisite to motherhood for millennia. It's a rite of passage. It's like, you know, the boys in those African tribes who have to scar themselves before they're considered men."

"Which tribes?"

"I mean, *all* of them, basically."

"Right," Florence said uncertainly.

"By taking away that *sacred pain,* the medical-industrial complex is effectively eroding the mother-child relationship. That pain bonds you. It's an honor and a privilege to become a mother. You have to earn it."

"I guess that makes sense," said Florence. "You know, I read online somewhere that sea lice eat their way out of the womb when they're ready to be born. They chew their way out of the uterus, through their mother's organs and flesh and stuff and come right out of her mouth. She's totally ripped apart. Dead."

Agatha nodded approvingly. "Exactly, Florence. Exactly."

Florence scooted back to her desk and decided to chalk that conversation up as a victory.

———

At a little past four, she went out to get a coffee at the Dunkin' Donuts on the corner. As she stepped off the elevator, she finally caught sight of Simon. He was on the phone walking into the building. When he saw her he smiled and held up a finger for her to wait.

"Mm-hmm. Sure. I couldn't agree more," he said into the phone. He rolled his eyes at Florence. "Alright, Tim, I've got to cut out here. Talk soon." He tucked his phone into the inner pocket of his suit jacket and gave Florence an aggrieved smile. "Sorry about that." He looked around. "Here, let's pop around the corner a sec." He led her outside, halfway down a side street.

"Well. That was quite a night," he said, forcing a laugh. "Listen, I just wanted to check in and make sure everything was alright here. That you felt fine about it. It's not something I make a habit of, obviously, but I don't know"—he let out a long breath and shook his head—"there's something about you, Florence. I broke all my rules."

Florence opened her mouth to respond but Simon charged ahead. "That said—." He stopped and tried a different tone: "That *said*, it was a mistake. On my part. A hundred percent on my part. I take full responsibility. But it can't happen again. I respect you too much to put you in that position."

"Simon," Florence said, "I'm not going to 'MeToo' you."

Simon laughed a little too loudly. "Ha. Ha. Well, thank you, thank you for that. Ha. No, I don't think it's quite a 'MeToo' situation."

He caught the eye of someone behind Florence and tossed off a nod and smile. "Right," he said, turning his attention back to her. "Okay. Great. Thank you."

Florence said nothing.

"So, we're all good here then?"

"Everything's fine, Simon."

He gave her a pat on her shoulder. "Good, good. And everything's fine upstairs? You're enjoying working for Agatha?"

Florence said she was.

"Good, good," he said again.

They parted ways at the corner. Simon went back into the building and Florence walked to the coffee shop. While waiting in line she replayed the conversation in her mind. She had told him the truth. She *was* fine. She had known Simon had a wife when she slept with him. She had known it would probably be a one-time thing. The sex hadn't even been that great. He had touched her tenderly, accommodatingly, in a way she found slightly revolting. (How sad, she thought, that even in his infidelities he fucked like a married man.) But she had to admit that part of her felt a tug of regret. It wasn't that she wanted his company, exactly. But she had liked the feeling of being in his orbit, even if for only a few hours. She'd liked the Bowery Hotel. She'd liked his collar stays. She'd liked attracting the attention of Ingrid Thorne's husband.

6.

Florence did not go home for Christmas. She told her mother the flights were too expensive, though there were fares on JetBlue from seventy-nine dollars.

On Christmas day, she took the subway to the Bowery Hotel. The lobby—a large, open room that stretched back to a glassed-in terrace—doubled as the bar, but most of the tables were empty. She sat in an armchair upholstered in worn yellow velvet and ran her hands up and down the fabric. When the waitress arrived, she ordered a fourteen-dollar glass of Glenlivet.

She placed her book—Renata Adler's *Speedboat*—and her notebook on the table in front of her but didn't open either. Instead she studied her surroundings. The hotel had the air of an abandoned British outpost in some exotic colony: sooty paintings, terra-cotta floors, antique carpets. There were wreaths and garlands strung up for the season.

Her eyes fell on an older man in a gray three-piece suit sprouting a purple handkerchief from its pocket. He was watching her. When their eyes met, he pushed himself up from his chair with effort and shambled over.

He leaned in close. He smelled of liquor and cologne. "Jew or misanthrope?" he asked in a crumbly growl.

She looked at him with distaste but said nothing. They maintained eye contact in silence. He broke first.

"Aw, don't be like that, honey. I meant no offense. I'm both, you know. I'm double the fun." He let out a hacking laugh that turned into a cough. He pulled out his handkerchief and held it to his mouth. Something wet settled in its folds.

Florence's waitress walked over and put a hand on his lower back. "Alright, let's let this nice lady enjoy her drink in peace, shall we?" She led him gently back to his seat by the fireplace while he mumbled, "She's no lady. Not that one."

Florence downed the rest of her drink and went to the bathroom. She looked at herself in the mirror. There were two spigots, one for hot water and one for cold. She held her hand under the hot one until she couldn't bear it anymore. She'd discovered in college that this particular ritual was the best remedy for anger and despair. Then she went back to her table, left a twenty, and started back to the subway.

———

Vera spent Christmas with her best friend, Gloria, and Gloria's two children. She told Florence about it that night:

"I'm sure they weren't thrilled about little old *me* hanging around all day but of course Gloria wasn't going to let me spend the day alone. Not that I blame you for not coming home. But, you know, Gloria doesn't want to see anyone suffer. And Grace, her oldest! You wouldn't believe it. She's the manager of the entire Tampa office at Gold Coast Realty. I mean, think about that: They're a national conglomerate. *Plus* four kids."

"I'm pretty sure Gold Coast Realty isn't a national conglomerate," Florence replied. "If it's called *Gold Coast*."

Vera exhaled loudly. "Alright. I guess that isn't impressive enough for you. Four kids and a six-figure job. Meanwhile she still found time to buy me a Christmas present."

"I got you a Christmas present," Florence cut in, sounding defensive. She'd sent her mother the collected stories of Lydia Davis. She knew her mother would probably never crack the spine, but there was still a part of Florence that desperately hoped Vera would change. It wasn't like Florence liked being ashamed of her.

"Well, honey, you're family, of course you did. Anyway, you'll never guess what she got me."

"What?"

"A zoodler!"

"I don't know what that is," Florence said in a flat voice.

"You do. You know. *Zoodles*."

"I promise you, I do not know what that word is."

Vera sighed again. "Alright honey, I'll let you go back to your fabulous New York lifestyle."

Florence rubbed her face roughly. She didn't want to act this way with her mother, but she had trouble controlling herself. "I'm sorry, Mom. I'm sure it's a great gift."

Her mother was appeased. It didn't take much. "It really is. The next time you come home I'll make you zoodles. They taste just like real pasta. It's incredible."

"Neat."

"Oh! And do you know who I ran into the other day? Trevor. What a nice boy. He came right up and said hello to me at the mall."

Florence's sense of contrition evaporated. "Mom, you literally despised him." Trevor was the high school boyfriend Vera had repeatedly encouraged Florence to break up with. Half the reason she'd stayed with him for over two years was to deny her mother the satisfaction. The only thing she and Trevor had really had in common was a deeply felt, if rarely voiced, conviction that they were smarter than everyone else. Not surprisingly, that bond had ended up being too weak to sustain them once they left home.

"Oh hush, I did no such thing," Vera said. "Anyway, he's some big deal engineer at Verizon, and he was asking all about you. He couldn't believe you were in New York."

"Yet here I am," Florence said dryly.

"You should give him a call."

"Why?"

"It'd be nice, that's all."

Florence knew that wasn't all, but she let it go. Not taking the bait would be her real Christmas gift to Vera. "Alright, Mom, maybe I will. I love you. Merry Christmas."

"Love you more, baby."

————

The Forrester office was closed between Christmas and New Year's, and Florence had planned to use the time to work on her own fiction. But for the entire week, she found herself beset by the same problem she'd had since moving to New York nearly two years ago: She couldn't write. Not a single word.

It was her first experience with writer's block. After college, she'd stayed in Gainesville and worked at a bookstore to devote herself fully to writing. Every minute she wasn't at the shop, she was typing feverishly at her computer. She often wrote through the night, sipping cup after cup of microwaved ramen. In college she had discovered Robert Coover and Donald Barthelme and Julio Cortázar. Reading them made her feel like she could step into another world where the strictures of normal life were loosened; the bonds between cause and effect were snipped; and all that lay ahead was freedom. She found the idea thrilling—a reality where she wrote the rules.

She finished several strange, unsettling stories during this period. Her favorite was about a woman who ate her husband bit by bit over many years until she'd consumed him entirely. When Vera read it, she pointed out what was, to her, a fatal lapse in logic: "Wouldn't the husband *realize* his wife was eating him and call 911?"

During this post-college stint, her mother had urged her nearly every day to get a real job. After almost two years and count-less rejection slips from various literary magazines, Florence had complied. She sent in applications to every publishing opening she could find and accepted the first offer that came her way: editorial assistant at Forrester Books.

Soon after this, her productivity came to an abrupt end. She could trace the origins of her condition to a single night during her first week in New York. Most of the younger staff members at Forrester gathered for drinks every Friday at the Red Lark, a bar near the entrance to the Holland Tunnel. It was a grimy place whose sticky counters assured the wealthy financiers who lived in Tribeca that, despite their suits and their nutritionists and the playrooms in their high-rise luxury condos, they were still cool. The junior staffers went because they had five-dollar pitchers from five to eight.

On Florence's first Friday, a group heading to the Red Lark had gathered at the elevators at six, and she and Lucy had silently appended themselves to its perimeter. As much as Florence hated to admit it, she was as intimidated as Lucy was. Their new coworkers were confident and well-read. They felt at ease at literary parties with brand-name writers. They wore sheath dresses and vintage jewelry. Among them, Florence felt like an imposter.

Amanda Lincoln was their self-appointed leader. She'd grown up in New York, the daughter of a *New York Times* columnist and a successful literary agent who sat on the board of the New York Public Library. After Dalton, she'd gone to Yale, followed by an internship at *The Paris Review*. Her pedigree, in other words, was immaculate. She'd probably never stepped foot in a place like Port Orange in her life.

When the group settled at a large table in the back, Amanda raised her glass and called out, "Chin-chin!" Florence and Lucy looked at each other unsurely, but mumbled "Chin-chin" back with the rest of them.

Simon's assistant, Emily, a friendly Midwesterner, had turned to the newcomers to try to draw them into the fold. "So where are you guys from?"

"Amherst," said Lucy in a barely audible voice.

Amanda cut in: "Did you go to school there? That's where my brother went. Stewart Lincoln?"

Lucy nodded but it wasn't clear which question she was answering, and she offered no further commentary.

Emily asked Florence, "What about you?"

"I went to the University of Florida. Gainesville."

"Oh cool," Emily said. Everyone at the table nodded supportively. She might as well have just told them that she had cancer, so aggressively tactful was their response. Nearly all of them had gone to Ivy League colleges or their equivalents.

"Have you been down to Hemingway's house in Key West?" Fritz asked.

Florence shook her head.

"It's awesome. They have these six-toed cats descended from his actual six-toed cat."

"God, don't tell me we're still pretending Hemingway is relevant," Amanda said. "What is this, ninth-grade English class?"

Fritz rolled his eyes. "Jesus, Amanda, all I said was that he had a six-toed cat."

A little while later, while they were on their second round, a middle-aged man in an orange kurta circulated the bar peddling roses. When she saw him, Amanda said, "There is literally nothing tackier than a single red rose. Someone should tell that poor man to start pushing peonies. Then he'd move some merch."

Everyone laughed except Florence, who stared quietly at Amanda, slightly awed. Who didn't like red roses? For that matter, who didn't like Hemingway? How could this girl, no older than Florence, hold such blasphemous opinions so cavalierly?

On it went. Throughout the rest of the night, Amanda dropped cultural references that, until Florence Googled them later, seemed like little more than a series of disordered syllables: Adorno, Pina Bausch, Koyaanisqatsi.

In Florida, Florence had grown used to being the most sophisticated person in the room. But in this grubby bar, she felt inadequate—stupid, really—for the first time in her life. She had been blithely walking around thinking she knew more than everyone and all of a sudden she realized she didn't know a thing. If you'd asked her that morning, she would have said that red roses were just about the most elegant thing she could think of. And she hadn't realized that maligning Hemingway was even on the table.

The next day, she stared at the blank page and felt an unfamiliar emotion: fear. If red roses were tacky, what else was she wrong about? How many other embarrassing errors would crop up in whatever she wrote? And for that matter, could she even begin to contemplate writing a novel without reading Adorno first?

She'd reread her old stories then and found them childish and clunky. She actually felt grateful to Amanda Lincoln, that smug bitch, for teaching her how little she knew before she humiliated herself.

The attainment of greatness now felt like just one possibility among many rather than her God-given right. It was entirely plausible that she would end up an editor rather than a writer. Or back in Florida, selling houses or bank loans. Nothing was guaranteed. Nothing was owed.

Her sense of self slipped from her as easily as a coat slips off the back of a chair. She'd outgrown the girl she'd been in Florida, but how did one go about building up someone new? She tried on moods and personalities like outfits. One day she was interested in ruthlessness. The next, she wanted to be an object of adoration. She put her faith in the transformative power of new boots, liquid eyeliner, and once—terrifyingly—a *beret,* as if an identity could seep in from the outside, like nicotine from a patch.

By the time she encountered Simon Reed at the Forrester holiday party, she had been in New York for two years and still a true self had not begun to solidify. She was a ship without ballast, tilting wildly in the waves. This very quality of unfixed-ness had probably attracted him to her in the first place. He was one of those men helplessly drawn to these young, shifting forms—for she was hardly the only twenty-six-year-old woman to find herself grasping in the dark for an identity.

He must have known that sleeping with a young assistant who worked for him had the potential to destroy both his career and his family. Why did he do it? Florence didn't flatter herself with illusions of her own irresistibility. She suspected, instead, that he had a pathological addiction, not necessarily to sex, but to the sight of his own reflection—powerful, confident, desired—in an insecure young woman's eyes. Plus, a nobody is less likely to kick up a fuss.

And he was right. She hadn't.

7.

The Forrester office reopened on January second. A few days after that Agatha sent Florence to deliver a bag of books she'd recently edited to an author she was trying to woo. The writer lived up on Eighty-Seventh Street, all the way east. It was an unseasonably warm day for January, and Florence was happy for an excuse to get out of the office.

After she'd dropped off the books, she took her time heading back to work. She turned south and walked the perimeter of a pretty park running along the East River.

She stopped at Eighty-Fourth Street, where a crowd of people were gathered outside a large mansion on the opposite side of the street. They were all women, most of them dark-skinned. One wore a gray maid's uniform under her parka, like a character in a play. The handful of white women among them chatted with one another or checked their phones.

The mansion's double doors opened and a stream of girls in red plaid skirts poured out like a nosebleed. Florence read the gold plaque mounted above the door: The Harwick School. Simon's daughters went here—she'd read it in a *Vanity Fair* profile of his wife. She looked back at the crowd of waiting mothers with more interest, but Ingrid wasn't among them. Florence stayed to watch, perching on a bench across the street.

Most of the children were herded into waiting buses; not the yellow school buses Florence had ridden in Florida, but the kind with velveteen upholstery and a bathroom in the back. According to a heavyset teacher with a whistle around her neck, they weren't even buses; they were *coaches*. "Coach One leaves in five minutes, girls!" she bellowed. "Let's go, let's go!"

Only after the coaches had pulled away, the nannies and mothers had walked off with their charges, and the teachers had been reabsorbed into the school did Florence stand up to begin her trek to the subway.

———

Back at the office, Florence was picking at her soggy, overdressed salad when Agatha called out, "Florence!"

Florence scooted to the door of Agatha's office. "Yes?"

"Are you sure this is extra chickpeas?" Agatha gestured skeptically with her fork to the bowl Florence had just picked up from the Sweetgreen down the block.

"Um, yep." She had, in fact, forgotten to ask for extra chickpeas.

"Clara is *not* happy about this," Agatha said. "Clara needs her chickpeas. Clara's going to force her mommy to mainline hummus when she gets home."

Florence nodded and smiled. Then, when Agatha seemed to be waiting for more, she asked, "Sorry, who's Clara?"

"Did I forget to tell you? Josh and I finally settled on a name."

"Clara? That's pretty."

Agatha smiled.

"I think that was Hitler's mother's name," Florence added.

Agatha froze, a piece of lettuce quivering on her plastic fork. "What?"

Florence tried to backtrack. "Oh, well, actually I think she spelled it with a *K*. Being Austrian and all..."

Agatha kept staring at her in silent perplexity.

"Or are you spelling it with a *K*? Because I like that too."

Agatha shook her head slowly. "No...a *C*."

Florence was silent for a moment. Then she said, "Yeah, pregnancy cravings are so weird. My mother said she couldn't get enough Filet-O-Fish when she was pregnant with me."

Agatha started nodding slowly. "Yes." This was a topic she could warm to. "Yes, well they say that eating fish makes your child smarter, especially salmon, as long as you watch your mercury levels. That's obviously why she was craving it. Mother Nature knows what she's doing."

"Or she's shilling for McDonald's," said Florence with a laugh.

"McDonald's?"

"Filet-O-Fish? From McDonald's?"

"Oh, I thought you were just talking about fillets of fish. I've never actually been to McDonald's."

"Come on," said Florence. "Yes you have."

Agatha shook her head guilelessly.

"You have to have been to McDonald's. Everyone's been to McDonald's."

"Not me. Do you know how many hormones are in that meat?"

Florence would have bet that every single person in America had eaten at McDonald's. How could Agatha so easily snub something millions of people did every day without ever having tried it, and at the same time refuse to get an epidural because a handful of African boys were flogging themselves with sticks?

Before the holiday party, it hadn't occurred to Florence that she might be in a position to judge Agatha. Florence was younger, less experienced, she made less money, she wasn't married, she had no children. She lacked nearly everything Agatha valued. But the dismissive way Simon had said her name at the bar—Agatha *Hale*—had pulled back a curtain and revealed something ridiculous about her. This new perspective was disorienting. If Florence didn't look up to Agatha, what was she doing? Why was she working here? Was this really helping her to become a writer?

"Unhappy the land in need of heroes," Amanda had said. But unhappy, too, was a land whose only hero was Agatha Hale.

———

Agatha left at five that afternoon, but Florence stayed on to finish a report on a manuscript she'd been given a few days earlier. At seven thirty, as she was emailing off her notes, her desk phone rang. It was Simon, and she could tell he'd been drinking from his ineffectively muffled ebullience.

"Florence! You're there! What are you doing working so late?"

"Um, working?"

"But that's absurd. You shouldn't be slogging away at this hour. Come meet me. Clearly I need to talk some sense into you."

"Meet you now?"

"Meet me five minutes ago. Meet me *yesterday*. Come as fast as those gorgeous legs will carry you."

Florence pinched her lips to squelch a smile. "I thought you respected me too much to put me in this position."

"That doesn't sound like me. No, in fact, I haven't the least bit of respect for you. I hold you in utter, total contempt. You and Idi Amin—that's my list. Let me show you just how little respect I have for you."

"Are you serious? Right now?"

"I'm dead serious. I'll meet you at the Bowery Hotel in thirty minutes. I'll reserve the room under the name Maud Dixon, how about that? Easy to remember."

Florence hung up and brought her hand to her face. It felt hot. She gathered her coat and her bag and hurried out of the office, half hoping someone would ask her whether she had any plans tonight. If she'd told Lucy about her first encounter with Simon, she would have relished apprising her of the second, but she'd kept it to herself, knowing the judgment and dismay Lucy would have tried—and failed—to hide from her expression.

Florence splurged for a taxi and beat Simon to the hotel. As promised, there was a reservation under the name Dixon. In the room, she sat on the chair by the window and tried to look casual. Should she undress? No, that was too ridiculous. She crossed and uncrossed her legs. She wished she'd worn nicer underwear.

An hour later, he still hadn't arrived.

She pulled out the notebook she always carried in her bag and began writing a short story about a young woman waiting for her lover. She tore out the page and tossed it in the trash. At ten, she got into bed. She set the alarm on her phone for six. She'd have to take the train home to change before going back into the office.

Several hours later the room phone woke her.

"Florence, I'm so sorry," Simon whispered on the other end.

"What happened?" she asked, whispering back for no good reason.

"My wife's father had a heart attack. I didn't have your cell number."

"Is he okay?"

"Who, Bill? No. He's dead."

"Oh."

"Yeah."

"Can you come now?"

"No, I have to stay here. Listen, this was madness. Total madness. I'm so sorry. I should never have pulled you into this."

"It's okay."

"It's not. But thank you for saying so."

They hung up, and Florence immediately felt like a fool. Why had she asked if he could come over now? She'd sounded so needy. Like her mother.

She lay back and stared at the ceiling. She prodded herself to feel some pity for Ingrid, but it was hard to muster sympathy for someone who'd lost something that she herself had never had.

There's a crucial difference between a loss and a lack. Florence, after all, had never gotten any sympathy for growing up without a father. On the contrary, she thought she'd seemed tainted somehow, like she didn't deserve one.

All Florence knew about her father was his first name, which she'd pried out of her mother one Thanksgiving after she'd drunk three-quarters of a bottle of Shiraz. She had hoped it would be something stately, like Jonathan or Robert. But no. It was Derek, which was about as stately as a vinyl-sided condominium. What was that *k* even doing there, all garish and naked without a *c* in front of it? Bill was a much better name for a father.

She sat up and fumbled for the remote. There was no way she was getting back to sleep now. Scrolling through movies, she came across *Harbinger*, a small indie film from a few years ago that Ingrid had starred in. She charged it to the room and pressed Play. When Ingrid appeared, Florence paused the screen on a close-up shot of her face, mouth spread wide in a beatific smile.

Florence regarded the woman on the screen in front of her. No, what she felt for Ingrid was not pity. It was something very, very far from pity.

———

She didn't bother to go home to change the next morning. She went to work in the same clothes she'd worn the day before. She doubted anyone would notice.

On the subway, she checked Ingrid's Instagram account. The most recent photo showed a sunlit vase of daffodils. The caption said, "Rage, rage against the dying of the light." Florence thought Bill probably hadn't raged against death all that hard—a heart attack sounded sudden—but she appreciated the sentiment. The post already had over four hundred comments and two thousand likes. She tentatively liked it, then panicked and unliked it.

An idea occurred to her. Perhaps Ingrid would pick up the children from school herself that day. Were they too emotionally fragile for the bus? For the *coach*?

When Agatha got into work, Florence told her she had a doctor's appointment that afternoon.

Agatha nodded distractedly. "No problem."

Florence was up at the Harwick School by ten of three. She sat on the same bench across the street where she'd sat the day before and read *The Driver's Seat* by Muriel Spark. When the school doors opened, she took out her phone and brought up an image of Simon's daughters that she'd found online. It had been taken at a fundraiser for shelter dogs the previous summer on the North Fork. In it, the younger girl, Tabitha, cradled a scrawny and frightened looking Chihuahua, while Chloe, the older one, flashed a peace sign. Behind them, Simon and Ingrid smiled serenely with their arms around each other. Florence zoomed in on each face one at a time.

Florence looked up to scan the crowd of students pooling outside. A young teacher was trying to usher them into the waiting buses, but her soft-spoken exhortations had no effect on the wild mob. Florence spotted Chloe in a huddle of girls crowded around an iPhone. She guessed they were in seventh or eighth grade. Chloe gesticulated grandly, like a stage actress, but she was chubbier than you'd guess Ingrid's daughter would be. Florence used the camera on her phone to zoom in for a closer look, and then, because she had it in her hand, she took a picture. She captured Chloe mid-laugh, her mouth thrown open grotesquely. Florence thought it slightly unseemly for her to be so giddy after her grandfather had just died. She wondered what Ingrid would say if she saw her.

But Ingrid did not show up. The girls scrambled onto Coach One, and Florence waited to watch it drive away.

8.

The rest of January unfurled in a series of mild, sunny days, as if atoning for the bitterness of December's chill. Florence was grateful for the reprieve—took it as an endorsement, for she was now spending one or two afternoons a week on the stone bench across from the Harwick School. If pressed, she wouldn't have been able to articulate a reason for these trips uptown; all she knew was that something kept drawing her back. On Fridays, when dismissal was at one thirty, she went up during her lunch break, even though it took close to an hour to get there. Other days, she invented appointments to explain her absences from work.

Sitting there, she almost felt like she was a part of that life. A life that was, simply put, better than hers in every possible way. She noted the two-hundred-dollar ballet flats on feet that hadn't stopped growing. The way the teachers lingered in the crowd, joking with the students. Florence had never joked around with her teachers. She had never even seen her teachers joke around with one another. Her seventh-grade teacher had gotten spit on, right in her eye. She didn't even yell at the kid. She just walked out of the room and didn't come back for the rest of the period.

The entire area around the Harwick School seemed insulated from everything ugly and vulgar in the world. Florence always left feeling cleansed and energized, like she'd breathed pure oxygen.

But the truth, if she could have admitted it, was that she was there to see Ingrid, who had thoroughly replaced her husband as a figure of fascination for Florence. Simon's collar stays did nothing for her anymore. He was an ordinary man with ordinary weaknesses. Ingrid, on the other hand, was a true artist: She twitched an eyebrow onscreen, she shed a tear, and somebody thousands of miles away, even years later, *felt* something. Someone's inner chemistry changed because of Ingrid. What power—to impose a new reality on a total stranger. To hold them in your thrall. That was what Florence wanted to do with her writing.

She had spent the past few weeks watching Ingrid Thorne movies on her roommate's Netflix account and poring over pictures online. She longed to see Ingrid in person. To convince herself that this woman was real, had flesh like hers, because she and Ingrid were inextricably connected; Simon, after all, had chosen both of them.

In early February, her persistence paid off.

Instead of getting onto one of the idling coaches like they usually did, Chloe and Tabitha ran ecstatically into the outstretched arms of their mother. Florence drew in her breath sharply. Ingrid wore narrow black pants and a white blouse with complicated folds. Her hair was newly short, and undoubtedly expensively cut. Her face had more wrinkles than it did onscreen.

The trio walked westward, Ingrid in the middle. Tabitha held her mother's hand and swung it back and forth with violent jubilance. Florence followed half a block behind on the other side of the street. When Ingrid and the girls caught the M86 bus on York, Florence had to sprint to make the same one. She was breathing heavily by the time she climbed aboard. A few people turned to look at her, but not Ingrid.

The family got off at Lexington and disappeared into a doctor's suite on Eight-Seventh Street. Florence forced herself to wait a full minute before following them in.

"Can I help you?" A fortyish woman with bleached blond hair smiled at her expectantly from behind the reception desk. Florence glanced at the pamphlets in front of her. She was in an orthodontist's office.

"Um, I have an appointment with Dr. Carlson?" she said. Dr. Carlson was the name of her dentist growing up.

"I'm sorry, there's no one here by that name."

"Oh. Hm. Do you mind if I just sit for a second and check my email? I have his information in here somewhere."

The receptionist smiled and nodded.

Florence sat across from Ingrid and the girls. They had briefly fallen silent during Florence's exchange with the receptionist, but Tabitha started talking again.

Florence scrolled through her phone and listened to the child tell a dull story about gym class.

Then Ingrid's phone rang and she said, "Hang on, goose, I have to take this."

She swiped the screen. "Hi, David." Florence could hear a man's tinny sing-song through the phone. Then Ingrid cut in: "That's absurd. I'm not doing that...No...No...Well, let's try to get someone else then...She did that show about felons?... Yeah, that's a good idea. Alright, call me back."

Ingrid hung up and sighed. She made eye contact with Florence and rolled her eyes. "Sorry about that."

"That's alright." Then Florence added, "You have a lovely family."

"Thank you," Ingrid replied with a pleased smile, turning it on her girls one after the other.

At the sight of Ingrid's white, even teeth, Florence pressed her lips together, suddenly ashamed of her crooked smile. She'd never been to an orthodontist. She forced herself to rise from the couch and surrender the warmth of the waiting room.

Outside, it was turning dark and a cold rain had begun to fall. She was tempted to wait for Simon's family to emerge, so she could follow them home, but she didn't want Ingrid to think she was stalking her. Besides, she had to get back to work. When she'd told Agatha that she was getting a cavity filled—she'd claimed an appointment for a dental exam last week—Agatha hadn't received the news as serenely as she had in the past. She had a tendency toward passive aggression that Florence didn't understand—she was already in a position of power; why didn't she just use it to ask for what she wanted? Instead, she had dropped a manuscript loudly on Florence's desk before she left for lunch and asked for her thoughts by the following morning, adding pointedly, "*if* you can find the time."

This performance was obviously supposed to generate a feeling of contrition in Florence, or at the very least a small quiver of anxiety. But she felt neither. Instead, she felt oppressed by Agatha's utterly commonplace expectations—email X, call Y—as if Florence were any low-level flack. She wanted to take those expectations and twist them like a pinkie finger until they snapped.

This was not the job, or the life, she wanted—which was precisely what Vera had been telling her for years.

Florence had thought Vera would be appeased after she landed the position at Forrester. Instead, she'd asked, with extra-sibilant force: "An *assistant*? Like a secretary?" Florence had tried to explain that this was the way things worked, that everyone in the literary world started out as an editorial assistant, but it was useless once her mother also found out that she would be making less money than Vera herself did.

And so the tension between mother and daughter had continued to escalate with every conversation. Florence felt like she was running a Ponzi scheme: Vera demanding an immediate return on her investment, and Florence paying her down as best she could in tiny installments of affection and apologies, biding her time until she could scrounge up the capital she owed.

But perhaps she had absorbed more of her mother's impatience than she thought.

9.

A few weeks later, Florence was on the elevator heading to work when Simon stuck his hand in the door just as it was about to close. He hesitated a moment when he saw her, like he wished he hadn't caught it after all, and then Florence saw why. Ingrid was with him. He recovered and said, "Hello, Florence. All's well?"

"Fine, thank you," she said. Ingrid stood with the expectant smile of a woman waiting to be introduced.

"Right," said Simon. "Have you met my wife? Florence, Ingrid Thorne. Ingrid, this is Florence Darrow, one of our most promising editorial assistants."

"Pleasure," Ingrid said, with a very firm handshake. She didn't seem to recognize her from the orthodontist's office. "I have a shirt just like that."

"Oh, really?" Florence blushed. She'd bought it after seeing Ingrid's.

Simon cleared his throat and said in response to a question that no one had asked, "Yes, well, Ingrid is actually here to meet a friend of yours. Amanda Lincoln."

"Amanda?"

"I slipped her a copy of Amanda's manuscript, and she thought she might be interested in turning it into a film. Trying her hand at producing."

"Amanda's manuscript?"

"Haven't you heard? Forrester just acquired Amanda's first novel."

"Amanda sold a novel?" Florence felt herself slipping in the dark, unable to find traction.

"It's an absolutely brilliant satire of Upper East Side mores," Ingrid said. She pronounced it *morays,* like the eel. Florence made a mental note to stop pronouncing it like *s'mores.* "It's wickedly funny."

Simon wrapped an arm affectionately around his wife's waist then abruptly removed it. The elevator pinged for Florence's floor. She moved toward the door and waited impatiently for it to release her. "Good luck," she said dully on her way out.

"Thank you!" said Ingrid brightly at the same time that Simon called out, "Keep up the good work!"

Florence walked directly into the handicapped bathroom and locked the door. She turned on the hot water, waited until it was scalding and held her hands underneath it until her skin glowed red. Amanda's novel? What fucking novel? She looked in the mirror. Tears were gathering in her eyes.

"Don't," she snapped at her reflection. She shoved the hot heels of her hands into her eyes. When she removed them, the tears had cleared, and she managed to put a smile on her face.

"Better," she said.

On her way to her desk, she detoured to talk to Lucy, who was hunched in front of her computer screen, clicking through pictures of dogs available for adoption on petfinder.com.

"You should just do it," Florence said behind her.

Lucy jumped in her seat and put a hand to her heart. "God, you scared me," she said.

"Seriously, why don't you just get one?"

Lucy looked at Florence like she'd suggested drop-kicking an orphan. "Oh, no, I couldn't. I work too much. It wouldn't be fair." Florence shook her head. She never understood people who denied themselves the things they wanted. Her problem was that the things she wanted constantly seemed out of reach.

"Have you heard about Amanda's novel?"

Lucy nodded.

"Why didn't you tell me?"

"I thought it might upset you." Lucy had no interest in being a writer, but she knew Florence did.

"Upset me!" Florence exclaimed more loudly than she'd meant to. "Why should it upset me? Believe me, *that* is not the type of book I have any interest in writing." She still knew next to nothing about it.

"No, of course not. It sounds super cheesy."

"It does?" Florence asked eagerly. "Have you read it?"

"No, but Sam has it."

"Douchebag Sam or ginger Sam?"

"Ginger."

Florence hurried off to find Sam, who promised to email her the manuscript. "It's actually not terrible," he said.

"That's what I hear," she replied grimly.

———

Florence spent the day reading the manuscript on her computer. It was ten at night by the time she finished. Agatha had left hours earlier, as had everyone else on her floor. Florence turned off her computer but made no move to pack up.

Sam was right. It wasn't terrible. Even worse—it was good.

Florence shoved the heels of her palms into her eyes until she saw sparks. It simply wasn't fair. Amanda already had everything. Now she got to be a published novelist too? The one thing Florence wanted more than anything else? *And* to work with Ingrid Thorne? She imagined Ingrid and Amanda having cozy working dinners. Talking about art and inspiration. Talking about fucking Brecht.

What did Florence get? A tiny room in a shitty Astoria apartment? A mentor who would rather talk about her doula than German playwrights? A one-night stand with Simon Reed, who probably wished it had never happened in the first place?

Something about that last thought snagged in Florence's brain. *Who probably wished it had never happened.*

A smile spread across Florence's face. She looked around the empty office and laughed out loud. Why hadn't she seen it before?

Of course Simon wished it hadn't happened. But it had. He knew it had, and she knew it had. Why hadn't she recognized the power in that? Why had she let him think that she was disposable? Why had *she* thought she was disposable? Poor Simon had lost the upper hand the moment he put it on her leg in that grimy bar.

If he could publish Amanda's novel, he could publish her book too. She could *make* him publish her. She would gather all the stories she'd already written into a collection, and there was her manuscript. It wasn't ideal, getting published through blackmail, but nothing in life is pure. You don't throw away a winning lottery ticket just because it gets a little dirty in your wallet.

Florence hurried home. She stayed up until three in the morning making minor edits to the stories she'd written in Gainesville. Reading them for the first time since Amanda had convinced her of her own ignorance, she could still see their flaws, but now she saw something else that she'd missed before: the sheer joy she'd felt while writing them. Hours had passed like mere seconds.

She had originally wanted to be a writer so that everyone would know that Florence Darrow was a genius. But during those years in Gainesville, what she'd loved most was the rush of *not* being Florence Darrow. For brief periods of time, in front of her computer, she'd left that self behind and become anyone she wanted.

It was an amazing thought: If she did this one thing well

enough—inhabiting someone else's life—her *own* life would finally be worth something.

———

The next day was cold and sunny. At nine thirty, when she knew Simon would be in his office, but before his morning meetings started, Florence took the elevator upstairs. His assistant Emily was displeased when Florence asked to see him. She was sweet—she'd been the one who'd tried to include Florence and Lucy in the conversation that first night at the Red Lark—but like many assistants, she had pinned her worth to her boss's prestige. Still, she dutifully stuck her head inside his office, and when she reemerged told Florence she could go in.

"Well, Florence, to what do I owe the pleasure?" he asked, holding out his hands like a magician with nothing to hide.

Florence told him about her stories and handed him the pages she'd printed out that morning. "Since you're taking submissions from the bullpen..." she said. He set them carefully on the desk and patted them gently. He looked relieved that this was the reason for her visit.

"Splendid," he said. "I'll try to start them this weekend. I'm looking forward to it."

Florence stood in front of his desk for a moment, unsure what to do next. They smiled at each other in silence.

"Okay, then," she said, and walked out.

———

That night Florence couldn't sleep. She was going to be a published author!

All weekend, she was visited by visions of herself in a beautiful apartment with casement windows, antique rugs, and gourd-shaped vases. She was at a party and everyone wanted to talk to her. She wore black and her cheeks were flushed in the candlelight. There was jazz playing. It was winter. Florence loved winter; it was as far from Florida as you could get. She liked going out with three or four layers between her skin and the sharp air, seeing her breath hover in front of her. Your soul made manifest, Pastor Doug from her mother's church used to say, even though the temperature in Port Orange rarely dropped below fifty.

On Monday she went back up to Simon's office, but Emily told her he was in a meeting. She returned to her desk but couldn't concentrate. Finally, at 5 p.m., an email from Simon pinged in her inbox. Florence scanned it quickly.

Some good stuff here.
You've got talent, but your writing needs more life experience behind it.
Find *your* story.

Florence read it again, certain she'd missed something. But that was it. He'd said no.

10.

Florence sat on the windowsill in her bedroom with her bare feet dangling outside. It was past 2 a.m., and the streets below were quiet except for a dashed line of cars running across Thirty-First Avenue. She tapped her heels against the gritty bricks and scrolled through photos on her phone. There were dozens of Chloe and Tabitha in their school uniforms and a handful of Ingrid from the day she'd picked up the girls herself. Florence zoomed in on Ingrid's face. The wrinkles around her eyes were smile lines, she realized.

By what algorithmic glitch had she ever come out ahead of Ingrid Thorne, even for just a night? What could Florence Darrow give Simon that Ingrid could not? She was weak and talentless and pathetic. She was the polar opposite of Ingrid Thorne.

Well, maybe that was the point. Maybe Simon had wanted a break. He'd wanted oatmeal instead of steak, just for a night. His jaw was tired.

What a glutton, she thought.

She could just imagine Simon's life. Sleeping in ironed sheets. Collecting first editions. Counting out tips for his doormen at Christmas. Fucking Ingrid. Fucking Florence. Fucking whoever the fuck he wanted. Simon's life was just how Simon wanted it. So comfortable. So well-curated. So safe.

He'd never really thought that that night—or Florence herself—would change his life one bit. And they hadn't. He

still woke up in ironed sheets next to his lovely wife. So...
unthreatened. Unblemished.

She took a sip of the glass of bourbon balanced next to her. As
it went down, she felt it warm her insides organ by organ, like
someone walking through an old house, turning on the lights.

If I could just mark him a little bit, she thought. Nothing
drastic. Just a scratch on the lens of his glasses, an annoying
little reminder that wouldn't let him look at life as something
unmarred and pristine and safe anymore. A reminder to be
grateful for what he has.

And without another thought, she emailed him all the photos
of his family. She smiled as she typed the subject line: *Some good
stuff here.*

11.

Florence woke the next morning with the sense that the person she had been until the night before had simply toppled off, like a dead toenail forced to cede its position to a new one growing underneath. In its place was something foreign and denuded, something that had been building for months without her even realizing it, until the pressure was simply too great to contain it.

She felt energetic and hopeful, though she wasn't deluded. She knew that Simon wasn't just going to change his mind about publishing her stories. It was just as likely that he'd forward her email to HR. But, for the moment, the thought of his face while he read it was enough for her.

As soon as she got into the office, she learned which choice he'd made. A blinking light on her phone indicated a new voicemail. It was the head of HR, asking her to meet him in his office immediately. Three days later, a courier arrived at her apartment at seven in the morning to serve her papers. Not only had she been fired, Simon and Ingrid had taken out a restraining order against her.

She should have been embarrassed, or frightened—she had practically no savings and had cultivated no other job prospects—but all she felt was relief and exhilaration. In a moment of rashness, she had kicked open an escape hatch from the life she'd been leading. Now that she stood outside of it, she could see how small it had gotten.

In college, she'd read *The Immoralist* and felt a rush of sympathy with Michel's disdain for "fireside happiness"—comfort instead of glory. But a small, cozy life was exactly where she'd been heading. Agatha's life, basically. She wanted something much, much more than that. With one outsized action, she had regained the conviction that it was out there, waiting for her. She just had to reach for it.

She sent out her newly edited stories to dozens of literary agencies. She was sure that with an agent on her side, publishers would finally see her talent. Her faith in her own potential had been restored. What type of cruel God would give her the deep, unwavering drive to become a writer without the ability?

She saw a lawyer about suing for sexual harassment, but he didn't think a jury would find her sympathetic. "Probably not," she'd agreed, chuckling lightly, to his obvious discomfort.

She had $1,100 in her bank account, and she owed $800 in rent at the end of the month. Still, she didn't worry.

It was the first time since she was sixteen that she hadn't had a job. And the first time in her life that she felt free from her mother's scrutiny; Florence still hadn't told her that she'd been fired.

She couldn't believe how happy she was. She felt, for once, in league with the universe. The universe, she believed, would look out for her. Fate would intervene.

And then it did.

Two weeks after her firing, she received a voicemail from Greta Frost at Frost/Bollen, one of the best agencies in the business, asking her to call back.

Before dialing, Florence took several deep breaths to tamp down any evidence of desperation in her voice. Greta answered in a flat, husky tone that Florence tried to match as she explained who she was.

"Thanks for getting back to me," Greta said. "I was reaching out because one of our writers is looking for an assistant and someone floated your name."

Florence was confused. "This isn't about my stories?"

"Hmm?"

"The stories I sent in?"

"Oh. Yes, they were very compelling; it's part of the reason we're reaching out to you for this role."

"What role?"

"Before I tell you anything more, I am going to ask that you keep what I'm about to say confidential."

"Alright."

"Are you familiar with the author Maud Dixon?"

"Are you kidding?"

"I am not."

"You're asking me if I want to be Maud Dixon's assistant?"

"I'm asking whether you'd like to *apply* for the position of Maud Dixon's assistant."

"Of course."

"Wonderful," said Greta in a voice that sounded like it had never found anything wonderful in its life. "Before we move forward, I need to make you aware of several caveats. Due to the rather unusual circumstances—I'm referring of course to her anonymity—the role has several unique qualifiers. Should you get the job, you will be required to sign a nondisclosure agreement. Not only will you be prohibited from revealing Maud Dixon's real name, but you will also be prohibited from ever saying that you worked for her."

"Okay."

Greta paused before speaking again. "I want to make sure you realize what that means, Florence. For the rest of your life, you will have a gap in your resume that you will be legally prohibited from explaining."

Florence paused. The whole point of being an assistant to a writer was to use his or her connections to leverage your next job, or, if you were lucky, get published. Without that, you'd be better off working as a waiter, where at least you earned tips.

But it would take more than an NDA to make her turn down the opportunity to learn from a best-selling novelist and, perhaps more importantly, to develop a relationship with her very powerful agent. "That's fine," she said.

"Alright. Well, that brings me to number two. She doesn't live in Manhattan. I can't disclose where exactly she lives at this point in the process, but she has offered to provide lodging to the successful applicant."

"Fine."

"Fine?"

"Yes. Fine." Florence knew—she just *knew*—that fate had intervened to send her this job, that it was the next step toward assuming the mantle of greatness herself. Greta could have listed physical mutilation as a job requirement and Florence still would have wanted it.

"Alright then. Let me tell you where you can email your CV. Do you have a pen?"

Florence sent her resume and a cover letter to Greta's assistant that night. The next day, she received a call to schedule a video chat with Maud Dixon.

12.

Hello? Can you hear me?"

"I can hear you," said Florence. "But I can't see you." Her own face was clearly visible in a small box in the lower corner of her screen, but the space where Maud's face should have been was blank.

"Well, yes, that is rather the point of anonymity, isn't it?" said the voice on the other end.

"Oh." Florence blushed. "Right."

"What's that light behind you? I can barely see your face."

Florence looked behind her. Her desk lamp was on. She switched it off.

"That's better," said Maud. "What pretty hair you have."

Florence reached a hand up to her head as if to check that she still had the same mop of curls. "Oh, thanks."

"So, tell me a bit about yourself."

Florence gave her spiel about where she was from, the writers she'd studied in college, how she'd ended up in New York.

"But you don't work at Forrester anymore?" Maud asked.

"No. I decided I'd learned everything I could there."

"Okay, what else?"

"Um. I'm a writer. Or rather, I want to be a writer."

"That's all well and good but I don't need a writer. I need an assistant. Can you type? Are you willing to run tedious errands? Can you conduct research?"

"Of course. Yes. To all of it."

"Okay. What else should I know about you?"

Florence struggled to think of anything that would make her stand out. "Um. I was raised by a single parent, like you." Florence realized her mistake. "Or rather like the character in your book, sorry. Like the Maud character in your book."

"Alright. What else?"

"I'm not sure. I loved your book. I love your voice. It would be a real honor to learn from you. And to help in whatever way I can, obviously."

There was a pause.

"And you wouldn't mind moving out to the sticks?"

"Not at all. To be honest, I'm kind of over New York."

"You know, I once heard a psychologist remark that whenever a patient used a phrase like 'to be honest,' it was a sign that he was lying."

Florence gave an awkward laugh. "I'm not lying."

"No, of course not. Although now that I think about it, a liar would be perfect for this role, considering that they can't tell anyone who they work for."

Florence didn't know what game Maud was playing, but she knew she wasn't keeping up. "I assure you, I can keep a secret," she said.

"Well, you've given me a lot to think about. Greta will be in touch."

That was it?

"Thank you so much for this opportunity," she said, but Maud had already signed off.

Florence shut her laptop and buried her head in her hands.

———

She was still in bed at eleven the next morning when her phone rang. It was Greta, calling to tell Florence that the job was hers if she wanted it.

"Seriously?" she couldn't stop herself from asking.

"Yes. Why would I not be serious?"

"No, of course. Thank you so much. I accept."

"You don't want to think about it?"

"No thanks."

"Fine. Maud has proposed a start date of March eighteenth. Are you able to make that work? I realize it's quite soon."

Florence opened the calendar on her laptop. "Wait, next Monday?"

"You will come to learn that patience is not Maud's strong suit."

She shut the computer. "That's okay. I can make the eighteenth work."

They set up an appointment to sign the paperwork later in the week.

After she hung up, Florence looked around her room in amazement. Had that actually just happened?

She remembered something from *Mississippi Foxtrot* that Maud says to Ruby after the murder: "Everyone's born with different amounts of living in them, and you can tell when someone's run out. That man had none left. If I hadn't of done it, he'd of died anyway."

Florence wondered if that's what Maud Dixon had seen in her: *life*. The will to *really live,* at any cost. That, ultimately, is what her stint at Forrester had left her with: a deep fear of insignificance and the understanding that one could slip into a flimsy, aimless life without even realizing it.

Just then her phone buzzed with a text from her mother: "I gave your number to Keith today. He has a gr8 idea for a book!!!"

A moment later it buzzed again: "Two words: Dragon. Catheter."

Florence frowned.

A third message came in: "Catcher!!! Not catheter."

Florence turned off her phone.

PART II

13.

Florence stood on the platform at the Hudson train station and watched her train tear away with more force and violence than she'd given it credit for. A scattering of leaves and food wrappers surged up in its wake then settled back down with a sigh. Florence tucked her chin into her scarf. It was colder here than it had been in the city.

Shielding her eyes from the bright, early-spring sun, she saw a wall of dark clouds mounting in the distance. Rain. She hoisted her duffel bag onto her shoulder and staggered briefly under its weight. It contained everything she owned, minus the furniture. She'd tried to sell her mattress and desk on Craigslist, but she'd only managed to offload them after reducing the price to zero.

Florence joined the surge of departing passengers streaming toward the parking lot, which was where she'd agreed to meet Helen.

Helen. That was Maud Dixon's real name: Helen Wilcox. Not a man, it turned out. A woman with, as far as Florence could discern, no publication history, no presence on the Internet, no traces of existence whatsoever. Unless she was a prodigiously talented teen gymnast from La Jolla, California.

The week before, Florence had met Greta Frost at the Frost/Bollen office in a gleaming Midtown high-rise. Greta was an imposing woman in her late sixties with a gray bob, thick-framed glasses, and impeccable posture. She'd watched silently as Florence signed a W-9, an employment contract, and a non-disclosure agreement.

"So how many people know who Maud Dixon is?" Florence asked when Greta stood up, signaling the end of the meeting.

Greta pointed a knobby finger at her own chest. "One." She turned the finger on Florence. "Two."

Florence was taken aback. "You're the only person who's known all this time?"

"As far as I am aware."

"How is that possible?"

Greta smiled coolly. "I'm very good at keeping secrets."

"What about her editor?"

"They mostly email. Deborah just calls her Maud." Greta paused. "In the spirit of honesty I'll admit that I can't for the life of me fathom why she decided to let you, a perfect stranger, in on the secret. I tried to talk her out of it. It seems like a wildly ill-conceived plan."

Florence wasn't sure how to respond. "I won't tell anyone."

"I should hope not. You just signed a legally binding document to that effect."

"Right."

Despite Greta's coolness, Florence had walked out of the Frost/Bollen office that day feeling heady with excitement. She had always been uncommonly secretive—her mother's exuberance had trained her early to build dark rooms within herself where she could be alone and free of scrutiny—but she was rarely invited into anyone else's secret. It gave her an unfamiliar—and intoxicating—sense of power. By its nature, every secret contains the power to destroy something. Simon could attest to that.

Florence looked out into the parking lot. The sun was behind her, and its glare reflected off the field of chrome in a thousand blinding bursts. All the cars looked dark and empty. Beyond the lot were warehouses and abandoned buildings instead of the picturesque town she'd expected.

Presently the driver's-side door of a beaten-up green Range Rover swung open and a woman stepped halfway out, leaving one foot inside. She had short blond hair and a long, bony nose with a jarring bump on the bridge. It was a nose no one would ever have called cute, even on a baby. Above it perched two frown lines between her eyebrows like a quotation mark. She wore a heavy wool fisherman's sweater over jeans and an unexpected swipe of bright-red lipstick.

Helen shielded her eyes with one hand, dropping a shadow across her face. With the other she waved at Florence. Florence waved back and walked toward the car.

"Hello, Florence," Helen said, extending a long, cold hand.

Florence smiled. "Nice to meet you."

"Likewise. Hop in."

Helen rotated her body in the driver's seat and watched Florence shut the door and draw the seat belt across her chest. Florence smiled nervously.

"How old are you?" Helen finally asked.

"Twenty-six."

"You look younger." It sounded like an accusation.

"I get that a lot."

"Lucky girl." Helen sat looking at her for another moment, then abruptly shifted the gear into reverse and pulled out.

Florence turned her face toward the passenger window and said nothing. The intensity of Helen's gaze had unsettled her. Helen revved the engine, and the tumbledown buildings abruptly gave way to a narrow two-lane highway.

"It's about a ten-minute drive," Helen said.

Florence had looked it up beforehand; Google had estimated that it would take almost twice that long, but she understood the discrepancy when she saw how fast Helen drove.

They turned right toward the bridge spanning the Hudson River. Florence noticed a sign for an "escort waiting area" but resisted the urge to make a joke. She could already tell that the woman sitting next to her would not find it funny.

As they crossed the Rip Van Winkle Bridge, Florence looked down and saw the train tracks on which she'd just arrived skirting the river's edge.

"Cairo's not really in the Hudson Valley," Helen went on, "though the real estate agents like to claim it is. It's more like the Catskills."

She pronounced it *Cay-ro*, not like the city in Egypt. Florence was glad she hadn't said it first. She stole another glance toward the driver's seat. Helen was smoking a cigarette and tapping two fingers on the steering wheel in time to a Lucinda Williams song.

Florence looked out her own window and frowned as they passed a junkyard. She had expected someplace more charming. A few minutes later, they passed a billboard announcing YOUR FUTURE HOMES towering over a dozen cheap, prefab houses raised on cinderblocks. It reminded Florence of Florida more than anything else she'd seen in New York so far.

"What brought you out here?" Florence asked.

"The solitude," Helen answered without elaborating.

Florence tried to think of something else to say, but her mind was blank. Her early comments seemed so weighted—it would signal something definitive about her character and determine whether or not Helen would respect her. She couldn't settle on the right tone, the right topic. She'd thought about telling her how much *Mississippi Foxtrot* had meant to her, but the words sounded trite and hollow when she rehearsed them in her head. Helen, for her part, seemed content to continue in silence.

Soon the clouds crossed the sky, blotting out the sun, and the light took on a jaundiced tint. Florence watched a flock of blackbirds descend on a single tree like a net thrown over it. A few fat drops splattered on the windshield as Helen exited the highway and took a series of turns that led them to an unevenly paved street called Crestbill Road. Florence recognized the name from the address Greta had sent her a few days before.

"It won't last long," Helen said as she flicked on the wind-shield wipers. "These spring storms come on strong but soon they get bored and move on." She added with a glance at Florence: "Perhaps not unlike writers' assistants."

"Oh, I don't plan on moving on anytime soon," Florence assured her.

"So where did you tell people you were going?"

"What do you mean?"

"Since you couldn't tell anyone about this job. And I trust that you didn't."

"Oh. I didn't really tell anyone anything."

Helen raised her eyebrows without taking her eyes off the road. "No? What about your family?"

"Well, it's just my mom. And she thinks I still work at the publishing house."

"You didn't tell her that you left?"

Florence shrugged. She didn't want to say anything that would hint at the circumstances of her departure from Forrester.

Helen pressed on: "You're not close, then?"

"Not really. She's—. I don't know. We're just very different."

"How so?"

No one had ever asked Florence to so starkly define her relationship with her mother, and she struggled to put it into words.

She finally said, "You know how Trump's always talking about winners and losers?"

Helen nodded.

"That's the way my mother is too. She's constantly cataloguing the world according to this very concrete hierarchical structure that she has built in her mind, and she has very specific ideas of where I should slot into it. Her whole investment in parent-hood has been about getting me up to a high-enough rung, and she gets upset when she thinks I'm sabotaging that effort. She doesn't understand that we just catalogue the world in very different ways."

Helen said nothing.

"She also voted for Trump," Florence added with an uneasy laugh. "In case that wasn't clear."

"And you didn't, I take it?"

"*Me?* God, no. Are you serious?"

Helen shrugged. "How would I know?"

"I'm not a sociopath."

"Not everyone who voted for Trump is a sociopath."

Florence had just spent two years surrounded by people who spent a lot of energy arguing precisely the opposite point.

"What liberals don't seem to understand," Helen went on, "is that rational, intelligent people are capable of separating his personal shortcomings from his policies. I mean, nobody's voting for him to be their best friend."

"So you . . . " Florence could hardly believe she was asking the question. Novelists don't vote for Trump! "So you . . . you voted for him?" she asked as mildly as she could.

"Lord, no. I never vote."

"Oh."

After a few more minutes Helen took a left onto a long driveway marked PRIVATE. It meandered through thick woods for nearly a quarter of a mile before depositing them outside a small stone house with green shutters. On its roof, a spindly copper weathervane jerked in the wind. It had nothing in common with the low, ugly houses they'd passed on the drive.

"It was built in 1848," Helen said, following Florence's gaze. "I bought it two years ago, after the royalties from *Mississippi Foxtrot* started to come in."

The rain was in a frenzy now, battering the rosebushes lining the front porch. Helen told Florence to leave her bag in the trunk, and they both dashed for the door.

On the covered porch, Florence dried her face on her sleeve while Helen jammed a key into the old lock. The door swung open with a creak and Florence found herself awash in brightness. The walls, the ceiling, the floors—the entire interior of the house as far as she could see—had been painted a rich, milky white.

They were in a small foyer. An old wooden table was pushed up against one wall and scattered with keys and mail. Two pairs of muddy boots sat underneath. Through a door on the left, Florence spotted a dining room. Helen led her the other way, into the living room, where she threw her purse down on a large linen-covered sofa. A full ashtray balanced nervously on its arm. In front of it sat a square ottoman piled with books and a brick fireplace where embers smoked desultorily. Helen tossed another log in, and a cloud of ash and sparks shot up in protest.

"Well, here it is," she said.

Florence's mother liked to imagine a life of diamonds and gilt for her daughter. But this, *this*, was the life Florence wanted. A blue-and-white teacup stuffed with clementine peels. A tangle of white ranunculus in a ceramic pitcher on the windowsill. Amanda had once put a vase of those same flowers on her desk at work. The whole place looked like a painting by Vermeer. And it was *cold*. Chilly gusts rattled the windows in their frames. Someone had told Florence once that glass was actually a liquid that settled slowly, over eons; that was why in old houses the windows were always thicker at the bottom than at the top. Was that true? Florence didn't care. In the same way she couldn't understand why people were so determined to expose Maud Dixon's identity, she couldn't understand why they needed to pin things down, turn poetry into fact. Wasn't poetry better? Why would you turn something beautiful into something quotidian?

Helen led Florence on a tour around the rest of the main floor: a dining room with a long wooden table obscured by books and a laptop, a small guest room with two twin beds covered in faded quilts, and a kitchen with a massive old farm-house sink. Helen picked up the pot from a battered Mr. Coffee on the counter and poured out two mugs.

"Upstairs is just my bedroom and office and a couple of spare rooms," she said, gesturing above her head. She set one of the cups of coffee down on the counter in front of Florence without offering milk or sugar. "You'll be staying in the carriage house out back. It's nothing fancy but I hope it will suit."

Florence said she was sure it would. She took a sip and watched the rain drip down the windows. All she could see beyond them was a gray-green field with some blurred brown smudges.

When the rain subsided, Florence went to collect her bag from the trunk of the car and met Helen behind the main house. They followed a path of gray slate slabs embedded in moss.

"The person who lived here before me was an arborist," Helen said. "He crossbred a lot of these trees. So I have some odd specimens out here—half one thing, half another."

Florence looked at one of the trees that Helen was gesturing toward. It didn't look like a mixed breed but rather like two trees grafted violently together.

Helen continued the tour. "Over there is a pretty modest vegetable garden, which I do my best not to destroy, and behind those pines is my deep, dark secret"—she turned to Florence with a mock grimace—"*the compost pile*. And before you say anything, yes, I realize I've become the full-on cliché of the Hudson Valley hippie."

Florence smiled, as she knew she was supposed to.

They reached the carriage house, which lay about a hundred yards from the main structure. Behind it, a dark line of trees marked the beginning of the woods. The front door stuck when Helen tried to open it but she popped it loose with a swift kick to the bottom corner. "I'll do something about that," she said. And then a moment later: "Actually, I probably won't, but there are worse things in life than a sticky door, right?"

Florence nodded and followed Helen inside to a bright, open space with a sitting area and a small kitchenette tucked away in one corner. A pink rotary phone was mounted on the wall next to the fridge. A peek into the bathroom revealed a deep, old-fashioned tub. Wooden steps, closer to ladder than stairway, led up to a lofted bedroom. She loved it. She'd never had her own space before—her own *building*—and this one felt right in a way no place she'd lived before ever had.

Helen left her to get settled and told her to come over for a drink before dinner around seven. Florence immediately started unpacking. She had always been orderly. She couldn't go to sleep unless her shoes were lined up properly in the closet.

It took only twenty minutes to put away all of her belongings and stow the duffel bag under the bed. She sat on the couch and opened up the brand-new notebook she'd bought that morning at Grand Central. It was for the novel she planned to write while she lived up here. She needed a bigger canvas than short stories, she'd decided. She stared at the blank page for a few minutes. She wrote the date and "Cairo, NY" at the top. After a few more minutes, she shut the notebook with an exasperated sigh.

Oh well, she'd have more to say soon. Having met Helen Wilcox, she doubted that life would be dull.

She opened a book instead—she'd been slogging her way through Proust for a month, pretending to enjoy it more than she actually did—but soon she shut that too. She felt restless and at loose ends. She thought about calling Lucy, but she hadn't returned any of Lucy's messages since she'd been fired. Florence hadn't wanted her sympathy; she preferred the balance of power to stay as it had been, firmly weighted in her own favor. Besides, she wouldn't even have been able to brag about her new job.

If she'd been back in the city, she might have gone for a walk or settled for chatting with Brianna and Sarah in the living room. Now she realized how truly isolated she was. She closed her eyes and listened. There was only silence. She was utterly alone.

14.

At five to seven, Florence knocked tentatively on the front door of the main house. Hearing no response, she opened it and went in. Music was playing from the kitchen, so she followed the sound.

Helen was wearing an apron over her clothes, drinking a glass of wine, smoking a cigarette, chopping tomatoes, and stopping every now and then to conduct the orchestra with her knife.

"Hi," said Florence.

Helen turned around and sang *"La tua sorte è già compitaaaaaaa"* in a husky alto, drawing out the last syllable. She finished with a swig of wine. "Do you like opera?"

"Um, I'm not sure." Pretty much the only time Florence listened to classical music was during car commercials.

"Oh, it's divine. *Divine!* I saw *Il Trovatore* at the Met last year. I'll take you the next time I go. Here, have some wine."

"Thank you." Florence took the proffered glass and tried to hide her delight at the thought of attending an opera with Maud Dixon. "Can I help with dinner?"

"No, I'm a total control freak in the kitchen." She held up a small cherry tomato between her thumb and index finger. "Do you know what they call these in France? Pigeon hearts. Isn't that fabulous? Isn't that just what they are? You'll never be able to look at a pigeon again without thinking of his little tomato-shaped heart beating away inside his puffed-up chest."

"My mother sometimes calls people pigeon-hearted," said Florence. "People she thinks are weak."

"Pigeon-hearted," Helen repeated, gesturing at her with the tip of the knife. "That's good. I may have to steal that. Remind me, are you a Southerner? All the best sayings come from the South."

"Florida. We're neither here nor there."

"That's alright. Here and there are overrated."

"I suppose."

Helen stopped chopping to say, "It's true. There's real power in being an outsider. You see things more clearly." Something in the oven snapped loudly enough to make Florence jump. "Chicken. You're not a vegetarian, are you?" Florence shook her head. "Thank the lord," Helen pronounced and resumed her quick thrusts of the knife.

"So you're settling in all right?"

"Yes, thank you."

"Good. We'll get started on work tomorrow."

"How is the new book coming?"

A shadow crossed Helen's face. "It's coming," she said vaguely.

"Is it a sequel to *Mississippi Foxtrot*?"

"No. Maud and Ruby's story is officially *finis*." She made a slicing motion at her neck.

"Oh." Florence felt her excitement deflate a little. Like most fans of *Mississippi Foxtrot*, she wanted to know what happened next. "People are going to be disappointed."

"Yes, my agent reminds me of that daily. Apparently I *owe* my readers an ending." Helen rolled her eyes.

"You don't agree?"

Helen laughed. "Owe them! Of course not. I don't owe anyone squat. She just wants me to write a sequel because it would make more money."

She pulled the chicken out of the oven and carved it expertly, placing a breast and a leg on each plate. These she set on the kitchen table with the bottle of wine and a bowl of salad. She gestured at Florence to sit.

Florence asked when she'd get to read the new work.

"Soon. Maybe tomorrow. If you can manage to decipher my godawful Mississippi-public-school chicken scratch." She wrote her first drafts longhand on yellow legal pads, she said. It would be one of Florence's jobs to type them up.

"I'm about a quarter of the way into my first draft. As soon as I started writing I realized that it was going to require a lot more research than the first one. That's where you'll come in. It takes place in Morocco. Have you been?"

Florence shook her head.

"There are a few authors who've written about it very well. Tahar Ben Jelloun and Paul Bowles come to mind."

"I'm sorry, I haven't read them. I can, though."

"No need to apologize. I'll give you a list of books that would be helpful for you to read. Let's start with nonfiction, actually. Forget Ben Jelloun and Bowles—they may be more of a distraction than anything else."

"What's it about?"

"I'm still working out a lot of the details. But it follows an American woman who drops everything and moves to Morocco to work for an old childhood friend. From there, of course, disaster ensues." Helen smiled.

Florence, more relaxed from the wine, saw her opening. "I wanted to tell you that I love the way you write about female relationships." That had been the line she'd been rehearsing in the car from the train station. Immediately after she said it, she worried that it sounded just as trite as she'd feared it would then.

"Well, it's only because men don't interest me very much," Helen laughed.

A weighted silence fell on them.

"I don't mean that I'm a lesbian," Helen clarified. "I sleep with men. Occasionally. But I don't care to have relationships with them. I've never found one . . . fascinating in the way I find women fascinating. Men are blunt objects. There's no nuance there.

"I was dating a man once," she went on, "and we went away for the weekend. At the hotel, I realized he didn't have a clue how to tip—not the bellman, not the housekeeper, not the concierge. He kept asking me how much to give, when should he give it, who should he give it to. I found it so off-putting. I realized then that I could never be with a man who didn't know how to tip. But then, later, I realized I couldn't be with a man who tipped easily and smoothly either. What smugness. What satisfaction. So who does that leave?"

"Maybe there's some middle category of tipper," offered Florence.

"No. There's no middle category of anything."

Florence could think of countless middle categories—the whole world felt like a middle category to her—but she left it.

"Middle categories are for middling people," said Helen, as if she could read Florence's mind.

Soon only the greasy bones and ligaments remained on their plates. But they stayed at the table drinking the last of the wine. Their conversation had lost some of its early stiltedness. Outside, crickets screeched in a pulsing drone.

"Doesn't it bother you that no one knows it's you?" Florence asked when she could no longer resist. "That you wrote *Mississippi Foxtrot*?"

"Bene vixit, bene qui latuit."

Florence nodded then said, "Sorry, what?"

"It's Latin, from Ovid. It means, 'He lives well who is well hidden.' "

"Oh."

Helen laughed at Florence's confusion. "Don't mind me; I'm being needlessly cryptic. The short answer is *no*, I don't mind that nobody knows I wrote *Mississippi Foxtrot*."

"Why did you do it, though? What's the point of all the secrecy?"

Helen lit a cigarette and turned her gaze toward the window. "Does it sound stupid? Not to me. But I was young. I wrote *Foxtrot* when I was in my mid-twenties. Your age, I guess."

Florence couldn't help interrupting: "So, wait. You're only...thirty-three? Thirty-four?"

Helen laughed. "So much for social niceties. I'm thirty-two."

Florence was surprised; Helen seemed older to her. Though now that she thought about it, there was a lot in *Mississippi Foxtrot* that had reminded her of her own adolescence. Some of Maud and Ruby's classmates had had cell phones; Bush had been president. This realization brought with it a sinking sense of her own inadequacy; she wasn't even close to having a story to tell, much less a best-seller. Maybe that's why Helen seemed older; she'd accomplished so much more.

"Anyway," Helen went on, oblivious to Florence's distress, "I was living in Jackson then, working as a proofreader for a textbook company. I wrote it almost entirely during my lunch breaks. The crazy thing is, all I wanted was to move to New York and become a famous writer...just not for *that* book. That book I had to write. I had to get it out of me so I could move on." She turned back to Florence. "Do you know how you get rid of a tapeworm?"

Florence shook her head.

"You go into a dark room, pitch black, and you hold a cup of warm milk in front of your face. Then the worm pokes its head out of your nose, and you have to grab it quick as you can and just start pulling. That's what the process of writing *Mississippi Foxtrot* was like for me: violent, painful, grotesque. But, ultimately, healing.

"I didn't want to arrive in New York associated with that book. I wanted a clean slate. I wanted to go somewhere where no one knew anything about Hindsville, Mississippi."

Florence noted the name of the town.

"I thought I could just write that one book under a pseudonym and then move to New York and make my brilliant debut as Helen Wilcox. I had grand plans to write this massive, multigenerational novel about a family crossing the American West in the early nineteenth century. But no matter how many ways I tried to start it, I always got stuck. I couldn't escape my own story."

Helen pushed out her chair roughly and went to a cabinet near the fridge. She pulled out a bottle of whiskey and two glasses. She poured them sloppily, splashing a bit on the counter, and handed one to Florence.

"Anyway," she went on, "I never foresaw the success of *Mississippi Foxtrot*. I couldn't imagine *one* person being interested in that dusty little corner of the country, much less millions. I sent it out to agents mainly to get it out of my sight, so I could finally be rid of it. When I got a call back from Greta Frost, you could have knocked me over with a feather.

"Later, after it really started to sell, Greta got me a ridiculous advance for a second book, on the basis of absolutely nothing: a one-page plot summary that I can barely remember. That was over a year ago now. And of course they're paying for the Maud Dixon name. That's who the audience belongs to. It would ruin everything if I came forward and admitted who I was. People think they want the truth but they're always disappointed. It is invariably less interesting than the mystery. Believe me, I've tried to convince Greta to let me do it under my own name, but she's right; it just doesn't make sense. I'm stuck with Maud Dixon for the rest of my life."

"Where did the name come from, anyway?" Florence asked.

Helen tapped the ash from her cigarette onto her plate. "The Tennyson poem, *Maud*. Have you read it?"

Florence shook her head.

"You should. It's wonderful. It's a love story with all these strange, dark undertones. He describes Maud as 'faultily faultless, icily regular, splendidly null.' I just love that."

"And Dixon?"

"My college roommate. It was her middle name." Helen shrugged. "Couldn't stand her, actually."

"And did you keep in touch with Ruby after you left home?"

Helen smiled a wide, closed-lip smile that Florence would come to recognize well. "Florence, it's just a novel."

———

It was past eleven by the time they finished their drinks. Helen waved off Florence's offer to do the dishes. "Go get some sleep," she said, stubbing out a lipstick-smeared cigarette.

"Likewise," Florence responded, pleased she'd found an opportunity to use the word. She'd admired its air of sophistication when Helen had used it at the train station.

Florence walked to the carriage house slightly drunk. Halfway there, in the still darkness, she looked back. Every window was lit up, and Helen stood at the sink in the kitchen. She had turned the music back on and was conducting again.

Florence smiled. Helen was everything she wanted to be, and she'd been handed the opportunity to study her at close range. She would not, she swore to herself gravely, waste it.

15.

Florence woke up at six. She showered and took a short walk in the woods behind the house as the sun rose. When she got back to the cottage, she discovered a new voicemail from her mother, which she ignored. At nine, she went over to the main house and found Helen reading the paper at the dining room table.

"There's coffee in the pot," Helen said without looking up.

When Florence returned with a mug, Helen pushed out the chair opposite her with her foot.

"Alright," she said. "Baptism by fire: I have over a hundred unread emails to respond to, and what that actually means is that *you* have over a hundred unread emails to respond to."

Most of them, she explained, were from Frost/Bollen—either from Greta or her assistant, Lauren. They were requests for interviews and appearances, responses to readers' letters, and so on. Helen opened the laptop on the table and signed into the account maud.dixon.writer@gmail.com. Then she swiveled the keyboard toward Florence. "Here, we'll do the first one together."

Florence opened the most recent email. It was from Greta:

Hi M.

How's it working out with Florence?

Florence laughed uncomfortably. "Maybe a different one?" she suggested.

"You handle my correspondence now," Helen said. "*All* of it."

"Okay…" Florence lifted her fingers to the keyboard, then stopped and said, "Wait. She called you M. Is that for Maud?"

"Yes. We didn't want anything hackable linking my real name to Maud Dixon's agent. You can never be too careful. Anyway, it's second nature by now."

"But I should sign my emails from me, right?"

"Actually, I hadn't thought about it. Yes, I suppose that's fine. The important thing is just make sure to never use my real name. Now write."

Florence typed a reply in the same dispassionately professional tone Agatha had taught her to use:

Hi Greta,
Things are working out well. Thank you for your concern.
Best,
Florence

She turned questioningly to Helen, who read it and rolled her eyes. She pulled the computer back toward herself and replaced what Florence had written with:

We're getting along like a house on fire.

She hit Send and turned back to Florence. "Something you should know: I deplore moderation."

Beyond Helen's correspondence, Florence's duties would include assisting with research and typing up Helen's rough drafts. Helen handed her a stack of pages covered in large, loopy scrawl. "I've been saving it up for you," she said. "I find typing painfully tedious."

"No problem," Florence said. She put the pages next to the

laptop and tried not to look at them while Helen continued to talk.

There was a woman who came in once a week to clean and buy the groceries, but the rest of the day-to-day management of her life would fall to Florence. That included paying Helen's bills—credit cards, phone, Internet, mortgage, everything, as far as Florence could tell. Helen handed over her passwords and bank accounts with a nonchalance that suggested either profound naivete or profound trust. Florence chose to assume the latter.

"I dislike entangling myself with the wider world," Helen explained. "I'd be a true hermit if it weren't so damn inconvenient. Besides, I'm hopeless with logistics. I once booked a flight not only on the wrong day but in the wrong *year*. I'll leave the small print to small minds."

Florence glanced at her to see if she realized the insult she'd just volleyed at her new assistant, but Helen went on with the lesson.

She had another Gmail account in her real name, which she showed Florence how to access in order to manage all her various online accounts. Florence took a quick glance through the inbox and saw mostly Amazon order confirmations, notifications from her bank, and daily digests from the *New York Times*.

At ten, Helen took her coffee upstairs to her office and told Florence to start on the emails for Maud Dixon. Florence opened the most recent unread message. It had been sent by Greta the morning before.

Hi M.

Deborah is on my case again about book #2. What can I tell her? We really should give them a show of good faith. A first chapter. A more detailed outline. A timeline. *Something*. Let's discuss. Call me.

G.

Florence glanced around guiltily. She had a feeling this was not an email Helen wanted her to see. She closed it quickly and marked it as unread. The next one was from Greta too, but it was more in line with what Helen had told her to expect.

M—

NPR wants you on Fresh Air. You can do it from up there. We can try that voice modulator they use. What do you think? It would be great to keep Maud Dixon's name fresh in people's minds—especially since the second book is going to come out such a long time after the first. Let me know. G.

Florence thought Greta made a good point, but Helen had been clear: The answer was always no. She tried to channel Helen's voice and forget everything she'd ever learned about professional courtesy. She wrote:

Greta,
The no-interview rule stands, no exceptions.

She hovered the mouse over the Send button but didn't click it. She couldn't do it. She couldn't send that email to Greta Frost. She erased what she'd written and typed instead:

Hi Greta,
Unfortunately, Helen won't do the interview with NPR. I hope you understand.
Best,
Florence

She pressed Send. By the time she was redirected back to the inbox, Greta's previous email—about Helen's second book—was gone. Florence glanced up at the ceiling. Helen must have just erased it. Did she have another laptop up there?

For the next several hours, Florence waded through the backlogged Maud Dixon emails. She allowed herself just one diversion: logging in to Helen's Morgan Stanley account. Her eyes widened when she saw the balance: just over three million dollars. She'd known that *Mississippi Foxtrot* must have made somewhere in that range, particularly after the TV rights were sold, but it was different seeing the actual number, made so concrete by the insignificant tally of cents tacked on the end. Florence tried to think about what she would do with that much money, but her imagination failed her. All she could think was that she'd do just what Helen had done: buy a house, retreat from the world, grow tomatoes.

By two in the afternoon, Helen had still not come back downstairs. Florence made herself a sandwich with some bread and turkey she found in the fridge, finished the coffee, and cleaned the pot. When she returned to her makeshift desk at the dining table, she finally allowed herself to pick up Helen's handwritten pages.

Here it was. The next Maud Dixon novel.

At the top of the first page Helen had scrawled what Florence assumed was a chapter title: "The Age of Monsters." She scanned the rest of it, and realized at once that she could barely read Helen's handwriting. She squinted at the first sentence:

In the night the wind something and the weather something, bringing a something sky and . . .

She flipped to the next page. It, too, was rife with words she couldn't decipher:

She listened, wondering if it had been a something noise which had something her back from sleep: she heard only the endless sound of the sea against the rocks, so far below that it was like a something being held to the something. She opened her eyes.

The room was bathed in brilliant moonlight. It came in from the something, *but on all sides she could see the glow of the* something *night sky out over the water. Slipping out of bed, she went and tried the door in the* something, *just to be positive it was locked.*

Florence put down the manuscript and bit her fingernail. She wasn't sure what to do. Transcribing this would be like doing a Mad Libs. She stood up and walked to the bottom of the stairway. Helen hadn't invited her to the second floor yet. She went up halfway so that she could see into the hallway. All the doors were open except one. She guessed that was Helen's office. She climbed the rest of the way up, cringing at every creak, and listened at the door. She heard nothing, until all of a sudden a crash sounded from within. Florence jumped. It sounded like something heavy had been hurled across the room. She stood for another moment or two, then turned around and started creeping back toward the stairs.

Just then the office door flew open, and Helen filled the frame. She looked furious.

"What are you doing up here?"

"I'm sorry. I—"

"I didn't think I needed to articulate this, but apparently I do: Do not disturb me while I'm working. I find it very hard to regain focus."

"I'm so sorry, I'll just go back downstairs."

"Well, you've already interrupted so you might as well just tell me what you want."

"It's your writing," Florence said, holding out the stack of paper. "I'm having a little bit of trouble reading some of it."

"Oh, for heaven's sake." Helen snatched the pages impatiently.

While Helen looked at them, Florence peeked into the room behind her and saw crowded built-in bookshelves and a worn Turkish-looking carpet.

"What can't you understand?"

Florence pointed. "There, and there. And there."

"That says *luminous*. And that—that's just an ampersand."

"And there?" Florence asked, pointing to another scribble.

Helen brought the page closer to her face and angled it toward the light. After a moment she exhaled and handed the sheaf of pages back to Florence. "I don't know, Florence. Just try to figure it out on your own. Write down your best guess and underline it or something. I'll figure it out later."

Helen shut the door crisply on Florence's repeated apologies.

Florence trudged back down to the dining room feeling foolish. She looked at the last word Helen hadn't been able to read. It started with a *P;* that was all she could glean. She reread the sentence:

When she heard the word "forceful" being used in connection with herself, even though she knew it was perfectly true and not intended as derogation, she immediately felt like some rather ungraceful something animal, and the sensation did not please her.

Florence tapped her lower lip with her finger. *Predatory?* Yes. She nodded definitively. She typed it into the manuscript and underlined it, praying that she'd picked the right word—not just because she was eager for Helen's approval, but because, she realized, she was slightly terrified of her.

16.

Over the next few days, Helen and Florence fell into a rhythm. Florence went over to the main house around nine or ten. She and Helen usually had a cup of coffee together while they went over the plan for the day. Otherwise, Florence would find a note on the kitchen counter listing her projects. There was usually some typing to be done, along with keeping up with Helen's correspondence. Helen also wanted Florence to read several books on Moroccan history and culture and write up a summary of her findings.

Twice Helen lent Florence her car so she could drive to Hudson and pick up a book she needed or a few bottles of the Châteauneuf-du-Pape she liked to drink. Each time she told Florence to take her time and enjoy herself.

Florence discovered that Hudson proper was actually just as charming and picturesque as she'd imagined; it wasn't until you crossed the bridge heading back to Cairo that things started to go to seed. The town's main street, which they'd bypassed on the drive from the train station, was filled with bakeries, home-decor shops, and sunny restaurants.

On her second visit, however, Florence started to see something artificial in the town's charm. It seemed designed for people who wanted to experience country living without feeling like they'd left Brooklyn. Plus, it wasn't like she could afford the hand-dyed Shibori tablecloths and reclaimed driftwood *objets d'art* the boutiques sold. She could understand why Helen had settled in less fashionable Cairo.

Helen rarely went into town herself. Most days, she didn't leave the property. It wasn't until Florence's second week on the job that she found herself alone in the house for the first time. Helen hadn't mentioned where she was going, just that she'd be gone for several hours.

A few minutes after the car pulled away, Florence did something she'd wanted to do since she arrived: She crept up to the second floor and into Helen's study. The sun streamed in from windows on two sides of the room, illuminating dust motes in the air. Florence sat down in Helen's seat. The chair was made of ribbed, caramel-colored leather that had been worn down by use. She ran her hands across the desk's scarred wood. She opened the top drawer and found a laptop in it. She glanced at the door, then took it out and opened it. The screen came to life but a dialog box appeared asking for a password. Florence quickly shut it and put it back where she'd found it. She leaned back in the chair and closed her eyes. She pretended that this was her study. That all she ever had to do was to sit in this beautiful room and write whatever she wanted.

Suddenly she heard a bang downstairs and bolted from the room, sending the chair careening across the floor. Downstairs, she realized that it had only been the wind blowing the kitchen door shut. She hurried back up to make sure she left the room exactly as she'd found it.

This aborted foray upstairs did nothing to allay her curiosity. If anything, it emboldened her. She sifted through Helen's emails, looking for something personal. She finally spotted, three pages in, a message with the subject line *Turandot?* She opened it.

Helen,

What do you think about Turandot on April 5th? I know we

just saw it last year, but this production is supposed to be spectacular. Let me know.
Sylvie

Florence Googled the name in the email address: Sylvie Daloud. She was an architect who lived in New York. Florence searched the inbox for more emails from her. There were dozens, nearly all of them concerning opera. Helen's replies were just as polite and formal as Sylvie's. So much for deploring moderation, Florence thought.

Florence had to skim through emails back until November before she found a personal email from someone other than Sylvie.

Helen!!! I hope this is actually you. I just ran into Daphne and she gave me your email address but said she hadn't used it in ages. How are you?? Married? Kids? Where are you living now? I'm still in Jackson, married to Tim. We've got two great girls, and we're waiting on a third. Let's just say Tim knows more about Disney princesses than he ever thought he would lol. Anyhoo! I just wanted to say hi. I still see the gang pretty regularly and we all realized we hadn't talked to you in forever. Do you ever come back to visit? We just built an extension on our house (don't ask me about it—I've barely recovered!) so there's a guestroom with your name on it...
Xoxo Tori

Florence searched the Sent folder. Helen had never responded, and Tori hadn't tried again. Florence thought it was little wonder that Helen hadn't wanted to keep in touch with someone who casually deployed "anyhoo!" in her correspondence.

She looked in Helen's search history and found a seemingly random collection of terms: Guerlain KissKiss Shaping Cream lip color in "Red Passion." How to replace a lost passport abroad.

Mississippi parole regulations. Someone named Lisa Blackford. A restaurant in a place called Semat, Morocco. Florence's own LinkedIn page and Instagram account. She flushed when she saw that. Florence was mortified at the thought of Helen looking through her Instagram account, which had barely thirty followers and featured mainly pictures of dogs she saw on the street and quotes from books she was reading.

But of course Helen had researched her before she'd hired her. Besides, Helen wasn't in a position to ridicule the size of Florence's social network; other than those emails from Sylvie and Tori, Helen didn't seem to have any friends at all. The landline at her house had only rung twice while Florence had been there. The first time it had been a telemarketer. The second time it had been Greta, and Helen had asked Florence to tell her she wasn't home.

A few days after Greta's failed attempt to reach Helen, she called Florence directly.

"I'm glad to hear you two are off to such a great start," she said.

"We are, thank you," Florence replied, still unsure why Greta had called on her cell phone.

"And I appreciate your slogging through all those old emails from my team. I know it's not exactly thrilling work, but it does need to get done."

"You're welcome," Florence said cautiously. Greta was treating her with a deference that had been entirely absent from their first meeting.

"So listen, I wanted to let you know that I read your stories, and I think you have a lot of potential. I don't think they're *quite* where they need to be yet, but we could work on them together, if you're interested."

We?

Greta went on, "As I'm sure you know, story collections—particularly by unknown writers—are incredibly difficult to sell, but that's not to say impossible."

"I know," Florence hurried to explain. "My plan is to write a novel. That's what I'm going to do up here while I'm working for Helen."

"Wonderful. Maybe you'd like to send me a draft when you have it."

"Really?"

"Absolutely. Call Lauren and set up a time to talk when you feel like you're ready. But listen, Florence, while I have you here, there's something you can do for me in return."

Florence frowned. What did *she* have to offer Greta Frost?

"I have no doubt that the novel Helen is working on is going to be brilliant, but she's being incredibly secretive about it and that is making it very difficult for me to do my job.

"I understand that this book is demanding more research than the first one, which is part of the reason she wanted an assistant. But she won't tell me how much research, or what kind or how long it's going to take or even *what* is being researched. I know next to nothing. I realize that Helen finds some parts of the author's job tedious—the typing, the interviews, the marketing—and for the most part I'm happy to leave her to the actual writing, but *someone* needs to take care of the other, less exciting details. Do you understand?"

"I think so . . ."

"What I'm saying is that I'd like to invite you to join me on the strategy side of things. I know you'll find it helpful for your own career in the future."

"The strategy side of things?"

"Basically what *we* can do to make the book a success, beyond the actual words on the page. Communicating with Helen's editor and various other stakeholders; coming up with the best timeline for submission and publication; putting together a marketing plan. For instance, it would be ideal if the second book were published around when the Mississippi Foxtrot mini-series premieres. But of course to do any of this, I need to actually know what the second book is about, and how far along she is in the process. That's where you come in."

Florence didn't say anything.

"Of course, I wouldn't ask you if it weren't in Helen's best interest," Greta said smoothly.

Florence stalled for time. "Well, I don't know much yet. I've only read a couple of chapters."

"That's okay. Why don't you just email me whatever you've typed up so far."

Florence chewed on her lip. "Umm. I'm not sure I feel comfortable doing that."

"Okay, forget that idea. We'll keep it casual. Can you tell me the gist?"

Florence lowered her voice. "Helen's upstairs right now. She could overhear."

"Ahh, I see." Greta paused. "How about this, why don't you just give me a ring tonight. We can talk about your novel too. This isn't just for Helen's benefit. I can't imagine you want to be a writer's assistant forever."

Florence wasn't a fool. She knew that Greta was playing her. But that didn't change the fact that Greta was right: In the grand scheme of things, Greta *could* do more for Florence than Helen could. And anyway, Greta and Helen were on the same side.

"I'm happy to help," she finally said.

"Wonderful. I knew you were a smart young woman. You know, you actually remind me a lot of Helen when we first met. Did she tell you about that?"

"She said she sent her manuscript to dozens of agents and she couldn't believe her luck when you took her on."

Greta let out a short bark of a laugh. "Yes, I imagine that is the story she'd tell. The truth is slightly more complicated. I initially wrote back to her and said her book was incredibly powerful and well told, but ultimately it was just too rough around the edges. I also told her that I didn't really take on this type of work; there were other agents who would be better suited to it. I think I even suggested a few names.

"A few weeks later, I heard my assistant, Rachel—this was before Lauren—arguing loudly with someone outside my office. I stepped out to investigate, and there was this steely-eyed woman with the strongest Southern accent I'd ever heard; I thought at first she was putting it on. This woman—Helen, obviously—kept saying she'd made an appointment and she wasn't leaving until I met with her.

"Rachel explained what had happened: Helen had phoned earlier in the week pretending to work for one of my well-known clients in order to make an appointment in that writer's name. Then she simply showed up as herself, convinced she'd be let in anyway.

"Well, I guess her confidence was warranted because I did ultimately invite her into my office. Mostly because I could tell that Rachel was starting to panic.

"Helen dropped her manuscript on my desk and told me she'd revised it based on my feedback, and she'd like me to read it again. Then she plopped down in a chair and said—I can still hear her twang—'I'll wait.'

"I didn't know whether to laugh or call security. Long story short, I eventually got her out of my office with a promise that I'd read it over the weekend, and I did, obviously, end up taking her on as a client. As you know, Helen can be quite . . . compelling. In fact, I see some of that same grit and ambition in you."

"Thanks," Florence said, unsure whether she was actually being complimented. She'd rather be known for her talent than her ambition.

"So listen, take another look through the manuscript this after-noon, and call me on my cell tonight. I'm always up late."

Florence said she would, feeling a mixture of elation and shame.

———

That evening, Florence struggled to give Greta answers that wouldn't disappoint. She'd only seen a portion of the work, and many of the sections weren't even in chronological order.

"I think she's probably written, like, sixty pages?" she said. "It's about a woman who travels to Morocco to work with a childhood friend. So far, not much has happened. I think something bad is going to happen though. The tone is very dark and foreboding. It feels like she's building to something, but I have no idea what. I don't think *she* even knows what it is yet. She gets really frustrated when she writes. I can hear her throwing stuff in her office and cursing."

"Well, Helen has never been what you would call placid."

"Few great writers are."

Greta paused. "Don't stroke her ego too much, Florence. It does her no favors." Then she seemed to check her tone. "How are you doing up there, by the way? Believe me, I know Helen can be a difficult person to work with. I can only imagine what she's like to live with, especially out there in the middle of nowhere."

"Actually," Florence said, "I love it."

She was telling the truth. The seclusion was a relief. She had grown up in an apartment whose door was constantly flying open or slamming shut. Her mother always had on the TV or the radio or both. And she was never quiet. She sang, she hummed, she talked to herself, she talked to Florence, she talked on the phone, she talked to the radio, to the TV, to her neighbors, to her frequent visitors. And what she talked about more than anything else was her daughter, her brilliant daughter.

Florence's sanctuary had been their small shared bathroom, which was covered in teal tiles and crowded with Vera's beauty products. Florence liked to take long baths in there. She would lie with her head underwater and her knees jutting up so she could relish the heavy, enveloping silence, shivering slightly with the beat of her heart.

Here, deep in the woods, there was silence all the time, except when Helen played music. But the opera didn't bother Florence the way her mother's radio did, with its car dealership ads and traffic reports and caustic DJs. If anything, opera was like a very noisy form of silence.

Florence found Helen's relationship with opera fascinating. How had she gone from Hindsville, Mississippi—population 3,200 (she'd Googled it)—to knowing the words to Verdi? Or what they call tomatoes in France?

When Florence had arrived in New York, she'd been overwhelmed by the diffuse, esoteric, truly foreign knowledge that had been accrued by seemingly everyone but her. She tried to look things up online, but the sheer volume of information the Internet provided—the combative free-for-all spirit of it—overwhelmed her. She didn't want everyone's opinions. She wanted the *right* opinions. She wanted to know that red roses were tacky. She wanted to know how to pronounce *mores*. People like Amanda Lincoln and Ingrid Thorne would never understand the innumerable advantages they had over others. This was how the social order was maintained. Someone who grew up with parents who read Philip Roth and went to the theater and told their children where to put their knife and fork when they were done eating could dismiss others as uncultured or impolite, and it accomplished the same thing as calling them white trash without the same taint of classism. But if your mother wore tight clothes and slathered on tanning oil and thought Philip Roth was a discount furniture store in Jacksonville, where did that leave you? What if you wanted a different life? How did you get from A to B? How did you become the type of person who *belonged* in B?

Florence didn't know.

But Helen did. Somehow, she had learned the rules.

Florence finally mustered up the courage to ask Helen how she'd done it, not sure whether Helen would understand the question or, if she did, be offended. But she had responded candidly.

"Exactly as you'd expect," she said. "I watched very closely and then I played the part. If you pretend for long enough, anything can become natural. And I mean truly natural. I wouldn't listen to opera or drink expensive wine if I didn't genuinely enjoy them."

Florence was reminded of a brief stint in her childhood when her mother had decided that she ought to be an actress. She'd signed Florence up for acting lessons and dragged her to countless auditions.

Florence had hated nearly every part of it—the ridiculous games they played in class, the hammy staginess of the other children, the attention—but she'd loved pretending to be someone else. She'd strip away all her own quirks and become clean and pure and empty. That's when she first realized that she could build herself into someone new. Someone better.

Living in near-isolation in upstate New York, Florence was starting to accomplish the first half of that process: the demolition. Her interactions with other people had always been the scaffolding by which she'd constructed her personality. Since those interactions had dwindled to nearly nothing, the old Florence, with no outlet for expression, seemed to be disintegrating day by day.

She was happy to encourage the process. She threw out clothes that didn't look like Helen would wear them, which meant most of her wardrobe had to go. Certainly anything bright or flouncy. With few exceptions, Helen wore clean silhouettes in shades of navy, black, and white. Occasionally she would throw on a discreetly patterned scarf or sculptural jewelry, but most of the time she went unadorned. Florence couldn't afford the labels Helen wore, but she ordered rip-offs from Zara and H&M online. She went through Helen's Amazon order history and took note of the books Helen had bought and the movies she had watched.

She devised a kind of curriculum for self-improvement. She even asked Helen to teach her how to cook.

She felt a strong desire to fade out of view, to ease off screen and then return, triumphant, in a new guise. She didn't want anyone to witness the process. It would be like showing someone a rough draft of her writing, which she—contrary to Helen—would never do.

———

Florence's first cooking lesson was coq au vin.

The two women stood side by side in Helen's kitchen, the pale, late-March sun filtering weakly through the window. Helen had poured them both a glass of red wine even though it was only 4 p.m.

"Okay, where's our beautiful little bird?" Helen asked. "Let's give him a little rinse."

Florence retrieved the chicken from the refrigerator and man-handled it into the sink. She shuddered as she felt the bones shift under the skin. "He feels alive," she said, realizing that now she was calling it a "he" too.

"You're lucky he isn't. My grandmother had me chopping heads off chickens by the time I was eight years old."

Florence glanced skeptically at Helen; that seemed like something that might have happened in rural Mississippi in 1945, not 1995. But Helen gave no indication that she'd been joking.

Florence placed the slippery bird on the cutting board, and Helen picked up a sharp, heavy knife with a scarred black handle.

"We've got to cut him up into parts," she said. "First, you slice through the skin that connects the leg to the body and then you just sort of—" She wrenched the chicken's leg back with such force that it popped off with a snap. "Here, you do the other one." She held out the knife for Florence.

Florence cut the skin, but when she pulled back on the leg nothing happened.

"*Yank* it," Helen ordered. "Half-measures won't get you anywhere."

"Seems like they might get you halfway," Florence joked.

"Well, who the hell wants to be there?" Helen asked as she put her cold, wet hands on top of Florence's and jerked the thighbone out of the socket.

Florence repeated the process with the wings, then Helen went at the body with a few loud thwacks of the knife to remove the breasts from the back and separate them in two. She dumped all the chicken pieces into a large bowl, washed her hands, and started pouring wine from the bottle they were drinking directly over the meat.

"How much wine is that?" Florence asked, picking up her pen to take notes.

"I don't know. How many times did it glug? Three?"

Florence tentatively wrote down "three glugs." She couldn't imagine that would be all that helpful if she ever attempted to make coq au vin on her own.

Helen took out a thyme stem and pulled it between her thumb and index finger so that the tiny leaves tumbled off into the bowl.

"Wait, how much thyme was that?" Florence asked.

Helen rolled her eyes. "One point three grams."

Florence started to write that down.

"Florence. I'm joking. I didn't weigh the herbs."

Florence set the pen down on the counter and closed her notebook, feeling stupid. But how was she supposed to learn if Helen just improvised everything? She needed *some* sort of framework.

"You seriously don't use recipes?"

"I can barely stand to read them. 'Caramelize the onions until they're golden and *jammy*.' 'Puree until *silky*.'" She rolled her eyes. "They're so pretentious, even when they're trying to be folksy and down to earth. If I'm told one more time to serve my dish with some good, crusty bread and a schmear of butter, I'll scream. I usually just glance at the ingredients and instructions, then figure out the rest on my own. If I mess up, I mess up. I find that people in general are way too scared of making mistakes. Sure, make a plan and do some research, but when it's time to act, my god, just *act*."

Florence, looking to prove herself, grabbed the knife and abruptly cleaved a mushroom in half. She barely paused before going at the rest of the pile with wild abandon. Suddenly, there was blood everywhere. She held up her finger in surprise. It had a deep, half-inch gouge in it, right above the knuckle.

Helen burst out laughing. "My god, I didn't know you were going to take my advice so literally." She tossed Florence a roll of paper towels. "Do you need a Band-Aid?"

Florence looked down at her finger. Blood was already seeping through the wad of paper towels she was pressing into the cut. It seemed pretty obvious that she needed a Band-Aid, if not stitches.

"Maybe?" she said.

"There are some in the upstairs bathroom cabinet, I think. Holler if you can't find them."

"The bathroom in your room?" She still hadn't been invited to the second floor.

"That's the only one there is."

Upstairs, Florence pushed open Helen's bedroom door tentatively, still nervous that she'd somehow misunderstood Helen's directions. The walls were painted deep indigo, nearly black. There was another worn, Turkish-looking carpet in shades of orange on the floor in front of a fireplace. On the queen-size bed, a thick white comforter had been halfheartedly pulled up and straightened. Florence tiptoed over to look at Helen's bedside table. A pair of reading glasses rested open on top of a stack of books and a yellow legal pad. The notepad was blank, but Florence could just make out the ghostly indentations left by Helen's pen on the page above. The book on the top of the pile was Emily Wilson's translation of *The Odyssey*.

Florence went into Helen's bathroom and opened the cabinet. She saw the box of Band-Aids, but her hand went straight to the prescription bottle next to it. According to the label, it contained .5-mg pills of clonazepam. Florence recognized the name; Lucy took it for anxiety. She was surprised. Helen did not seem like someone prone to nervousness. She hastily replaced the bottle and proceeded to bandage her bloody finger.

When Florence returned to the kitchen, a blue Le Creuset pot was simmering on the stove and Helen was at the table drinking her wine. She patted the seat next to her.

"Your mother doesn't cook?" she asked when Florence sat down.

Florence shook her head. "She works at a restaurant. She says she couldn't bear to spend a minute of her own time in another kitchen."

"What did you eat growing up then?"

"I don't know. A lot of Lean Cuisine, I guess. My mom is always on a diet."

"Lean Cuisine?" Helen grimaced. "That's bleak."

"Their barbeque chicken isn't that bad," Florence mumbled.

"Oh, Florence." Helen smiled at her with something verging on pity. "I'm sure it is. I'm sure it's very, very bad." Florence tried not to wince as Helen patted her injured hand.

That night at dinner, Florence peered into her dish of coq au vin and noticed several of the mushrooms she'd bled all over bobbing on the surface. She wondered if Helen had even bothered to rinse them off before tossing them in the pot. She also realized that she still had no idea how to make coq au vin.

17.

In the first week of April, the cherry blossom tree outside Florence's window bloomed, and she finally met one of Helen's neighbors. She had taken to walking in the woods behind the house most evenings before dinner. Despite covering only a couple dozen acres, these woods felt limitless to her. Every time she crossed the threshold from the grassy, dusk-lit field into the darkened wood she got a flutter of foreboding. Deeper inside, she sometimes wondered if she'd ever find her way out. But she loved being in there, completely alone, encountering the same landscape an eighteenth-century settler might have seen. She'd once come across a Cheetos wrapper in the dirt and felt as startled and dismayed as if it had been a dead body.

Her life in Florida had always felt claustrophobic. The small apartment. The dingy classrooms. Even the places that must have once, centuries ago, offered a sense of expansiveness were ruined now. The harbor clogged with boats, the beaches strewn with bodies.

New York had been even worse.

The only place she had ever gotten a sense of the world's beauty and magnitude was in books. She'd been obsessed with *The Lord of the Rings* in middle school. She'd loved escaping into a universe entirely unlike her own. It was part of what made her want to be a writer. She wanted to hold that immensity in her hand. To mold entire worlds according to her vision.

On that chilly April evening, during her regular stroll, she sensed a rustling behind her in the woods. She paused to listen more closely. At first she heard only the sound of her own heavy breathing, but then another set of ragged breaths joined in, followed by the pounding of footsteps getting louder. She told herself to run, or hide, but she couldn't move. It was like one of those dreams where something is coming after you but you're frozen in place, helpless to change your fate. She was terrified.

Just then a bush in front of her parted, and a yellow blur shot out, coming right for her. She put her hands up in front of her, and a low, involuntary whimper escaped her throat.

It was a golden retriever.

He loped toward her excitedly, his wagging backside pulling him off course every few steps. He shoved his snout gleefully into her crotch. His tail swooshed back and forth in broad strokes, picking up leaves and twigs from the ground.

Florence exhaled a phlegmy, manic-sounding laugh of relief and reached out her hands to scratch his ears.

A man in his sixties came running after the dog. "Bentley! Down, boy!" he shouted. "I'm so sorry, miss. Bentley, down!"

Florence waved off his apologies. She rubbed the dog's head and neck vigorously. He raised his eyes toward the sky in ecstasy.

"Looks like he likes you," the man said, slowing to a stop in front of her. He was wearing a blue golf shirt tucked into cargo shorts and panting lightly. In his hand was one of those plastic toys that hurl tennis balls great distances. "Bentley can smell a dog person from a mile off."

"Hi, Bentley," said Florence quietly. "Hi, buddy."

The man watched them for a moment with a fond smile on his face. Then he said, "You staying at the old house down the road?" nodding in the direction of Helen's. Florence said she was.

"So she didn't warn you about big, ferocious Bentley?" he asked with a chuckle.

"No, she's never mentioned him." Bentley was licking her hands with his wet, sandpaper tongue.

"He got into her garden once or twice, and she nearly lost her mind. Now whenever Bentley sees her his tail goes right between his legs."

Florence felt obliged to defend Helen. "Maybe she's just not a dog person."

"Oh no, she is definitely not that. But I guess she's a dog-person person and that counts for something. You're her second visitor in as many months who Bentley's gone nuts for."

Florence looked up in surprise. "Second? When was the first?"

"Oh, I don't know—maybe it was longer ago, come to think of it. There was definitely snow on the ground."

Bentley suddenly froze and cocked his ears. A second later, he disappeared into the brush as abruptly as he'd arrived.

"Oh boy, there he goes again," the man said, shaking his head. He headed after the dog with a wave goodbye at Florence.

Later that night at dinner, Florence related the encounter to Helen and asked who her visitor had been.

"I have no idea," said Helen. "Must have been someone staying at another house. No one's been here."

"Huh."

"God, that dog's a terror."

"Bentley? He was so sweet."

"Talk to me after he's dug up all your roses."

Suddenly the silence was pierced by what sounded like a woman shrieking.

Florence looked up at Helen in alarm. "What was that?"

Helen shrugged. "Probably just an animal."

"Probably?"

Florence walked to the window and looked out. She saw only

her own rippled reflection. Then she heard it again coming from somewhere in the direction of the road.

She said, "I'll just go see."

She walked out into the cold night. After the brightness of the house, it was like slipping on a black hood. She approached the edge of the driveway and peered out into the darkness. She heard the shriek again and walked toward it.

An owl lay on the ground, peering up at her with panic in its large yellow eyes, its pupils like liquid drops of ink. There was no blood or sign of injury. He screeched again, insistently.

She walked back to the house.

"It's an owl," she said. "He's in bad shape. Do you have a towel or something I could use?"

"For what?"

"To carry him inside. Do you know if there's a vet in town we can call?"

"You're not bringing that thing into my house."

"I think he's going to die if we don't help him."

"It happens fairly often. They eat mice that have ingested rat poison."

"What? That's horrible."

"So is finding mouse pellets in your pillowcase," said Helen with one of her grim, toothless smiles.

Florence looked intently at her.

"Oh for god's sake, Florence, it's an owl," Helen said in exasperation. "I can barely muster up enough empathy to cover the humans I know. Every day we're asked to feel sorry for refugees from Syria and gay men in Chechnya and Muslims in Myanmar. It's too much. The human mind wasn't built to assimilate so much suffering. It was designed to produce just enough empathy to cover its own little community. So please don't ask me to expend my dwindling reserves on *an owl*."

"Okay, sorry," said Florence quietly. She sat back down. Then she said: "It's just that I feel like the owl *is* a part of our community. He's right there." She gestured weakly toward the door.

"You misunderstood me, Florence. I said nothing about any actual community. Haven't you heard? We killed them all off. My community is *me*. And I don't feel accountable to anyone outside of it—human, avian, or otherwise."

Florence was taken aback. Was that really something you could just decide? That you didn't owe anything to anyone? She could never tell when Helen was taking a position just to add a little jolt to the conversation and when she actually believed what she was saying.

She tried to imagine what her life would look like if she abdicated all responsibility.

She couldn't picture it. And after a few minutes, the shrieking stopped.

18.

By mid-April, about a month into the job, Florence had started doing something that she knew she really, *really*, should not be doing.

The more she read of Helen's new novel, the less impressed she was. The sentences were well written, and the plot was compelling, but for all that it lacked the spark, the life, of *Mississippi Foxtrot*.

When that book first came out, Florence had still been working at the bookstore in Gainesville. A coworker had bestowed it on her with closed-eyed reverence, as if it were Christ's teenage diary. Later, at Forrester, Amanda had summed up Florence's feelings exactly, saying of Maud Dixon: "I could *kill* her." They were jealous, of course—jealousy being a natural corollary to ambition.

Florence had been blown away by the confidence and vitality of the writing. She had tried typing out a few of its sentences because she'd read that Didion had done that with Hemingway. She'd felt transfigured, like she'd been writing her own work with arthritic fingers and had suddenly found the cure.

But when she typed out Helen's handwritten draft of her second novel, she felt none of that. In fact, she thought—with a different type of exhilaration—*I could write this.*

That was how it started.

When she couldn't decipher a word that Helen had written,

she made decisions more swiftly and surely. At first, it was just to avoid another terrifying encounter like the one in Helen's study on her first day. But soon it became her favorite part of her job. Every time she chose a word to type into the manuscript, she got a small rush. She felt like Helen's collaborator rather than just her assistant.

From there, she grew bolder. She started adding words that she knew were not what Helen had written. But they made the book *better,* they just did. Surely if Helen noticed, she would agree. Maybe she would even thank Florence.

But Helen did not notice. Every time she finished typing up more of Helen's draft, Florence saved a new version of the manuscript on the laptop and emailed Helen the file. She assumed Helen was reading over it and making edits, but she never gave her back anything to retype, and she had yet to comment on any of Florence's additions. Florence began to suspect that her own words might actually end up in the novel.

One morning, she had just typed a word—*catastrophic*—that bore only a loose resemblance to the scrawl on the page when she heard tires crunching on the gravel. She sat up. They'd never had a visitor before.

She stood and peered out the dining room window. A police car was in the driveway. She felt a brief and irrational suspicion that they'd found out what she was doing to Helen's manuscript. She whipped around guiltily when she heard footsteps creaking down the staircase.

"The police are here," Florence told Helen.

"What'd you do now?" Helen asked. "Rob a liquor store?"

Helen walked calmly to the front door and slipped outside just as the car door slammed shut.

Florence craned her neck to get a better view out the window. An overweight cop with gray skin and thinning hair hitched up his pants before waddling as authoritatively as one could waddle toward Helen's erect figure at the foot of the steps. She was shielding her face from the sun, just as she'd done the first time Florence met her.

Florence couldn't hear what they were saying. The man gestured toward the house. Helen raised her eyebrows and laughed lightly. She turned then and gestured at the house too. As she did, she caught sight of Florence's face in the window and rested her gaze on it for a brief moment. Florence stepped back. She sat down at the table again and tried to look absorbed in her work.

Helen reentered the house a few minutes later.

"Everything okay?" Florence asked.

"Good god, if *that* is what I'm spending my taxes on, maybe I should be hiding my money in the Cayman Islands."

"What did he say?"

"Oh, some foolishness about speeding tickets."

"He came to your house for speeding tickets?"

"Well, I do have a lot of them."

Florence remembered the drive from the train station. She could believe it.

"Do you want me to deal with them?"

"Hm? No, that's okay. I can handle it. I think they're stuffed in my desk drawer somewhere."

Florence, feeling unusually chagrined, erased the word *catastrophic* letter by letter.

19.

The night after the policeman's visit, Helen looked up from her dinner and put down her fork and knife. "Florence," she said, "I've been meaning to ask you something."

Florence froze. She'd been caught; she knew it.

What on earth had compelled her to tamper with Helen's manuscript? It was beyond stupid.

She was so hemmed in all the time by timidity and insecurity that every once in a while some self-destructive impulse in her demanded brash action. It was the same impulse that had made her send those photos to Simon. She had no control over it.

There was a flavorless, over-chewed piece of lamb in her mouth that she couldn't swallow. She'd braised the meat herself under Helen's direction that afternoon. She lifted her napkin to her mouth and quietly spit it out.

"Do you have a passport?" Helen asked.

Florence was taken off guard. She shook her head.

"Can you get one?"

"Yes. Why?"

Helen composed a perfectly proportioned bite of lamb, rice, and tomato confit with her knife and fork. She chewed it slowly and thoughtfully. It was a performance, Florence knew, designed to keep her waiting.

"I thought you might like to join me on a research trip to Morocco. Would that interest you?"

It took Florence a moment to regain her bearings. "Yes, absolutely." She was flooded with relief.

"Great. Why don't you go to the passport office Monday and see if you can get it expedited. I'll pay any fees, obviously."

"Why, when do you want to go?"

"As soon as possible. I feel stuck on the novel, and I think being there will help. Besides, I'm getting a little sick of sitting around in cow country, aren't you?"

Florence didn't answer. She had, in fact, never been happier. Every morning she woke up awash in pink sunlight filtering through the cherry blossom tree and thought that she had finally landed where she was meant to be. "Should I look into flights?"

"Yes, do. Today is—what?—Saturday? Let's go at the end of next week, maybe Wednesday or Thursday, if we can find seats."

"Wait, *four* days from now?"

"Why not? What's the point of waiting? We can fly into Marrakesh then drive out to Semat the next day." Semat was the small town on the coast where Helen's novel took place.

"Should I book hotels too?"

"Book any place that looks good to you in Marrakesh, but the hotels in Semat are a bit dicey. See if there are any villas available to rent. Something nice."

"For how long?"

"Let's say . . . two weeks?"

Florence nodded.

Just then her phone buzzed on the table next to her. She looked at the screen. It was another message from her mother: "CALL ME!!!!!" Ever since moving in with Helen, Florence had gotten into the habit of waiting two or three days before returning her mother's calls. She'd started to find her mother's flaws even more glaring now that she'd gotten to know women like Helen Wilcox and Greta Frost.

"Sorry," Florence said as she turned the phone over.

"Feel free to take it."

"I'd rather not. It's just my mother."

"Everything alright? You can talk to me, you know. I'm no stranger to family drama."

"I mean, nothing happened. I just—. Well, at first I was avoiding her calls because I didn't want to tell her that I'd left Forrester. And then I started realizing how much happier I was not talking to her." Florence let out a soft, uncomfortable laugh.

Helen nodded. "I was in a similar position myself when I left Hindsville. I tried to keep in touch with my family, but they always felt like this weight that was dragging me down, pulling me backward. My mother was dead by then, but my father and my grandmother both resented me for leaving. They thought I'd become this hoity-toity city girl—in Oxford, Mississippi, of all places. I mean, it wasn't like I had jetted off to Paris. So they picked and picked and picked, trying to bring me back down to size. It was the same thing every time I spoke to them. So finally I just stopped."

"You just stopped?"

"I stopped calling. I stopped writing. I stopped visiting. And it felt like the weight had been lifted. I felt unshackled. And that's when I was finally able to write *Mississippi Foxtrot,* when I stopped worrying about what they'd think. I stopped worrying about them at all. It created this wide open space that I was able to fill with something else. The words just erupted from me in a torrent."

Florence thought of the paralysis that beset her every time she tried to write. Could *Vera* be the problem?

"Mark my words," Helen said, gesturing with her fork, "cutting them off was the best decision I ever made. I wouldn't be a writer today if I hadn't done it."

That night Florence lay in bed and stared at the ceiling, which was only four feet away from her face up in the lofted bedroom.

Could she do it? Could she cut her mother out of her life?

What she'd told Helen was true—she *had* been happier since she'd stopped talking to her as much. The distance enabled her to see that every conversation they had left Florence feeling anxious and inadequate.

It was almost as if there were two different Florences in her mother's eyes: the potential Florence, the great one, whom Vera adored, and the real Florence, who constantly thwarted Vera's hopes and dreams. Perhaps this was why her mother had never shown her much tenderness. Her language was warm—full of "honey"s and "darling"s—but she had always called her customers "honey" too, even after management asked her to stop. And all those empty "Who loves you?"s were worse than nothing at all.

What Florence wanted to do was prove to her mother that *this* Florence, the one she really was, could be great on her own terms: as a writer; as an artist. She was sick of being made to feel like she was falling short of Vera's ideal.

Perhaps this was a test. If she could cast off her mother, her reward would be the same as Helen's: an unblocking. A violent unleashing of her talent, a torrent of brilliance. Her own version of *Mississippi Foxtrot*.

Mark my words, Helen had said. I wouldn't be a writer today if I hadn't done it.

Florence looked at her phone, glowing in the darkness of her room. She held it in her hands briefly like an amulet. Then she wrote a message to her mother: *I'm going out of the country for a while for work. I won't be in touch while I'm traveling.* It was nothing final, she told herself. Just a trial separation.

Almost immediately after she sent it, her mother called.

She silenced the ring and turned off the phone.

20.

On Monday afternoon, Florence stood outside the Dunkin' Donuts a block from the Forrester office, chewing on the straw of her iced coffee. She'd just taken the train into Manhattan from upstate. The closest place to expedite a passport was the US passport office on Hudson Street—which happened to sit directly across the street from Forrester's building. According to Simon's restraining order, she wasn't allowed within five hundred feet of it, but this risk, she'd decided, was worth taking.

She studied the building and tried to find his window. Was it five hundred feet as the crow flies? Simon's office was on the fourteenth floor, so the elevator ride would take up nearly a third of that distance.

"Florence?"

She turned. Amanda Lincoln was walking toward her, smiling in amazement.

"I thought that was you. What are you doing here? Are you back at Forrester?"

"No. I have a meeting nearby," Florence said automatically. She gestured vaguely toward the west side. The only thing that lay west of Forrester was the UPS plant, she realized.

"Are you still living in the city then? You disappeared so completely we thought maybe you'd left."

Amanda was clearly fishing for some piece of gossip she could relate breathlessly to her colleagues upstairs. ("You guys won't *believe* who I just ran into.") Florence couldn't imagine what they'd said about her when she was fired. She knew the story about the photographs had gotten out because Lucy had made a vague reference to it in one of her voicemails.

"No. I'm up near Hudson now. I love it. It's such a relief to be out of the city. To be honest, I always found New York slightly overrated." And then, recklessly: "You should come up to visit."

"I'd love that." They maintained eye contact in silence, each aware that such an outcome was absurd. They had never been friends. They were playing a game of chicken.

Florence broke first. "I can't put you up, unfortunately—I'm in a guesthouse that belongs to a sort of mentor of mine, but it's really small."

"That sounds amazing. I need to get a mentor with a guest-house," said Amanda with a laugh. "How do you know him?"

"Her."

"Oh, sorry, I just assumed."

Florence felt a familiar prickling in her fingers, the heat in her gut. She wanted desperately to humiliate Amanda. To make her feel ridiculous. Amanda had probably never felt ridiculous a day in her life. She dug the fingernails on her left hand into her palm. They weren't sharp enough.

"I have to go," Florence said. "I'm going to be late."

"Oh no. Well it was so good to see you!"

Amanda leaned in to kiss her on the cheek as Florence awkwardly responded with a hug. She ended up with a mouthful of Amanda's hair.

Later, in line at the passport office, she replayed the encounter in her mind. Amanda could report her to the police for violating the restraining order. Or to Simon. Yes, that's what she would do. Florence supposed she could deny it. Anyway, she was leaving the country in a few days.

She had never traveled farther than LA, where she'd flown

for an audition when she was nine. Her mother had been giddy with excitement on the way there, then grim with disappointment on the way home.

Florence had a sense that she, too, would return a different person, that travel would change her. Change is never a smooth curve; it comes in leaps and jolts, plateaus and remissions. And in the periods after an old identity fades away but before a new one is fully installed, there is a certain sense of impunity. As if nothing quite matters. You are not quite yourself. You're not quite anyone.

She was running out the clock on *Florence,* on the person she currently was. It was a pleasant thought. She was sick to death of herself. That was one of the problems of always being stuck in your own head; the outside world isn't loud enough to drown out the constant monologue on the inside. The same shit, day after day. Does she like me? Do I look okay? Will I ever be happy? Will I ever be successful? It was like listening to the same song over and over every day for years. Didn't they torture people that way?

"Florence Darrow?"

It was the man who'd taken her form and photograph twenty minutes earlier. Florence heard nothing. She was perched on a hard wooden bench watching an old woman fill out a passport application with a slow, shaky hand. Florence had a sudden urge to snatch the pen from her arthritic fingers and hurl it across the room. *Tired old crone,* she thought. How was she going to navigate customs and security when she couldn't even fill out a fucking form? Florence's body was rigid with unexpected fury. She didn't even know why she was so angry. Something about the woman's fragility struck her as offensive.

She forced herself to look away and take several slow, deep breaths. She knew from experience that the rage would pass. She tried to put Simon and Amanda and this old woman she didn't even know out of her mind.

"Florence Darrow?"

She had to prod herself to call out, "That's me."

PART III

21.

They landed in Marrakesh with a violent thud and skidded into an unnerving leftward veer. They had been traveling for more than sixteen hours: New York to Lisbon, Lisbon to Marrakesh. Helen had flown business class while Florence sat in coach.

As the plane taxied toward the terminal, the short Arab man next to Florence turned to her and said, "You see the wind in the trees there?" He leaned across her and pressed a well-manicured finger onto the plastic window. "It's the *chergui*. It blows in from the Sahara. It doesn't usually come this early."

"What does it do?"

"It brings heat and dust." He smiled. "And if you ask my grandmother, bad luck."

The plane stopped some distance from the terminal, and two men wheeled a rickety set of stairs up to the side of it. As soon as Florence disembarked, she felt it—the *chergui*. It whipped her hair around her face and into her mouth. Its roar was joined by the whir of the plane's engines winding down. The sudden heat and noise had a disorienting effect on Florence. Helen, on the other hand, seemed invigorated by the hot, violent gusts. Her eyes glowed, and she smiled wildly at Florence.

"Bonjour, l'aventure!" she called into the wind.

On the tarmac, two men in fatigues and green berets cradled automatic weapons and followed the line of passengers with bored eyes. There were two terminals. On the right, an old, pink two-story building with a rickety sign spelling out AERO-PORT MARRAKECH MENARA in both French and Arabic. Next to it stood a gleaming new construction, a swoop of shiny white plastic like an Ikea table, with a punched-brass facade.

They were ushered into the second building, where the kaleidoscopic carpets and shiny surfaces could have belonged to any conference center in middle America. Florence was disappointed. She had expected something more exotic.

Florence had never been in public with Helen before they'd arrived at JFK. There, the impatience and occasional severity Florence had grown used to in Helen's temperament manifested itself for the first time physically. She'd scattered crowds like buckshot while Florence tagged behind, trying not to trot. This aggressive efficiency was, in truth, a relief to Florence. She felt herself settle into the role of Helen's ward. For the time being, she would take a respite from responsibility. She kept her focus on Helen's back and blocked out everything else.

In Marrakesh, Helen once again charged to the front of the herd of passengers shuffling from their flight. But in the large customs hall they encountered a snaking line containing hundreds of people. It bulged here and there with families and tour groups, as if the snake were digesting several mice whole. Helen stopped short when she saw the crowd, then changed course and made a beeline for a woman in uniform.

"I'm pregnant," she said to her in English with no elaboration. The woman shot a split-second glance at Helen's flat stomach, then said, "Of course." She led them to a shorter line of six or seven people surrounded by strollers and wheelchairs and crutches. Florence shot a glance back at the people who would be waiting an hour, maybe two, in the longer line. She was glad she wasn't among them. She no longer wanted to be hampered by a petty obsession with rules. Something about it seemed vaguely low-class and pathetic to her now.

Florence had hired a driver through the hotel, and they found him outside of baggage claim holding a sign that said WILCOCK. He wore a long dust-colored tunic over black jeans and Reeboks. He introduced himself as Hamza before guiding them outside toward a late-model Fiat in the parking lot. Again, Florence was disappointed. Though, really, what had she expected—a camel?

They cruised down smooth modern roads, past floodlit billboards—many in English—and around orderly traffic circles planted with neatly groomed flower beds. They passed large, gaudy buildings with neon signs and elaborate fountains. It looked like Las Vegas.

Finally, they approached the ramparts surrounding the medina—the old city—and the Marrakesh of guidebooks appeared before them. The walls, Hamza told them, had been built in the twelfth century. The clay was a warm ochre color that glowed in the afternoon sun. The wall itself was pockmarked with huge holes, some of them jammed with wooden struts. Marrakesh, Florence had read, was known as the Red City, because its buildings had originally been constructed out of reddish clay from the surrounding plains; later, the government required newer structures to be painted the same color.

They drove through Bab El Jdid, one of the busiest gates leading into the medina, and above them rose the towering minaret of the Koutoubia mosque, carved with impossibly intricate fretwork. Topped by four gilded spheres, one on top of the other, it was visible from everywhere else in the city. As part of her research, Florence had learned that after the original mosque had been built there in the twelfth century, the whole thing had been demolished and rebuilt to correctly align with Mecca. Their hotel, Florence knew, wasn't far from it.

The roads here were more chaotic than the modern highways outside the city walls, but the cars, donkeys, horse-drawn carriages, and mopeds darted around one another without incident. Florence peered out the window. The buildings had a delicate beauty entirely absent from those in Florida, or even New York. The geometric carvings and colorful tilework looked extraordinarily labor-intensive. Florence loved the romance of it, eschewing the practical for the magical. Palm trees marked the facades with swaying shadows.

After driving through the old city for ten minutes or so, Hamza stopped at a busy intersection and put the car into park.

"What are you doing?" Florence asked.

"We're here," he said.

Florence looked around. They had passed several picturesque side streets on the way in, but this was not one of them. Music blared from a restaurant on the corner. The store next to it sold tires and car batteries. A dozen or so men were draped over white plastic chairs on the side of the road; to call it a sidewalk would have been an overstatement.

"Charming," said Helen flatly.

"No," said Florence, shaking her head. "No." She unfolded the printout of their hotel reservation and showed it to Hamza again. She had chosen it after hours of research. According to TripAdvisor it was a "tucked-away oasis oozing local charm."

"Riad Belsa," she said, stabbing the paper with her finger. "A tucked-away oasis oozing local charm."

"Yes," he said agreeably. "It is a very nice hotel." He stepped out of the car and moved around to the trunk. He handed their bags to a tall, thin man standing idly near their car. That man, in turn, tossed them into a large wheelbarrow beside him and started pushing it toward a narrow, poorly lit alley.

"Wait," she said uselessly.

"I cannot go any farther with the car," Hamza explained patiently. "This man will take you the rest of the way."

"This doesn't seem right," Florence said quietly to Helen.

Helen shrugged as she dug in her wallet for a tip for Hamza.

"I'm sure it's fine. He had the name of the hotel on his uniform."

Florence reluctantly followed Helen down the gloomy passageway.

"I'm not sure this is a good idea," she whispered.

"Panic is a waste of energy, Florence."

They followed the man with the wheelbarrow through the labyrinth. Every turn revealed another dim corridor, empty save for a few skinny cats slinking against the walls. Florence tried to look for street signs, but all the alleyways seemed to be unmarked. They'd never be able to find their way out.

Just then the call to prayer issued from the direction of the Koutoubia mosque. It sounded like a sad, moaning lament to Florence. She looked up, but found that the walls were too high and close together here to see the minaret.

Finally, they turned into a dead end and saw an elaborately carved wooden door with a gold plaque announcing it as Riad Belsa. Florence recognized the entrance from the photos on TripAdvisor. The man swung a large brass knocker, and the door was opened by a smiling, heavyset woman in a headscarf. She greeted them warmly, saying "Salaam alaikum, good afternoon, bienvenue," and ushered them through a small courtyard into a larger, second courtyard surrounding a burbling fountain. It was filled with citrus and pomegranate trees with lush, drooping branches. The floor and walls gleamed with black, red, and green tiles. She seated them at a table tucked under a knot of vines and then returned with a plate of dates and two small glasses of milk scented with orange-blossom water. Florence looked around in relief.

Soon a man in a three-piece suit arrived and sat down with them.

"Good afternoon," he said in British-accented English. His comb had left stiff ridges in his shiny black hair. "Welcome to Riad Belsa. I am Brahim, the manager."

He asked them where they were from and how their trip had been. Then he said, "My apologies, but let's move on to the formalities, if you don't mind. Then you can enjoy the rest of your visit without concern." He slid two slips of paper across the table. "We need some information for the police. They require us to file these every night about new guests. We have taken the liberty of filling out most of your information from your booking, but you will need to add your profession and your signature, there, and there." Florence examined her form. It was labeled *Bulletin Individuel d'Hotel,* and her name, address, and passport number were already written out.

"May I ask what you do for a living?" Brahim requested.

Helen and Florence answered "writer" and "assistant" at the same time.

"Assistant, that's very good," he said, nodding at Florence. "But please," he turned to Helen, "you must not put writer. The police will become very interested. They will think you are writing political articles or something unflattering about our country. They will ask us to tell them where you have been, what you have been photographing. It will become a headache, I assure you. Please, just write 'sales' or 'manager.' That is best."

Helen seemed delighted by the demand for farce. "Manager, then," she said. "What should I manage? A factory?"

"Just manager is fine," Brahim said mildly.

"I manufacture cogs, mainly," Helen went on, nearly giddy. "For boat engines. All seagoing vessels, really. If you can float it, we can power it...with cogs. We might need to work on that slogan, what do you think, Florence?"

Florence smiled unsurely. She wasn't used to seeing this playful side of Helen.

"Just manager will suffice," Brahim said again. "And you are staying for just one night, I see?" he asked, consulting his iPad.

They nodded. The next day, they'd drive west to Semat.

"In that case, might I suggest an itinerary for your brief time with us? El Badi is a ruined palace not far from here. Very magnificent. Well worth a visit. And you must take a quick walk through the souks. We will be happy to provide a list of the most reputable salesmen. Leather, jewelry, anything you're looking for."

"Mm. Perhaps," Helen demurred. Florence knew that she didn't like plans being dictated to her; she'd found that out when she'd suggested a detour to the Atlas Mountains on their way to the coast. Helen had stared at her for an uncomfortable few seconds then walked out of the room.

"I assure you it is quite safe, Madame," Brahim said, mis-interpreting Helen's reticence. "There are dozens of plainclothes policemen in the souks whose only job is to protect tourists. They pretend to be drunks, lowlife types, leaning against build-ings, sitting on the ground, but the moment they see something, they strike." He clapped loudly, and the sound echoed around the courtyard.

Florence raised her eyebrows. "Really?"

"Oh yes. Everyone in Marrakesh is pretending to be someone they're not," he added with a wink.

"I think we'll go to our rooms now," Helen announced, rising. She seemed to have abruptly deflated. Florence had to remind herself that Helen was not much more accustomed to international travel than she was. It was just past four in the afternoon in Marrakesh and they had been awake for more than twenty hours. Any curiosity they'd felt about the city had been blunted by fatigue and jet lag.

"Of course, Madame." Brahim led them up a spiral stair-case to the second floor. "This is a traditional Moroccan riad," he explained. "It's built around the open-air garden on the ground floor." Upstairs, Florence peered over the edge of the wrought-iron railing down to the courtyard below, lit by the late afternoon sun. Their rooms faced each other across the drop.

They stopped at Helen's first. She and Florence agreed to meet downstairs at seven for dinner.

Brahim then led Florence to her room. As she walked through the arched doorway, she noticed a looped bracket on the wooden door and a matching one on the doorframe. It looked like the kind of thing you could slip a rod or a broom handle through to lock someone in.

She wondered briefly why anyone would have installed that there, but she was too tired to care. All she wanted was sleep; if someone wanted to shut her in, let them.

22.

Florence woke with a headache and a dry, sour mouth. She struggled to emerge from a dense fog. Her sheets were tangled and damp. She felt the aftereffects of adrenaline pulsing through her veins. She tried to remember her dreams, but they darted away like fish. She had been running, she thought. Pursued.

She forced herself to sit up and rubbed her face roughly. She looked at her phone. It said 6:14 a.m. How was that possible? Had she actually been sleeping for fourteen hours? She heaved herself out of bed and walked to the bathroom on stiff legs. She splashed handful after handful of cold water on her face.

Gradually the reality of her surroundings became more concrete. She was in Marrakesh. She had been planning to meet Helen for dinner last night, but she must have slept through it. And today they were driving to Semat.

Florence took a shower and dressed in the first clothes she found at the top of her duffel bag: jeans and a wrinkled T-shirt. In the hallway, she listened at Helen's door but heard nothing. She looked over the railing into the courtyard below. She spotted Helen at a table under an orange tree, a black coffee in front of her. She was wearing a crisp black linen dress and leather sandals that wound up her ankles.

Florence sat down heavily across from her.

"I thought you were dead," Helen said cheerfully.

"So did I."

"It really would have ruined my plans."

"Ha, ha."

"Coffee," Helen said, pointing at the silver urn on a buffet table laid out in the shade.

Once Florence had returned with a cup, she apologized. "I don't know what happened. Did you end up getting dinner?"

Helen ignored her question. "I thought before we leave town today we could hit El Badi. I was talking to Brahim again this morning and it really does sound spectacular. El Badi means 'the incomparable'—isn't that fabulous? It's apparently one of Allah's ninety-nine names, which makes me feel quite impoverished, having only two. Let's go right after breakfast, then you can go get the car."

When they were planning the trip, Florence had suggested hiring a driver to take them to Semat, but Helen had insisted on renting a car. "Arabs can't drive," she'd said in the same matter-of-fact tone someone might say, "I grew up in Boise."

After breakfast, they both went back to their rooms to get a few things and then met again in the corridor. Helen held out her wallet, cell phone, and cigarettes to Florence and said, "Do you mind? I don't feel like carrying a bag."

"Oh. Sure." Florence stuffed them into her already full purse.

It took some time to find their way out of the dark maze surrounding the hotel. The walls were too high to allow much sunlight in and so close that Florence could touch them both at the same time. Some of the buildings, she noticed when she looked closely, were covered in a synthetic wrapping printed to look like stone.

Brahim had assured them that El Badi was only a short walk from their hotel, but they hadn't counted on how long it would take to orient themselves. They eventually came to the large intersection where their driver had dropped them off the day before, which sprouted wider, busier roads. Cars, mopeds, pedestrians, and donkeys all competed for space. The donkeys looked skinny and miserable, pulling nearly identical carts of construction materials—bags of concrete, bricks, and long rods of rebar that hung down and scraped the dusty ground behind them. A few taxis, old ochre-colored Mercedes sedans from the '80s, stopped for them, but they waved them on and kept walking. It was barely 9 a.m. but it was already hot. Florence wished she hadn't worn pants.

Many of the stores they passed had laid out their wares on the ground outside, and these too tumbled into the clogged streets, an odd mix of the exotic and the pedestrian: live turtles, plastic-wrapped socks, children's umbrellas, sacks of pigment and spices and beans, diapers, sunglasses, glistening piles of raw meat. Everything was overseen by somber men in djellabas. A cat darted past them with a bird's head in its mouth.

By the time they reached El Badi, Florence was overheated and on edge. They paid seventy dirhams—around seven US dollars—to enter and found themselves in a large, open-air complex that was shockingly silent and still. The palace had just opened, and they seemed to be the first people there apart from the guards.

Florence read from a pamphlet they'd been given with their tickets and summarized it for Helen: "The palace was commissioned by the sultan in 1578 and finished fifteen years later. A hundred years after that a new sultan stripped it and used the materials to build his own palace in Menkes—no, wait, sorry, Meknes—in the north."

Helen snatched the pamphlet from Florence's hand and began fanning herself with it. "It's hot as blue blazes in here," she said.

"It's the *chergui*," Florence replied.

Helen walked away, toward a sunken garden in the center of the courtyard. Florence retreated to the high walls where there was a sliver of shade. She ran her hands along the rough surface, which was pocked with the same large holes as the walls of the medina. Here, though, they were filled with cramped, huddled pigeons—hundreds of them. Their cooing had the aggressively soothing tones of a nursery rhyme in a horror movie. A few pieces of straw floated down to the ground in front of Florence. She looked up. Huge storks stared down impassively from shaggy, shedding nests they had erected on top of the walls. There was bird shit everywhere.

Florence turned down a set of steep stairs into a series of destroyed, roofless rooms with cracked tiled floors. The birds were even louder in here. She found a recess in the wall that was shaded from the sun and pressed her cheek against the surface. The stone was surprisingly cold. A few moments later, another tourist entered. Florence was not immediately visible to him. When he moved farther into the room he saw her and jumped.

"Christ," he exclaimed. "You scared me."

"Sorry," she said, moving out of the shadows.

"Hiding?"

"Just from the sun."

"Yes, he's a bastard today." The man had the accent and toothy look of an Englishman. "On holiday?"

"Not really," Florence said. "Working."

"Oh yes? Let me guess." He looked her up and down slowly. "Archaeology student," he pronounced, pointing a long, spindly finger in her direction.

"Novelist," said Florence. The man raised his eyebrows. "Oh, well done," he said. "Brilliant."

After lying, Florence had the same feeling she got when she stepped past the point in the ocean where you can still run from the waves, so deep that you have to rush headlong into them. She felt, absurdly, that he might begin to quiz her.

She moved abruptly away from him and climbed back up into the brightness. She crossed the complex, past the sunken gardens of orange trees and the algae-covered pool. On the opposite side, she found another staircase leading downward. She took it and found herself alone in a series of dark passageways. She entered a room with display cases filled with primitive-looking chains and neck shackles. On the wall hung faded black-and-white photographs of prisoners hunched over in despair. She hurried back up into the sunlight.

Helen stood peeling a small orange in the shade, her resin bracelets clacking in time with the motion.

"Where did you get that?" Florence asked.

Helen nodded her head at the orange trees in the sunken garden.

"You just took one?"

Helen shrugged. "Why not? Who's it for, the storks?"

Florence looked enviously at the juice running down Helen's wrist but she lacked the temerity to pick one herself. She glanced at one of the guards, an acne-scarred twenty-something tapping at his phone. He seemed to sense that he was being watched and looked up. Florence abruptly turned away.

"Are you about ready to go?" she asked.

Helen ejected an orange seed from her mouth and held it up to the sun between her thumb and forefinger before flicking it away. "Let's hit it," she said.

They parted ways at the entrance to the palace and agreed to meet in an hour at the intersection by their hotel.

"Oh wait, I need my things," Helen said, turning back.

Florence pulled Helen's phone, wallet, and cigarettes from her bag and handed them over. Helen slipped the cigarettes and phone into the pocket of her dress, but opened the wallet and pulled out her driver's license. She handed it to Florence.

"What's this for?"

"For the car rental place. I assume they'll need a license in the same name as the credit card the reservation is under."

Florence looked at the picture on the driver's license. She

tipped the card and watched the hologram catch and repel the light. "You think I'll pass?" She and Helen both had blond hair and small builds, but she'd never dared to presume any stronger resemblance.

"I guess we'll find out."

23.

Florence set off westward with the sun at her back. The rental agency was located outside the medina walls. Brahim had told her it was about a twenty-minute walk.

"Go through Jemaa el-Fnaa square," he'd suggested, pointing at the map he was marking up for her. "It's one of the most famous spots in Marrakesh. It's where they used to shoot prisoners. Afterward, their heads were"—he snapped his fingers a few times—"what is that word? You know? With the hot dogs? You eat them with the hot dogs—they're long and green and crunchy?"

"Pickles?" Florence offered doubtfully.

"Pickles! Their heads were, just as you say, pickled and hung from the city gates. As a warning."

"Oh."

"Also, you can get henna on your hands, very beautiful."

Jemaa El-Fnaa square turned out not to be a square at all, but a large, irregularly shaped plaza, anchored by the Café de France at one end. She and Helen had passed through it early that morning, when it was still empty, without knowing what it was. Now it was just starting to come to life. On tables shaded by tarps and umbrellas, towers of oranges waited to be juiced. An old man speaking in a hoarse voice held an audience of camera-toting tourists captive. Florence assumed he was one of the public storytellers that she'd read about. Still more tourists sat in the shade while their hands and wrists got painted with intricate patterns.

A man approached Florence holding aloft a skinny black snake and attempted to drape it across her shoulders.

"No, thank you," she said, edging away.

He persisted.

"No," she said more forcefully.

He laughed at her. "Don't be scared."

Florence bristled. She wasn't *afraid*. Was that the only acceptable reason for refusing a snake around one's neck? She veered around him and kept walking. His laughter echoed gratingly behind her.

Here, finally, was Marrakesh's exoticism, albeit an exoticism made palatable to tourists, but she was no longer interested. She was hot. She was tired.

She reached the edge of the medina. A grand building sat in front of one of the gates, flanked by a trio of guards in different colored uniforms. She took out her phone to take a picture of it and they all started shouting at her at once. One of them started to cross the street toward her, still yelling. Several bystanders turned to watch. She felt the blood rush to her face and she put the phone back in her bag. She waved her hands in apology, and the guard retreated. A passerby in a full-body burka inspected her, the light glinting off her glasses. Florence walked away quickly and stepped in a pile of what she guessed was donkey shit.

It took Florence thirty minutes to find the car rental agency, and by the time she got there she was caked in dust. It clung to her damp skin and trembled on her eyelashes. She felt its grittiness between her teeth.

"De l'eau?" she asked the skinny teenager at the desk, her college French clunky on her tongue. She made a drinking motion with her hands. "Water?"

The teenager shook his head somberly. Florence sighed and handed over the printout of her reservation.

"Un moment," he said and disappeared behind a splintered plywood door.

There were two folding chairs against the wall. Florence sat in one and leaned her head back. A fan rattled above her.

The teenager returned with an older man who greeted her in English. She handed over Helen's driver's license. He gave it a cursory glance and slid it back across the counter.

"Come," he said. She followed him out through the door to the street. The man's plastic sandals slapped noisily against the soles of his feet. His heels were riven with deep, dry cracks.

The garage was next door. The man led her to a white Ford Fiesta and gestured at it grandly. "Brand new," he said, patting the roof. She thanked him and he stood aside and watched her climb into the car. She turned on the AC as high as it would go. At first the air was hot and rank, like someone's breath, but soon it began to cool off and dry the perspiration on her skin. It also started to clear the addled, heat-warped vagueness that had clung to her since she'd woken up. The man from the office was still standing there watching her. She jammed the gearshift into reverse and narrowly avoided hitting an old woman as she maneuvered the car out into the frantic stream of traffic.

24.

When Florence finally pulled up, fifteen minutes late, Helen was standing at the intersection next to the same man with the same wheelbarrow, their bags piled inside. She was wearing a broad-brimmed straw hat, which she placed on her lap as she climbed into the car.

"New?" asked Florence, gesturing to it.

"Yes, I got it on my walk home. Forty dirhams. Brahim was right—the souk was incredible."

Florence nodded and smiled. She leaned her head back against the seat briefly. Her entire body was tense. She hadn't understood any of the street signs on the drive. She'd nearly collided with a horse-drawn carriage containing two alarmed tourists. The man from the hotel shut the trunk and patted it lightly. Florence didn't move.

"Florence, let's go." Helen snapped her fingers at her, maybe facetiously but probably not.

"Sorry," she said, sitting up. She gripped the steering wheel and shifted the car into gear.

———

About an hour into the drive, the air conditioner conked out. Helen leaned forward and flicked at the vent a few times then threw herself violently into the back of her seat and closed her eyes. They had another two hours to go.

Florence shut off the broken AC and rolled down the windows. The wind howled through the car, and their hair spun and whirled as if underwater.

Florence swerved slightly as a truck passed them.

"Jesus, Florence—careful," exhaled Helen.

Helen's eyes were still closed, and she wasn't wearing her seat belt. She never did. Florence wondered what would happen if she were to slam on the brakes. Helen's head would probably bounce off the dashboard like a soccer ball.

There weren't many other cars on the road. She pressed her foot down on the accelerator and watched the needle climb upward. Soon they came to a curve and she had to ease off the gas. The sun had dipped lower, and its rays flickered through the trees. Helen opened her eyes and turned the radio on, then off. She lit a cigarette. She had to hold it inside the car so the wind wouldn't snatch it from her fingers. The smoke clung to Florence's throat.

They drove another hour in silence. The landscape became drier and dustier the farther they went. Marrakesh, Florence had read, was actually an oasis in the desert. Here, on the highway, there was none of the city's lushness or color. The heat and steady *thump-thump* of the wheels on the road lured them both into a trance. They started to awaken only after noticing that the air rushing into the car felt different. It had cooled off a few degrees, and it felt fresher and brighter. Florence thought she could smell the sea. The area around them was getting greener too. Florence glanced at the map on her phone. It looked like they were about ten or fifteen kilometers from Semat.

The road approached a steep drop and continued along the cliff's edge. Below, the Atlantic foamed and churned. The sun glinted off its surface in the distance. It was hard to believe it was the same body of water Florence had grown up beside. How disappointing the ocean must have found the flat-topped warehouses of Florida, she thought, after the ramparts and minarets of Morocco.

The cliffside road was barely wide enough for two lanes and every once in a while, when a car or a motorcycle raced toward them from the opposite direction, Florence felt compelled to slow to a near halt. She kept wiping her palms on the upholstery to dry the sweat.

A truck with canvas flaps closed in on her back bumper and let out a keening moan. It finally swerved around her, barely making it back into the right lane before a car on the other side zipped around a curve. Their competing horns created a distracting din in Florence's head.

Finally the road pulled away from the cliff's edge and soon after that Florence took a left onto a small road whose name matched the one on their rental papers. She breathed deeply through her nostrils as they bounced up the quiet street. It smelled like wet soil.

The road pulled them upward at a sharp incline, and soon a white house with vivid blue trim—another riad, Florence knew—loomed before them. It was perched, alone, at the top of a steep hill. They drove past a large boulder that had been painted white with VILLA DES GRENADES spelled out in blue.

"Des Grenades?" Florence had wondered aloud when they'd booked it. "Like hand grenades?"

"Pomegranates," Helen had corrected.

Florence drove through the gate and parked the car in the driveway. She leaned back in her seat. Her entire body was sticky.

A stout, gray-haired woman in her sixties emerged from the house. She walked down the path toward them with a hitch in her step. Helen and Florence climbed out of the car to greet her.

The woman stepped forward and shook Florence's hand. *"Bonjour, mesdames, bienvenue,"* she said.

"Do you speak English?" Helen responded.

"Yes, little," she said with a shy smile.

She introduced herself as Amina and explained that she had worked at Villa des Grenades for more than twenty years. She would do all the cooking, shopping, and cleaning. Anything they needed, just ask her. She lived right down the road, she said, gesturing somewhere down the hill. She tried to take their bags, but Florence insisted on carrying them herself.

Stepping inside the house, Florence felt a wave of panic. The floor was missing large chunks of tile, and mold had found refuge in every corner. Creepers stretched their long tendrils inside the windows, crawling up walls and across ceilings. There were brown stains where the weeds had made gains before being hacked away. They reminded Florence of the sticky wakes left by slugs back home.

Upstairs, the walls and floors were in similarly bad shape, but at least the sheets looked clean, and the water ran hot and cold. As in the hotel, the second floor was open in the center, dropping down to the sunny courtyard below.

Behind the house, a large slate-paved terrace stretched back toward a small pool shaded by palm trees whose shaggy trunks of loose, burlap-like bark made it look like they'd been caught in the act of undressing. The pool itself was only three-quarters filled, and a thick layer of green algae filmed the water. Bugs marched fearlessly across the surface. Three mangled lounge chairs were arranged around the edge, trailing broken vinyl straps on the ground below them. Amina pointed to a stack of clean towels folded neatly on a nearby table, which made Helen laugh.

"I'll call the rental agency," Florence said. "Let's see if there's anything else available. I promise the photos did not look like this on their website." Helen had seen the photos too and had okayed Florence's selection.

But Helen just said, "It's fine. It's absolutely fine."

———

Helen wanted to get some writing done that afternoon, so they settled in the large, bright living room on the ground floor, which had doors leading both to the terrace out back and to the tiled courtyard in the center of the house. Helen wrote in quick, frantic bursts, the pen careening wildly across the paper and occasionally digging a divot in the page.

Florence watched from the couch across the room. She, too, had a notebook on her lap and a pen in her hand, but she had not written anything.

One sentence, she told herself. Just write one sentence.

She wrote: *I am*.

The second shortest sentence in the English language.

I am ... what? I am what?

She put the cap back on the pen. She looked again at Helen, her brow furrowed in concentration.

Florence slapped the notebook on the table in front of her, eliciting an annoyed glance from Helen, then stood up and moved outside to the terrace. She lay down on one of the lounge chairs and closed her eyes. It was nearly 7 p.m., but the air was still warm. She listened to the rustling palm leaves and chattering birds.

She felt betrayed. She'd given up her mother, hadn't she? Why was she still unable to write? Where was the great torrent she'd been promised? Or was that only Helen's reward?

The shrillness of the bird calls started to annoy her. She went back inside and checked Helen's email on the laptop, which she'd set up at a carved wooden desk in a corner of the living room.

There were a few emails from Lauren, Greta's assistant, but nothing pressing. And one personal message in the Helen Wilcox account.

"You have an email from Sylvie Daloud," she said.

Helen looked up and blinked a few times. "Sorry, what? I was miles away."

"You have an email from Sylvie Daloud. She says she's getting her Met subscription for the upcoming season and wants to know if you're interested in coordinating your dates for some of the performances."

Helen set her notepad and pen on the table next to her. "Okay, I'll write back later."

Florence nodded and shut the laptop. "Helen, I know this is a stupid question...but how do you know what to write about?"

Helen frowned. "How do I know what to write about? I think that's getting it backward. When I wrote *Mississippi Foxtrot,* it wasn't like I decided to become a writer and then sought out a plot. I had a story that I needed to tell, so I wrote it down."

"Oh," Florence said, deflated, though she wasn't entirely sure what Helen meant: she'd had a story *in mind,* or one that had actually happened? Well, Florence didn't have either, so what did it matter. "What about now?" she added. "Is it the same process with your second book?"

"Well, no. Not exactly."

She paused for so long that Florence thought the conversation was over. Then Helen said, "Sometimes you have to make your own story."

"What do you mean?"

"All stories have to have some basis in reality, otherwise it won't feel authentic. But of course reality is malleable."

"Is it?"

"How could you even ask that? Of course it is. You make your own decisions. You act. This"—she gestured around her—"travel, is a way of changing your reality."

"I guess so," Florence said. She supposed she *had* altered her reality. She wouldn't be in Morocco with Helen if she hadn't sent those photos to Simon. Was that a story? Maybe her journey from Florida to New York to Morocco was enough of a plot. What did she know about wives who ate their husbands? She knew her own life. Maybe it was finally becoming interesting enough to write about.

————

Amina served them dinner on the back terrace among the rustling palms. They'd bought a bottle of whiskey at the duty-free shop in Lisbon, and they each poured a large glass.

Amina brought out plate after plate of food—harira soup with chickpeas and lentils, spiced puréed pumpkin, mashed eggplant, a dish of oily olives, flat sesame bread that reminded Florence of the bottom of an English muffin, and finally, a steaming lamb tagine with prunes. They kept their napkins tucked under their plates as they ate, so that the wind wouldn't snatch them away. The moon was a bright, crisp crescent in the sky.

"God, wasn't El Badi beautiful?" Helen asked, pouring them each more whiskey.

"I'm not sure I would call it beautiful. It was in ruins."

"But you can imagine what it must have looked like in all its glory. The scale of it; the sheer folly of it. Three hundred and sixty rooms. Marble from Italy. Gold from Sudan. What an undertaking. It certainly makes a persuasive case against democracy."

"How so?"

"Well, it obviously could never have been built under a democracy. Same as the pyramids of Egypt or Versailles. But aren't we happy to have them? Aren't we happy to know what feats of beauty men are capable of when they act without limitations? I suppose democracy is *fair*"—Helen put the word in air quotes—"but why is fairness always the goal? What about greatness? Sometimes you can't have both."

"I don't know. Isn't there something to be said for equality?"

"There's something to be said for everything, Florence. But when everyone is equal, everyone is interchangeable. It's a flattening out."

Florence didn't know how to respond.

"Tell me this—when you were growing up, did you really think the people around you were your equals?"

Florence shrugged noncommittally.

"You didn't, Florence. I know you. You thought you were better than them." She paused. "And my guess is you were right."

"Maybe," Florence mumbled. She took another sip of her whiskey and turned away to hide her smile.

"Take my word for it," Helen went on. "If you spend your life looking for fairness you'll be disappointed. Fairness doesn't exist. And if it did, it would be boring. It would leave no room for the unexpected. But if you search for greatness—for beauty, for art, for transcendence—those are where the rewards are. *That* is what makes life worth living." Helen set her glass of whiskey down roughly, splashing some on the table. "I'm sure there are people in my past who don't think it's fair that my life turned out like it did. And who knows, maybe it isn't. But I want you to understand this: I wouldn't change a single thing I've done. Not a single thing."

Florence loved when Helen spoke to her like this, like a worthy disciple. She was flattered that she'd brought her along on this trip. True, she was just here as her assistant, but there wasn't actually that much for her to do. Helen was spending a lot of money to have her here to type for an hour a day. It was possible, she thought, that Helen had just wanted her company. That she *liked* her.

"Helen," she said, before she could stop herself. She was feeling reckless.

Helen was humming and tapping her fingers lightly on the tabletop. She glanced up. "Hm?"

"How much of it is true?"

"How much of what?"

"Mississippi Foxtrot."

Helen shook her head. "What does it matter? I've never understood people's obsession with 'the facts.'"

"I don't know." Florence shrugged. "It won't change anything, I guess. I just want to know."

Helen stared at her for a moment without saying anything. Florence was worried she'd overstepped. Then Helen said, "Oh, fuck it. It's not like you're going to tell anyone."

"Of course not."

Helen looked at her with a brief, amused smile. "Ruby," she finally said.

Florence waited for her to elaborate. She didn't.

"Ruby *what*? Ruby's real?"

Helen nodded slowly. "Ruby is real. Except her name." She grimaced. "God, I hate the name Ruby. I don't know what I was thinking. It doesn't suit her at all."

"What's her real name?"

Helen smiled in a far-off, dreamy way. "Jenny. She was my best friend." She paused to light a cigarette. "My father, as you might have gathered from the book, was a worthless bastard and my mother was just, I don't know, barely there. She was beaten down. She was just waiting to die, I think. Which she did, when I was eight. So it was just Jenny. Me and Jenny." Helen sighed. "And then she killed that man, and it all ended." She snapped her fingers. "Our friendship. Childhood. Everything. My whole world ended."

"The murder was real?" Florence asked, eyes wide.

"Well, not all the details. He wasn't some guy just traveling through town; he had lived there for longer than we had. Then when Jenny turned fifteen, he developed this sick fascination with her. He used to follow her around, ask her on dates, wait outside her house. Finally she'd had enough. She shot him with her daddy's shotgun."

"That's horrifying."

Helen looked up in surprise. "Is it? To tell the truth, I've never been horrified. Far from it. I was—what? I was proud. Jealous, too, maybe. She'd gone somewhere no one we knew had ever been before. She told me that after she decided to shoot him but before she actually pulled the trigger, everything was heightened—all her senses, her emotions, everything. She could hear his lungs expanding, she could hear the blood pumping in his veins. And she felt this phenomenal power coursing through her body, like electricity. And I knew nothing about it; I couldn't relate at all. It was like she had been initiated into a club that wouldn't have me. I felt like an imposter. I had been pretending at being an adult, being knowing, being cold, being cynical. But she was something else. She was the real thing. And it cowed me. I couldn't tag along after her anymore. She had gone somewhere I couldn't. She'd left me behind."

Helen patted the table absently for her pack of cigarettes. She took one out and lit it with the stub of the one in her hand. Florence stayed silent, willing her to go on, but she didn't. She just smoked and stared.

"What happened to her?"

"She got twenty-five years."

"But in the book—"

"The *novel*."

"Right, the novel. In the novel, it was *you*. You made the Maud character the murderer."

Helen waved her hand. "Oh, it just makes a better story. Well, maybe it was the jealousy a little bit. I wanted to try and experience a faint shadow of what she had."

"So is Jenny still there?"

"Where?"

"Prison."

Helen's eyes refocused. Florence had broken the spell. "Yes, of course."

Then Helen exhaled loudly and opened her eyes wide. "Well!" she said, effectively ending their conversation. "That went in a direction I wasn't expecting." She laughed lightly and placed her hands on her thighs to push herself up to standing. "And now this old sack of bones needs to get to bed. See you in the morning? We'll go into town, do some exploring."

Florence nodded.

At the door, Helen turned back. "I don't need to remind you that this stays between us, do I?"

Florence shook her head.

"Good girl." She paused. "I'm glad you came, Florence."

Then she disappeared into the dark house without waiting for a response.

25.

The tangled vines in the window filtered the early morning light, leaving rippling shadows on the wall beside her. Florence looked at her watch. It was a little after eight. She swung her legs off the bed and planted her feet on the cool terra-cotta floor.

Downstairs, Amina had laid out breakfast on the terrace. There were fresh brioches in a basket covered with a clean dishtowel. Sweating butter in a ceramic ramekin and three kinds of jam. A bowl of honey so thick that a wooden spoon stood up straight in it. There were dishes of dates, almonds, pomegranate seeds, and slices of navel orange. There were three different pitchers of juice.

Florence sat down and startled a small, sparrow-like bird pecking at the breadbasket. It fluttered to a nearby chair.

"Sorry, little guy," she said, throwing him a bit of brioche. A bird's feathers weigh more than its skeleton, she remembered from somewhere.

Helen came down shortly afterward. She paused in the doorway and turned her face up to the sun.

"God, that feels good," she said.

They ate slowly and spoke very little. They were both slightly hungover. After breakfast, Florence checked their email at the laptop in the living room.

"You have a new message from Greta," she called out to

Helen, who was still on the terrace, smoking a cigarette and staring into the distance.

"What does it say?" she asked without turning her head.

"Hope the trip is going well, blah blah blah, and she wants to talk to you about something when you have a sec."

"About what?"

"It doesn't say. She just says to call her."

"Okay."

"Should I write back?"

"Nah. I'll give her a call in a little bit."

Florence logged into her own email. She had just one, from her mother. She scanned it quickly. She caught the word *betrayal* before closing the window.

———

They left for town around ten. At the door, Helen once again handed Florence all her belongings.

"You're bringing your passport?" Florence asked.

"Life lesson: Always keep your passport on you when you're abroad. You never know what's going to happen. Besides, I don't trust that woman."

"Amina?" Florence asked, laughing. "Come on."

"Don't mistake naivete for compassion. Your own I mean. You know nothing about her."

Florence rolled her eyes but still trudged back to her room and grabbed her passport.

Semat proper was a fifteen-minute drive from the villa, in the opposite direction from which they'd come. The town was huddled on a hill above the coast and encircled by ramparts the same color as the sandy beach. The wall helped block the fierce wind that blew in off the water and whipped up frothy waves on its surface. Inside the medina, where there were few cars, a tumble of white buildings were silhouetted against the bright blue sky. It had been founded by Berbers in the first century, and in the ensuing years, it had been occupied in turn by the Romans, the Portuguese, and the French. The guidebooks called it a fishing village, but now its economy depended mainly on tourism, making do with whatever visitors hadn't been snared by the more popular seaside resorts of Essaouira and Agadir.

Florence parked near Place Hassan II, close to the heart of Semat, just outside a building with an arched door painted a brilliant blue. In one direction lay the harbor and the beach; in the other, the town. As they stepped out of the car, Florence noticed a grittiness beneath the soles of her shoes. She looked down. It was sand, blown in from the shore.

She asked if they could stop in the souk; she'd wanted to go shopping since seeing Helen's hat. Inside the marketplace, which was a fraction of the size of the one in Marrakesh, sunlight flickered through rattan matting strung up overhead to block it. Several tables held tall piles of spices; Florence saw labels for saffron and cumin and harissa. Another held colorful ceramic tagines lined up in neat rows. She wandered over to a man selling tooled leather purses. Behind him, his partner was carving an intricate design into a flap of raw leather with a knife. Florence picked up a small, stiff red bag and opened it.

"Two hundred dirhams," the man behind the table said. "Twenty dollars."

Florence rotated the bag in her hands. She turned to Helen to ask her opinion, but Helen was a few paces away, watching a man pull feathers from a chicken carcass.

"Okay," Florence said to the man. "I'll take it." She fished the money out of her wallet.

She transferred the contents of her purse into her new bag and put it over her shoulder. She was happy she'd have a souvenir from the trip. She imagined getting compliments on it, and telling people where she'd found it. She walked over to Helen, who had moved on to inspecting the tagines, and showed it to her.

"You like?"

"How much?"

"Twenty dollars."

"Down from what?"

"Down from nothing. Twenty dollars seemed like a bargain."

"You didn't haggle?"

Florence shrugged. "He probably needs it more than I do."

"That's not the point. They respect people who know how to negotiate. Now he has one more reason to think all Americans are spineless, coddled buffoons."

Florence was briefly exasperated by Helen's determination to always cast her as a fool. "Exactly," she insisted, "wouldn't it be wrong to mislead him?"

Helen laughed, a begrudging snort.

They left the souk and passed through Place Hassan II again, toward the harbor. Vendors were grilling fresh fish at stalls up and down the street. Smoke billowed up into the air before being tugged away by the wind. There were dozens, maybe hundreds, of boats bobbing in the water, mostly beat-up rowboats painted a brilliant blue and single-man fishing operations, though there were a few tall wooden ships and a handful of small, ugly yachts. In a way, it reminded Florence of home. When she was in high school, she and her friend Whitney used to sneak onto empty boats at the harbor. You couldn't actually get inside, but you could lie on the deck and pretend it was yours.

They came across a man slapping an octopus on the ground over and over. They stopped to watch.

"What is he doing?" asked Florence.

"Tenderizing it," said Helen. "It's too tough to eat if you don't slap it around a little first."

They ate lunch outside at one of the seafood places on the harbor rather than walk back up into town. The breeze coming off the water seemed to blow in more of the same hot, heavy air. They each ordered octopus fresh from the ocean, or advertised that way, with a variety of grilled vegetables and bottles of the local beer, Casablanca. As the sun climbed toward its apex, the shade of their umbrella shifted and exposed Helen's bare legs. She asked Florence to switch seats with her.

"Your young skin can handle the sun," she said.

Florence frowned at this justification; she was only six years younger. But then she reminded herself that she wouldn't even be here if not for Helen and quickly stood up.

Under the sun's glare, Florence felt herself wilt. She held the bottle of beer to her forehead and neck. She could barely look at the octopus. She thought of it being pounded to death on the ground. She pushed the plate away.

"You're not eating?" Helen asked.

Florence shook her head.

Helen pulled the plate toward her. "I'm starving."

When Helen finished her meal, she lit a cigarette and tapped the ash onto the uneaten tentacles on her plate. Florence looked away in disgust.

The walk back up to the square under the scorching sun was steeper than Florence remembered. She recalled that she had wanted to buy a hat. "It's hot as blue blazes," she said under her breath.

"What was that?" Helen asked.

"Nothing."

Florence hadn't thought to park in the shade, and they had to bunch up their dresses in their hands to grasp the door handles. The air-conditioning was still broken.

———

That afternoon they both retreated to their rooms. Florence tried to nap but she slept fitfully and woke up feeling less rested than she had before she lay down. It was past eight by the time they left for dinner. Florence was wearing a white cotton dress and a pair of leather sandals she'd splurged for in Hudson along with her new bag. Her face was pink from the sun.

She knocked on Helen's door. "Ready?"

"One minute," Helen called from inside. "Just finishing up some work."

Florence heard a drawer slam roughly then Helen swung open the door. She was wearing a navy dress that buttoned up the front, with a blue-and-white-striped scarf over her shoulders. "Let's hit it," she said, with the short stub of a cigarette sticking out of the corner of her mouth. Her whole room reeked of tobacco. So much for the no-smoking clause in their rental agreement, Florence thought.

In the hallway, Helen flicked her cigarette butt over the side of the railing with ink-stained fingers. It floated down fifteen feet or so to the hard tiled floor below. Florence grimaced at the thought of Amina stooping to pick it up later. At the door, Helen handed her belongings to Florence once again.

The night was nearly as warm as the day, the air scented with jasmine. They drove with the windows open and the sea air whipping their faces. They were going to a restaurant up in the hills, just north of Semat, which a friend of Helen's had recommended to her.

"What friend?" Florence had wanted to ask, but didn't.

"So you haven't really explained what type of research you want to do for the book," she said instead.

"Hm?" Helen asked, looking out her window.

"I mean, is there anything you want me to do while we're here? Talk to anyone? Visit anyplace? I'm still not exactly sure what I'm supposed to be doing."

"Oh, nothing so regimented. I just want to get a feel for the place, that's all."

The car's engine hummed as the road climbed upward. Both the town and Villa des Grenades receded in the rearview mirror. The road clung to the coastline even as it rose ten, then twenty, then thirty feet above the churning Atlantic below. Florence gripped the steering wheel tightly. It was a windy night, and sudden gusts kept buffeting the car. She inched it closer to the right side of the road, as far from the drop as she could.

"This is rather treacherous, isn't it?" Helen said.

Florence just nodded without taking her eyes off the road in front of her. She hadn't wanted to betray her nervousness; she'd assumed Helen would mock her for it.

They arrived at the restaurant without incident fifteen minutes later. Florence rubbed a tight knot in her shoulder as Helen pulled open the door, fighting against the wind.

The restaurant was empty except for two other patrons, a British couple in their sixties who were already on dessert.

The host greeted them warmly. "Bienvenue, welcome," he said.

"Two whiskeys," said Helen in response, holding up two fingers.

Florence had discovered only after they'd booked their trip that they were missing Ramadan by just a few days. It would have been nothing short of a disaster if Helen hadn't been able to drink.

They were led to their table by a waiter who looked like he was pushing ninety. A few moments later, the whiskey arrived in glasses smudged with greasy fingerprints.

"When in Rome..." Florence said with a shrug, reaching for her drink.

"...get salmonella," Helen finished.

They tapped their glasses together. "To new beginnings," Helen pronounced. They both took a long swallow.

———

Helen had ordered them both the house specialty, camel, but when their food arrived, Florence was put off by the pile of meat in front of her. She was feeling the effects of the sun and the heat, and she suspected she had drunk too much on an empty stomach. Tinny Arabic music played from a speaker mounted above their table, and it seemed to be getting louder, strobing in conspiracy with the lights.

Helen was talking but she seemed very far away. Everything felt very far away. Florence felt as if her whole self, her whole consciousness, had shrunk down to the size of a pebble and was knocking around inside her skull. Her insides felt dark and vast, the outer world too distant to matter, like a movie projected on a remote screen. The meat on her plate seemed to be sweating. Do you keep sweating after you die? No, no, that was toenails and hair that kept going. Growing.

The music quieted down then. Everything got quieter. As if underwater. Sounds were swallowed up by the water. She felt lulled by a swift current, swept away by the waves, pulled back by strong hands, then swept away again, and all the while Helen's voice was deep and pulsating, like a whale's song, like an echo, like a shadow in sound, like it had all been said before and would be said again but deeper and richer until it faded away entirely and all that was left were the waves. Lapping softly, softly, softly—

PART IV

26.

M adame Weel-cock?"

The next time Florence woke, she was more lucid. She'd been in a car accident, she remembered the doctor had said. And she remembered, too, that he had called her Madame Wilcox. What did that mean? Where was Helen? Perhaps in another bed, in another room, being called Madame Darrow?

When the nurse returned, Florence asked, "The woman who was with me in the car, is she here?"

The nurse looked at her blankly.

"Is there another American at the hospital? A woman?" She struggled to find some basic French vocabulary in the foggy recesses of her brain. *"Autres américaines? Ici? A l'hôpital?"*

The nurse shook her head. *"Il n'y a que vous."* Just her.

"There was a woman in the car with me. Do you know what happened to her? *L'autre femme?"*

The nurse smiled helplessly and shrugged.

"Have I had any visitors? *Quelqu'un visite,* um, *moi?"*

The nurse shook her head. *"Personne,"* she said before leaving.

Florence contemplated the ceiling. No one. No one had been to visit her.

She turned her head toward the window and noticed for the first time a wrinkled plastic bag on the table next to her bed. She reached for it and a jolt of pain shot through her ribs. Grimacing, she pulled it onto her lap.

Inside were the clothes she'd been wearing the night before: the white dress, her underwear, and the purse she'd bought earlier in the day. It was all soaking wet. Zippered into the side pocket of the purse were Helen's passport, wallet, phone, and a sodden pack of cigarettes. Well, that explained why everyone was calling her Madame Wilcox. There was nothing else in the purse. Her own wallet and phone and passport were gone.

She pressed the power button on Helen's phone. Nothing happened.

27.

Florence woke with a start. She was out of breath and her heart was beating too fast. As she rubbed her eyes, she realized that there was someone else in the room with her. It was the man in the uniform she'd seen the first time she woke up in the hospital. The one the nurse had shooed away. Why did he only appear when she was asleep? He was like a figure conjured by her dreams.

"Madame Weel-cock," he said. "Do you remember me? I am Hamid Idrissi of the Gendarmerie Royale. It is important that I now ask you questions about the accident." His English was slightly off, but better than she would have expected from a small-town policeman in Morocco.

Florence looked around, hoping the nurse might appear to provide another reprieve, but no one came. She nodded at the policeman.

The man patted his pockets until he found a small beige notebook, which he pulled out along with a chewed-up pen. All his movements had a jerky abruptness to them, as though his joints were brand-new and he was still getting used to them.

"The first. Do you remember the events of last night?"

Florence shook her head.

Idrissi flipped back a few pages in the notebook and said, "Your car went off Rue Badr into the ocean at around twenty-two and a half hours. Luckily, there was a fisherman out late who saw this happen. He pulled you from the car and brought you to safety. You arrived at the hospital at twenty-three hours. Unconscious."

An inappropriate smile came out of nowhere and spread across Florence's face. She felt like the butt of a joke.

"My car went into the ocean?" she asked skeptically. "And someone pulled me out of it while it was sinking?"

"That is what happened, yes."

Florence kept looking at him, waiting for the punch line. He stared back at her. He had a wary, tired look in his eyes. Her smile faded. She struggled to process this new information. It seemed absurd that something like that could have happened without her having any memory of it. The single most dramatic moment of her life, and she'd missed it. Typical.

That road, Rue Badr, was the one they'd taken to get to the restaurant. She remembered the way the shoulder of the road had simply dropped off the face of the earth. It seemed incredible that just a few hours later, their jaunty Ford Fiesta had hurled it-self into the night sky and crashed into the blue-black water.

She tried to imagine herself and Helen suspended in midair, between land and sea. Had they known what was happening?

And more importantly: Where was Helen now?

She started to ask, but the policeman spoke at the same time: "Madame, what is your last memory of the night?"

Florence tried to think back. The camel meat. The tinny music. "Dinner," she said. "The restaurant."

"What restaurant?"

"It was up in the hills. Dar Amal? Something like that?"

He wrote this down in his notebook.

"And were you drinking alcohol?"

Florence willed herself to stay very still. "Pardon?"

"Did you drink alcohol at dinner?"

Florence said nothing. Was he suggesting that the accident was *her* fault? His expression gave away nothing.

"Madame Weel-cock?"

"I don't remember," she finally said. "I can't remember, I'm sorry." She shook her head.

"Are you aware that it is illegal in Morocco to drive after drinking alcohol? Even just one alcohol?"

She remembered the two greasy glasses of whiskey. How good that first sip had felt going down after the nerve-wracking drive. And then what? What had happened after that first glass? She couldn't remember. There was just darkness.

Her unanswered question returned: Where was Helen?

And others: Why hadn't Helen been to visit her? Why did she still have Helen's passport and wallet? How could Helen *not* have been in the car? Of course they would have driven back from the restaurant together.

So, where was Helen?

She circled around this question slowly. Even after an answer had arrived, she continued to seek alternatives, as if a few more moments of uncertainty could change the outcome.

The policeman continued to look at her significantly.

Was it possible? Had Helen been killed in the accident?

"Madame Weel-cock, I'll ask again: Are you aware that it is illegal to drive after drinking alcohol?"

Florence forced herself to answer. "I am aware of that. I wouldn't have had anything to drink if I knew I was driving home."

He nodded slowly, watching her.

"So—." She wanted to ask this man something, but she didn't know what. Why hadn't he mentioned the other person in the car?

"Wait, but who? Who rescued me?"

"Fisherman."

"But who?"

"You want his name?"

"His name? I guess I do. I should thank him, right?"

The policeman rubbed his temples. He copied a name and phone number from his notebook onto a clean page, ripped it out, and handed the paper to Florence. "I doubt he speaks English," he warned.

She placed it on the bed without looking at it and shut her eyes tightly. When she did, she saw, as if projected on her eyelids, an image of Helen banging furiously on the car window, watching helplessly as Florence was spirited to safety. Is that what happened? Did the fisherman leave Helen there? Did he just not see her? Or did he only have enough strength or time to save one of them, and he'd chosen her? My god, what a fool. He'd picked the wrong one.

She shook her head to dislodge the image of Helen drowning. Certainly, she would know if she'd killed Helen.

Wouldn't she?

She felt her conviction wobbling. She remembered that she hadn't eaten lunch or dinner the day before. Maybe she really had gotten drunk and driven the car off the road. It was the only explanation that made sense. Helen would be here with her if anything else had happened, either as a patient herself or as a visitor who'd somehow emerged from the accident unscathed.

Florence felt tears stinging her eyes and blinked them back.

The policeman uncrossed and recrossed his legs and asked her where she was from.

"What?" she asked, surprised to suddenly get such an easy question.

"Where are you from?"

"The US."

The policeman continued with a series of benign questions. How long had she been in Morocco? Where was she staying? What was the purpose of her visit?

"Research," she said.

He glanced up severely at that. "You're a journalist?"

"No," she said quickly, startled at his tone. "No. For a book. Fiction."

He seemed appeased. "You're a novelist?"

Florence looked down at her hands. She nodded, once.

He stayed for close to half an hour but never mentioned Helen. Finally, he stood up to leave, and said, "You are very lucky" in a way that made it sound like an accusation. As he turned and grasped the curtain, Florence said, "Wait."

He looked back.

"What about the car?" she asked. "Was it dredged?"

"What is 'dredged?'"

"Pulled out of the water?"

"Yes, of course. But it is finished." He spoke as if she were a child. "The engine is all wet. There is no windshield."

"No, that's not..." Florence paused.

There was no windshield. It must have shattered on impact. And Helen, Helen who never wore a seat belt...

He continued to stare at her intently.

"So there wasn't any...thing else in the car?"

"What else?"

She paused.

"My shoes," she finally said. "I'm missing my shoes. They were expensive."

Idrissi flared his nostrils. He pulled his phone out of his pocket and made a call, speaking rapidly in Arabic. When he hung up, he said to her, "No shoes. But they found a scarf."

"A scarf?"

"Yes. A blue-and-white-striped scarf. Were you wearing something like that?"

In her mind's eye, Florence watched Helen flick her cigarette over the edge of the railing, her striped scarf slipping from her shoulders as she did.

"Yes, that's mine," she whispered.

"Okay, I will collect it for you."

"Thank you." She stared resolutely at the thin blanket covering her legs. She wanted him to leave. And with a violent yank at the curtain, he obliged.

She forced herself to breathe more slowly.

He didn't know there was someone else in the car. He didn't know she'd killed someone. He didn't know. Helen must have just . . . floated away.

Florence put her hands over her face. She stayed like that for several minutes, until she realized that what she was doing was a type of performance, and that she had no audience. She put her hands back on the bed.

28.

Early the next morning, a nurse brought Florence some forms to sign; she was being released. The forms were written in Arabic, but Florence didn't care. She printed the name Helen Wilcox where the nurse pointed and scribbled an illegible signature underneath.

And just like that, the chance for Florence to tell them that she was not Helen Wilcox came and went.

Her legs almost collapsed beneath her when she stood up. The nurse helped her to a communal bathroom in the hallway. It was small and filthy. For the first time she felt grateful for the bedpan she'd been using until then.

She dressed stiffly, avoiding a brackish puddle on the concrete floor. Afterward, she spent a long time looking in the mirror. Her face was swollen and discolored. She had a strange feeling of disassociation, as if the mirror were in fact a window or a photograph of someone else. She remembered when people were drunk in college they would draw with Sharpie on the faces of friends who had passed out. She felt like someone had done that to her—painted on bruises and blood with stage makeup while she slept.

But of course they were real. They were tender and raw. The salt-stiff fabric of her dress stung when it scraped against the abrasions on her body. The heavy tape wrapped around her torso pulled at her purpled skin.

She turned on the hot water tap at the sink and held her hands underneath the uneven stream. It stayed a disgusting tepid temperature even after several minutes. She shut it off in frustration.

Before she was released, they handed her a bill. It came out to ninety US dollars. She put it on Helen's credit card. Then the policeman, Idrissi, arrived to drive her back to Villa des Grenades. She would rather have taken a taxi, but she didn't want to raise suspicion. What innocent person would refuse a policeman offering a ride? Especially someone without any shoes.

In the car, she turned to ask him, "Am I in trouble?"

"As I said, it is against the law, alcohol and driving."

"But why do you think I was drinking? Was I Breathalized?"

"What is that?"

"I mean, do you have proof that I was drinking?"

"The restaurant says yes."

"You talked to them?"

"Of course I talked to them."

Florence shifted uncomfortably in her seat. The seat belt was hurting her ribs. "What will happen?" she asked.

The car in front of them stopped suddenly, and Idrissi punched the horn. He leaned his head out the window and shouted angrily at the other driver. When they were moving again, he leaned back in his seat and took a deep breath. At the next stoplight he turned to Florence and said, "What will happen? Probably nothing. Tourism is important here. You understand?"

Florence nodded. She felt ashamed, as she was sure he'd intended her to.

"My nephew was in jail for six months for this. But my nephew, of course, is not American."

"I'm sorry," Florence said lamely. She didn't ask, although she wondered, why he hadn't been able to use his police connections to help get his nephew out of it. Maybe that didn't happen here.

"Your English is very good," she said, hoping flattery might soften him.

"Yes, I'm chosen for the new *brigade touristique*," he said through gritted teeth. "Police. Just for tourists."

"Congratulations," Florence said unsurely.

He scoffed and pressed harder on the gas.

When they arrived at the house, Amina started down the foot-path to meet the car. She stopped when she saw the policeman behind the wheel. He nodded at her. She just looked at him.

As Florence put her hand on the door handle, Idrissi suddenly asked, "Where is your friend?"

She spun to face him. "What friend?" she asked sharply. She thought she saw a shadow of a smile on his face, as if he'd been waiting to spring that question on her.

"The one you ate dinner with at Dar Amal."

Of course. He'd spoken with the restaurant.

Florence wondered if it was too late to come clean; to tell him about the whiskey and the scarf and the dark hole in her memory. She opened her mouth and shut it again.

"She took a taxi home early," she said so quietly that Idrissi had to lean in to hear her.

"Why's that?"

"She wasn't feeling well."

"Did the restaurant call the taxi?"

Florence shook her head. "She did it on her phone."

"And where is she now? She didn't come to see you in the hospital?"

Florence shrugged. "Her plan was to go back to Marrakesh the next morning. I assume she still went. She probably doesn't even know about the accident."

Idrissi stared at her and said nothing.

Florence hesitantly returned her hand to the door handle. When Idrissi made no move to stop her, she opened it and climbed out.

As she started to walk away, Idrissi rolled down the passenger window and called out, "Madame Weel-cock?"

Florence turned.

"Tell me if you have plans to leave Semat." He held a business card out the window. She slipped it into her still-damp purse then stepped gingerly across the driveway in her bare feet to where Amina stood. The two women watched Idrissi drive away down the hill.

When his car was out of sight, Amina turned and gestured at the bruises on her face and the cast on her wrist. "You are okay?" she asked.

"I'm fine," Florence reassured her. She felt a rush of relief to be someplace familiar. She was grateful for this woman's kindness, in stark contrast to Idrissi's anger and suspicion.

She followed the older woman into the house and went straight upstairs. Her body ached and she longed to lie down. But before going into her own room, she went to investigate Helen's. All of Helen's clothes were still hanging in the closet. Her jewelry was scattered on top of the dresser. Even her toothbrush was in its place in the cup on the sink. It all looked as if their owner were due back at any moment. A small part of Florence had been holding on to the hope that Helen really had left Semat on her own, but now she saw how foolish that was. Helen wouldn't have left without her clothes, her toothbrush, her passport.

Florence ran her hand lightly across the dresses hanging in the closet. The hangers responded with a quiet tinkling.

She sat down heavily on Helen's bed and pulled the pain medication she'd been given at the hospital from her purse. She swallowed two hydrocodones with water from a half-empty glass that had been sitting there for two days. She collapsed backward and stared up at the shadows on the ceiling. It had been a mistake to lie to the police. But she couldn't have told him that there was someone else in the car. They might look the other way when a tourist drove drunk, but they certainly wouldn't if she'd killed someone in the process. Manslaughter was manslaughter.

Besides, what was the point? Helen was clearly gone. It wasn't like she was hanging on a piece of flotsam, waiting to be rescued. She was dead. Nothing could change that.

Florence tried to consider the implications of this fact. She would never see Helen again. She now had no job and no home. No one would ever read another word by Maud Dixon. Florence waited for the tears to come. But the painkillers were starting to kick in and her head felt cloudy. Everything was muffled.

Her thoughts kept returning to Helen's body. Where was it right now? She knew from the sensationalized Florida news shows her mother liked to watch that bodies became unidentifiable after just a few days in the water, bloated with water and eaten away by fish. She also knew that in some cultures—most cultures—the treatment of dead bodies was of sacred importance, but Florence had never understood that, and she suspected Helen would not have sanctioned such sentimentality either. The dead were dead. The rites were just a salve for the living.

She rolled over onto her side and looked around Helen's room. It was much bigger than hers.

Without another thought, she was asleep.

29.

Florence spent the next day in bed. Even if she hadn't been in too much pain to get up and do anything, she was paralyzed by crushing anxiety. *What had she done?* How was it possible that in the last sixty hours she'd killed her boss—one of America's most respected novelists—and lied to the police about it? It was like it had happened to someone else.

She tried over and over again to remember the night of the accident. She shut her eyes and saw the drive to the restaurant, the whiskeys, the camel meat.

And then what?

She couldn't keep the narrative going. She tried to gain enough momentum from the beginning of the story to sail through the point at which her memories stopped. Drive. Whiskey. Camel. Drive. Whiskey. Camel. *Then what?* Then...nothing.

There was nothing there.

Had she really drunk that much? She'd blacked out from drinking before, but not for years. Not since college. Of course, she had been drinking on an empty stomach. Stupid.

She shut her eyes tightly again. *Drive. Whiskey. Camel.*

And all of a sudden she remembered a rush of water. Was she just imagining it? No. There it was again—cold water, rising quickly.

And there was more: A hand gripping her arm tightly. Whose hand? The fisherman's?

She opened her eyes and pushed up her sleeve to inspect her upper arm. Much of the skin on her upper body was discolored, but she thought she could discern four small bruises—each the size of a fingerprint—that were distinct from the rest.

Just then Amina knocked on the door.

"Come in," Florence called out hoarsely.

The older woman entered with a tray of toast and eggs. She returned a minute later with a large brass teapot and poured Florence a steaming cup of mint tea. It would have been easier for her to pour it in the kitchen, but Florence appreciated the ceremony of it. Her mother had rarely been able to take off a day from work when she'd been sick as a child, and she was enjoying Amina's ministrations.

Amina watched with satisfaction as Florence sipped the sweet tea. "Your friend is gone?" she asked.

Florence hadn't said anything about why she'd swapped rooms or what had happened to Helen. She hadn't even explained where her bruises had come from. She could have blamed the lapse on confusion from the pain medication, but the truth was that she couldn't stand the thought of Amina looking at her in the same way that policeman had. She nodded.

"She will return?"

"I don't think so. She went back to Marrakesh."

"Without..." Amina gestured around the room that was strewn with Helen's belongings.

"She brought a few things in a small bag. I'll bring the rest when I go."

Amina nodded.

Florence spent much of the day dozing. She kept waking up in a confused panic. Maybe she'd gotten food poisoning, she thought at one point, eager for an explanation that would shift the burden of responsibility. Maybe Helen had somehow forced her to drink too much. She'd certainly been liberal with the wine back in the States.

Finally, as dusk was falling, Florence reached over and took a double dose of her pain medication. The next time she woke, it was morning.

————

The heat had thickened overnight, and Florence could feel it lying heavily on her like another blanket. It might already have been ninety degrees. She kicked off the covers, pushed two pillows against the headboard, and shimmied herself up as gently as she could to a sitting position. She was sore, but the pain had lost its sharp edges. She reached for her phone before remembering that she didn't have one anymore. She looked at the hydrocodones on the bedside table but decided not to take one. Yesterday had been a swirl of confusion and frustration and paranoia, fueled in part, she felt sure, by the pain medication. She couldn't do that again.

Sitting there in the hot, bright room, she could smell the sourness rising from her body. She hadn't showered in more than two days. She smelled deeply, grotesquely of herself—flesh marinated in its own excretions. How much effort we have to put into concealing our own scent, she thought.

She walked into Helen's large tiled bathroom on shaky legs and took a long shower, holding the wrist with the cast on it outside the stream of water as best she could. Her scrapes stung, but it felt pleasantly bracing. The pain reinforced her physicality. She didn't want to be in her head right now.

Afterward, still wrapped in a towel, she patted on some thick moisturizer from a glass jar on the counter. She combed her hair back and looked at herself in the mirror.

She understood how she could have been mistaken for Helen at the hospital, at least in comparison to the photograph in Helen's sodden passport. The major points matched—slender build, blond hair, dark eyes. And her face was swollen and bruised, which obscured most of its individuality. She was reminded of a piece of writing advice Helen had once given her: You only need to give one or two details about a character's physical appearance. It's all the reader needs to build an image in her mind. Anything more is a distraction.

Florence put on a pair of Helen's underwear—gray silk. She opened the door to Helen's closet and pulled out a beige linen dress with horn buttons running down the center. She slipped on a few of Helen's bracelets.

She remembered suddenly that Helen had been wearing chunky bangles on the night of the accident. Had she tried to swim out of the car? Could they have weighed her down?

She patted her cheeks lightly. It doesn't matter, she told herself. It doesn't matter. Don't get sucked into an endless stream of questions again.

Downstairs on the terrace she ate heartily. She slathered brioches with butter and jam and asked Amina to make her fried eggs. She drank three cups of coffee with cream. Afterward, she flopped down in one of the lounge chairs. Amina brought her some cold water with mint and lemon in it. The glass had already started sweating before she set it down. Florence closed her eyes and felt the heat press on her.

Helen was dead.

She rotated the thought around, like she was holding it up to the light, inspecting it on all sides. Helen was dead.

She waited, again, to feel something: grief, maybe guilt. But neither came.

Death is the most transformative event in anyone's existence, she thought, yet once it has happened, it doesn't matter to that person anymore. There's no person left. At that point, any significance it has fragments and scatters. Its impact is diffused among the survivors.

And who were they, for Helen? Her mother was dead, and she was estranged from the rest of her family. Who else was there?

Her editor? By Helen's account, they were not close. Greta? She might feel the sting of losing a client, but everyone has their share of professional disappointments.

Really, the only person to feel sorry for was herself. She was the one who'd been injured, left alone in a foreign country, shorn of a job, a home, and a mentor in one fell swoop.

Yet she didn't feel anything. No pity, no regret, nothing.

And in the lack of this emotion, of any emotion really, Florence was able to view the facts in a clearheaded way. And what she found so interesting about the facts, so *very* interesting, was that no one knew what had happened. She was the only person on earth who knew that Helen Wilcox was dead.

30.

It's possible that some part of Florence knew what she was going to do the moment she heard Officer Idrissi whisper that name in her ear: Madame Weel-cock. Or maybe it was earlier—maybe it was the first time she walked into Helen's cold, whitewashed house five weeks before and saw the ranunculus in the window, the glowing fireplace. Certainly by the time she found herself lying under Semat's glaring sun on that unseasonably hot morning there was little doubt in her mind.

She was going to become Helen Wilcox.

And why not? Helen's identity was just waiting there, unused, like a big, empty house. Meanwhile, she was living in a small, ugly, Florence-size hovel. Why shouldn't she move into the abandoned mansion? Why should she let it fall into disrepair instead? She could go in and do some upkeep. Clean the gutters, wash the floors, make sure it stayed in good shape.

She already had the keys; that was the amazing part. She *knew* how to be Helen. She was more experienced in the minor bureaucracy of Helen's life than Helen was herself—she lived in her house and paid her bills and wrote her emails. She certainly thought she could pass, physically, for Helen; she already had. Helen's passport and driver's license photos were small and outdated anyway, obscured by both holograms and, now, water damage. Helen's most prominent feature was the sharp bump on her nose, but it wasn't really visible in a photograph taken straight-on. Besides, who really looked all that closely at these photos anyway?

She remembered then that she didn't even have her own passport; it had, like Helen, been swept away in the current. In the normal course of events, she would go to the embassy and get a new one, but the normal course of events had done nothing but disappoint her for her entire life. Besides, what did she need Florence Darrow's passport for anymore?

Florence couldn't help letting out a quiet laugh: a small, whispery exhale. This situation was so bizarre, so unlikely, that it seemed to her that it *must* be a gift from some higher power, maybe even the one her mother had promised her for all those years. *This* was her chance at greatness. She could simply step into the void Helen had left behind. It all just hinged on not telling anyone that Helen had died.

Florence flung an arm across her eyes. She lay very still for several minutes.

She felt light, light in her bones, light in her soul. All those old doubts and insecurities and anxieties, her constant companions—those belonged to Florence Darrow, and she could finally let them go. She didn't have to try so hard to change anymore. Change? What a hoax! Nobody changes. They spend years tweaking their habits, taking small incremental steps in the hopes of altering the course of their lives, and it never works. No. You just have to know when to cut your losses. And Florence Darrow was, without a doubt, a write-off. She had no one. She'd published nothing. What would even be worth saving? She would purge it all. She would shrug off Florence Darrow in one swift motion and clothe herself in Helen Wilcox. An extraordinary life. The life of an artist; a writer.

And Maud! She hadn't even considered Maud Dixon yet! She was getting two identities for the price of one. Helen Wilcox *and* Maud Dixon.

She could be Maud Dixon.

Could she?

She could never come out publicly as Maud Dixon aka Helen Wilcox—that would invite too much scrutiny—but she could certainly publish her own work under Maud Dixon's name. The next book was already under contract; all she had to do was finish it. In fact, Greta hadn't even seen the beginning yet; she could write the whole thing herself. Then she'd finally see her work in print. And it wouldn't just be a handful of words here and there, like she'd been toying with in Cairo; it would be the whole thing. *Hers.* She didn't even care that it wouldn't be under her real name. "Florence Darrow" already felt like a relic from the past. She had no attachment to it. And she was sure that under Maud Dixon's name, people would finally see her talent. It's all about packaging—how often had Agatha told her that?

Helen was right: Fame didn't matter; it was about pride. *She* would know that the words everyone was reading were hers.

Though maybe, one day, years from now, the world would find out that she was Maud Dixon. . . .

She shook her head. Stop. She was getting ahead of herself. She forced herself to take a breath. She needed to make a plan for the immediate future.

She would stay here in Morocco for the remainder of the trip they'd booked—one more week. She didn't want to do anything that would raise suspicion for any reason. She would proceed as if everything were normal. And then what? She would go home to Helen's house. *Her* house. Move into the master bedroom. Light fires in the big fireplace. Read all of the books that lined the walls of Helen's study. Learn to cook. Grow tomatoes.

She'd have enough money to never work again, especially if she lived as frugally as Helen had. She could devote all her time to writing. She could write upstairs in Helen's beautiful study. She'd play opera and wait for her genius to flow. Surely it just needed a hospitable environment. Of course it hadn't wanted to poke its head out in her small, dark room in Astoria, surrounded by cheap Ikea furniture and empty yogurt containers.

She felt a surge of energy. Yes, yes! She was finally getting what was owed her.

Florence had been so cautious her whole life, working hard and following the rules, because she knew that that offered her the best chance of getting out of Florida—and away from Vera. And it had worked. Her discipline had taken her first to Gainesville, then to Forrester, and finally to Helen.

It had only been in the last few months—starting with that first encounter with Simon—that she'd begun to push against those self-imposed restraints. The old rules, she'd decided somewhere along the way, no longer applied.

Helen had told her once—referring to her writing, though it could also be applied to the way she lived her life—that the important thing is always to move the plot forward. Momentum matters. In general, she said, women tended to spend too much time considering consequences; by the time they finally made a decision, the men were already there, forging alliances, crossing battle lines, breaking things.

Mistakes, Helen said, can always be rewritten.

Well, fine. Florence would act too. She would break things and, if necessary, fix them later.

She smiled. Yes, this was a good plan. It was a very good plan.

Then she stood up and brushed some dried leaves off the back of her dress. She found Amina in the kitchen and asked her to call a taxi. She'd been cooped up too long. Far longer than the two days since the accident. She'd been cooped up for twenty-six years in Florence Darrow's small, cramped life.

"Feeling better?" Amina asked.

Florence smiled. "Much."

31.

The taxi dropped her off at the northern tip of the long, crescent-shaped beach. It lay just south of the harbor where she and Helen had watched the fisherman pound his octopus against the ground only four days before.

Florence stood at the top of a set of uneven stairs leading down to the sand and stared out at the water. The waves rolled in in low, steady curls like ice cream under a scoop. The wind whipped across the sand, picking up snatches of it here and there before tossing it away. By the base of the stairs, three camels sat in the sun under colorful blankets. A man dozed nearby, their leads in his hand.

Florence hadn't been to a beach in years. The last time had been in Florida during college. She'd gone swimming alone and been stung by a jellyfish. She'd staggered up to the shore, and a woman on the beach had poured cold Evian water into a towel and held it against her reddening skin.

"Jellyfish are actually ninety-five percent water," Florence had told her confidingly, woozy from the pain.

"But how can you tell which water belongs to them and which water belongs to the ocean?" the woman had asked. It was a good question.

Florence took off her sandals and walked down the beach. When she reached a relatively open space, she spread out the threadbare towel she'd taken from the house and buried the corners to hold it down. It rippled and pulled at its moorings but stayed put.

Even through the thin fabric, she could feel how hot the sand was. There were no clouds in the sky—just a few white contrails left by airplanes that were long gone. She stripped to her bathing suit—a black bikini of Helen's—and walked down to the water's edge. It was colder than she'd thought it would be. She waded in up to her waist. She wanted desperately to dive in but the doctor had told her to keep her cast dry. How was she going to get it off? She'd have to go to a doctor in New York. She plunged her head under the surface, holding her broken wrist up in the air. She emerged feeling reinvigorated.

As she walked back to her towel, a few people turned their heads to look at the purple bruises mottling her stomach and chest. They quickly glanced away in embarrassment, as if it were indecent of her to so brashly expose the frailty of the human body. She had used Helen's makeup to cover her face as best she could, but there wasn't much she could do about her body. She pulled *The Odyssey* out of her bag and lay down on her stomach gingerly. But instead of reading she let her head collapse onto her arms. Her skin had already grown hot again, and it smelled like Helen's moisturizer. She closed her eyes and breathed in the deep, musky scent.

She wasn't sure whether or not she'd been asleep when a shadow fell across her face. She opened her eyes. A girl who looked to be around twenty loomed over her. There was a phone tucked into her sagging orange bikini bottom and a dolphin tattoo on her stomach.

"Hi," she said. She was chewing on her lower lip, which was chapped and swollen.

Florence just looked at her.

"Sorry, I know this is annoying, but would you mind putting some sun lotion on my back?"

Florence stared at her for another beat. "How did you know I spoke English?"

"Your book."

Florence glanced at the incriminating evidence. "Oh."

"Do you mind?" The girl brandished a greasy-looking bottle of sunscreen in front of her.

Florence pushed herself up a little, wincing. She took in the girl's dark roots, the loose flesh on her stomach, the pimples mottling her chest. She shook her head. "I don't think so."

The girl let out a small, unsure laugh. "What?"

"I don't want to put lotion on your back."

"Oh." Her smile faltered but prevailed. "Okay." She started to turn away, but then her roving eyes found the bruises on Florence's torso.

"Whoa. What happened?" The girl squatted down and reached out her fingertips toward the purple skin. She held them inches away, fluttering lightly.

Florence frowned. Her injuries had upended the balance of power. It was like something primordial—she was a wounded animal, therefore no threat at all. For this girl, the injuries were an invitation, a physical weakness that rendered irrelevant social niceties and abstract hierarchies.

"I was in a car accident," Florence said curtly.

The girl widened her eyes. "That was *you?*"

"What do you mean? You heard about it?"

"A car going off Rue Badr? Yeah, everyone heard about it. Was it super scary?"

Florence couldn't help but laugh. *Super scary?* "I don't even remember it," she said.

"I know most of the expats around here—it's a pretty small town and I've been here for a while now—but nobody had ever heard of you. We figured you must have just gotten here. Helen something, right?"

Florence paused. Well, she had to begin somewhere. "That's right," she said. "Helen. Helen Wilcox."

"I'm Meg. Did you just get here?"

Florence nodded.

"Well, welcome! If you have any questions or anything just let me know because I'm like an honorary local, that's what everyone says."

Meg, who was still squatting, thumped down heavily at the foot of Florence's small towel.

"So you're on vacation?"

"Sort of. A working vacation."

"How so?"

"I'm doing research. For a novel."

"Wait, really? You're a writer? That is so cool. I love reading. I was obsessed with Harry Potter when I was a kid. Like, *obsessed*. I had the scarf, the glasses, everything." She watched Florence, waiting for a reaction. "The wand," she added significantly.

"Cool," Florence finally offered.

Meg nodded enthusiastically. Then without warning she heaved herself up with great violence and much sand displacement. "Hey, do you smoke?"

"Yes," Florence said emphatically. She had put a pack of Helen's cigarettes in her bag that morning. The thought of actually smoking one in this heat made her sick, but it had seemed like a helpful talisman, the way actors use a cane or a pipe to channel their characters.

Meg bounded over to her own towel a few paces down the beach and began rustling in a dirty tote bag. She returned holding out a joint triumphantly.

"Oh," said Florence. She had never smoked pot before, an embarrassing emblem of her social status in high school and lack of friends in college. Nonetheless, she took the joint from Meg and held it delicately between her thumb and forefinger. Why not? *Bonjour l'aventure.*

Meg held out a lighter. Florence put one end of the joint into the flame and sucked long and hard on the other, as she'd seen it done in movies. She was immediately wracked with coughs. She handed the joint back to Meg, eyes streaming.

"Yeah, the *kif* here is kinda evil," Meg said, laughing.

"Kif?"

"The hash."

"Yeah, I guess this isn't exactly what I'm used to."

"You probably get, like, Harry Potter weed."

Florence laughed. "That doesn't even make any sense." She lay back on her towel and covered her face with her arm. She felt Meg thud down at her feet again.

"So where are you from?" Meg asked.

"New York." Then she added, "But originally Mississippi."

"Really? You don't have much of an accent."

"I left a long time ago."

"Oh."

"Where are you from?"

"Toledo. Ohio."

There seemed to be no obvious response to this. The sand was swaying beneath Florence's body like a hammock. She was lulled into a pleasant state of relaxation. She felt looser than she had in months.

A bird called out repeatedly from somewhere in the distance.

"I love those birds that sound like owls," Meg said dreamily.

"You mean—owls?"

Meg started laughing loudly and recklessly. "Is that what they are? They're actually owls?"

Florence didn't answer. She didn't know what Meg was talking about. Her voice seemed very far away.

Meg kept repeating the word with slight variations. "Owl. Owl. *Owl.* What a weird word. Is it one syllable or two? I can't even tell."

"What?" Florence had lost the thread of the conversation.

"Two, I guess. Ow. Wull. Ow. Wull."

Florence's feeling of wellbeing slid away. She opened her eyes and looked at the girl next to her. When Meg laughed, the dolphin on her stomach looked like he was having a seizure. Dark hair sprouted jaggedly from her toes, like the upturned legs of a mosquito. Florence felt exposed and unclean. She wanted to be home. She wanted to be in Helen's room, among Helen's things. This is not the type of friend Helen would make. This was not right at all.

She stood up abruptly and began gathering her belongings. "I have to go," she said. She tugged the towel out from under the younger girl's body roughly. Meg rolled passively onto the sand like a log.

"Alright," she said cheerfully. "But hey, you should come to this party tonight."

"Party?"

"I mean, it's not like a *party* party. But there are a bunch of expats who gather at this house with a lot of, like, super interesting, creative people. I think you'd like it a lot."

It didn't occur to Florence to wonder how Meg might know what she would or would not like. She simply felt flattered that someone would consider it at all. She envisioned herself surrounded by poets and artists wearing colorful kaftans while candles flickered in brass lanterns.

"Yes," she said, nodding. "I *would* like that."

Florence explained that she didn't have a car, and Meg offered to pick her up at Villa des Grenades at eight.

Florence trudged across the hot sand back to the road. She had planned to go into town for lunch, but instead she walked into the first restaurant she saw, a dismal tourist trap advertising "American-style hot dogs," and drank a Coke while they called a taxi to take her home. She watched the hot dogs roll around in their greasy excretions and thought of pickled heads.

32.

Florence pulled at her lip. She was sitting at the dining room table, still in her damp, sandy clothes, looking at an email from Greta Frost. She read it several times, but the words never changed.

> Hi M. Checking in again. Give me a call. I want to discuss TPR in further detail. G.

Florence tried to draw some nuance from the words on the screen. She came up with nothing. She Googled TPR. It was either the stock symbol for a large fashion company or the acronym for a method of teaching foreign languages to children. Neither of those made any sense in this context. She drummed her fingers lightly on the keyboard for a moment. Then she pressed Reply and wrote:

> I've unfortunately come down with a bad case of food poisoning.

She reread what she'd written and erased it. She sent instead:

> Can't talk today—I've been poisoned by a thoroughly rancid piece of octopus. The upshot: I'm getting more insight into Moroccan toilet bowls than I ever thought I would...
> M.

An answer immediately pinged back:

What a shame. Get better soon. Stay in touch.

Florence wiped a smudge off the screen and shut the laptop gently. There, she'd begun being Helen Wilcox with someone who actually mattered. The charade was on. She knew that a reckoning with Greta was inevitable, but at this point she just hoped to delay it for as long as possible, at least until she had a clearer idea of how to handle her.

Greta was the major hitch in her plan: She interacted with Helen on a regular basis, she was thoroughly invested in the progress of Helen's work, and she already wanted to talk to her on the phone.

Florence supposed she could try to convince her to go along with the plan. Greta certainly did have a professional interest in keeping the Maud Dixon name alive and kicking. But enough to ignore the death of someone she had worked with—very successfully—for three years? To aid and abet identity theft? It was hard to say. How could she even broach the idea without admitting everything? It was a tell-all-or-nothing kind of proposal.

Well, there were other avenues besides collaboration. Florence had time. She had options. She was certain of one thing: Now that she'd been given this gift, no one—*no one*—was going to take it from her.

———

That afternoon Florence slept long and deeply. The sun was setting by the time she got up and showered. She was putting on makeup when Amina knocked gently on the door.

"Come in!" Florence called from the bathroom.

Amina hovered in the doorway. Folded in her hands was

Helen's blue-and-white-striped scarf. Florence froze, mascara wand in hand.

"Where did you get that?"

"Le gendarme," Amina said. The policeman.

"Idrissi? He's here?"

"He left. You were sleeping." She added, looking uncomfortable, "He asked about your friend. When she came home, when she left."

"What did you tell him?"

"The truth. I don't stay nights here."

"Good," Florence said quietly. "Thank you."

Amina made no indication that she'd heard. She placed the scarf on the bed and smoothed out a wrinkle. Just then, the doorbell rang, and Florence jumped. She looked at her watch. It was a few minutes before eight. It must be Meg.

Amina went downstairs to answer it. Florence followed a few minutes later and found Meg in the courtyard, looking at her phone. When she saw Florence she exclaimed, "Wait, you look so nice!" Florence was wearing a silk dress and a pair of espadrilles. She had also put on the red lipstick that Helen always wore. Seeing herself in the mirror, she'd felt like she was wearing a mask. She looked utterly unfamiliar to herself. She'd raised her hand to see if the reflection waved back.

"Thanks," she responded. "You too." Meg was wearing short jean cut-offs and a blousy embroidered peasant top.

Outside, Florence climbed on the back of Meg's rickety-looking Honda motorbike and tentatively put her arms around Meg's soft middle. She gripped the cast on her left wrist gently with her right hand.

"You okay back there?" Meg asked.

"I'm great. *Bonjour, l'aventure!*"

Villa des Grenades lay on a narrow, twisting road. From above, it must have looked like a piece of hair strewn on the ground. The whine of the scooter's motor rose and fell as it tore around the curves. Florence found herself enjoying the ride, the dangerous tip of the bike as it took the turns. She recalled the sensation of revving the engine on the drive to Semat, when she had imagined Helen's head bouncing off the dashboard like a soccer ball. She shook her head to dislodge the memory.

After about fifteen minutes, Meg pulled into the parking lot of a charmless modern apartment building just outside the medina walls. She told Florence that four Australian guys had rented an apartment here, and various expats moved in and out every few weeks. Mostly kiteboarders, here for the wind. She pressed the buzzer on the intercom, which produced a jaunty little tune.

"Yeah?" crackled the speaker.

"It's me," Meg sang out, leaving a smear of lip gloss on the intercom.

There was a pause, then another crackle: "Who?"

Meg laughed and said, "Meg!" She rolled her eyes at Florence good-naturedly. She seemed like a woman used to being forgotten. At length the intercom buzzed and the door unlocked with a thud. As they climbed up to the third floor, Florence asked Meg how old she was.

"I'll be twenty-two in September. Why, how old are you?"

She decided to split the difference between Helen's age and her own. "Twenty-nine."

Upstairs, a blond guy in board shorts and nothing else opened the door. He turned around and walked back into the room without saying a word. Following Meg inside, Florence took in the scene with mounting dismay. There were eight, maybe nine people draped around the room, which was dominated by an enormous black leather sectional couch patched with masking tape. A scummy table was scattered with full ashtrays and empty beer cans. Nobody was wearing a colorful kaftan. There were no lanterns.

"Hey, guys," Meg said cheerfully. She walked around the room and introduced Florence to everyone with a formality that the setting didn't warrant. "Helen is a writer," she said every time. "A *novelist*."

Most of the crowd wore the same bored, impassive expression as the guy who'd opened the door for them, but Florence noted with satisfaction that their masks seemed to slip a little when Meg introduced her as a writer. Something—if not respect, at least curiosity—flickered in their eyes.

"I'm a writer too," confided an emaciated girl in a bikini top as she sucked on a vape pen. "I mean, it's just like a travel blog right now, but I'm hoping to turn it into a book."

"That's great," Florence said.

"Yeah, so if you have any tips on like getting an agent or anything..."

Florence smiled magnanimously. "Of course."

"What about you? Have I read anything you've written?"

"Well, I don't know what you've read."

The girl smiled and shook her head. "Sorry, that was such a dumb question. What have you written?"

Florence wondered what Helen said when she was asked this question. She had so rarely seen Helen interact with people. Maybe she didn't tell people she was a writer at all. But it was too late for that now. "To be honest," she said, "I write under a pseudonym. And I don't really share it."

The guy who had opened the door for them looked up from rolling a cigarette and said, "Christ, don't tell us you're Maud Dixon."

Florence laughed forcefully. "I wish."

"Oh my god, I looove Maud Dixon," said a sunburned American girl on the couch. She turned to the guy whose lap her legs were draped over. "Jay, aren't I always talking about her?" He gave no indication that he'd heard her. She jiggled her legs. "Babe—aren't I always talking about that, like, killer redneck?"

"Mmm," Jay said. He was scrolling through his phone.

"I'm gonna stab *you!*" she said merrily, pretending to plunge a knife into his stomach.

"Stop," he said dully.

Meg reappeared from the kitchen holding two bottles of Casablanca, and they settled on a pair of white plastic chairs on a balcony overlooking the parking lot.

"So!" said Meg cheerfully.

"So," said Florence less cheerfully.

"This is fun."

"Mm."

"Tell me about how you became a writer."

"I don't know. I always wrote. And then one day I guess I just got lucky."

"That's so cool. I'd love to be a writer."

"Do you write?"

"Not really. I'm super left-brained. Like, really logical and stuff?"

"So what's your plan?"

"I don't know. My parents really want me to go back to college. But I don't know if I'm into that. I might want to act?"

"Like movies? Or the theater?"

"Yeah, I think I'd like movies. I don't know. Maybe. I might also become an actuary? That's what my dad does."

"So, an actress or an actuary. Those are really different."

"I know, right?" Meg said with wide eyes. She took a cigarette from a pack on the table and offered it to Florence, who shook her head.

"So why do you write under a fake name?"

Florence tried to remember what Helen had said when she'd asked her that. Had it involved . . . tapeworms? "It's complicated," was all she could come up with.

Meg nodded. "Totally."

One of the apartment's inhabitants ambled out to the balcony swinging his limbs loosely. Nick, he'd said his name was. He was tall and tan and would have been strikingly good-looking if not for his long, blond dreadlocks, which nobody seemed to find as embarrassing as Florence did.

"Got one of those for me, Megs?" he asked.

Florence thought she saw Meg flush slightly as she slid him the pack of cigarettes. He was the first person at the party who'd actually used her name.

After lighting one, he turned to Florence and said, "So you're the wild woman who drove off Rue Badr a few nights ago?"

"So I'm told."

"You know, if you're looking for thrills, I can just lend you my board."

Florence smiled. "Thanks, I'll keep that in mind."

Nick shook his head. "Seriously though, that road is a death trap. I wrecked my moped up in those hills a few weeks ago."

"There's been like four accidents already this year," Meg chimed in.

Florence felt somewhat cheered by the news. Maybe the accident wasn't her fault after all. "How did you guys hear about it again?" she asked.

"I saw it in *Le Matin,*" Nick said.

"You speak French?" Florence asked, surprised.

"Un peu," he said in an appallingly terrible accent.

"I'm gonna go get another beer. You guys want?" Meg asked. Nick and Florence both shook their heads. Nick collapsed into the chair Meg had vacated and rubbed the scruff on his neck. "So you're a writer?"

Florence nodded.

"Very cool."

Nick reminded Florence of someone, but she couldn't think who.

"What about you?" she asked. "What do you do?"

"I'm still in school."

"Really? You look older."

"I'm twenty-four. I took a few years off. I'll finish up at UC San Diego in the fall."

"And then what?" Florence didn't know why she was playing the role of career counselor. The truth was, she wouldn't have known how to act in this situation—surrounded by strangers at a small, shitty party in a foreign country—even if she hadn't been pretending to be someone else.

"I'll probably go into real estate. My older brother Steve is a real estate agent and he makes *bank*."

"That's what my mom keeps telling me to do."

"Oh yeah?"

"Yeah. Her friend's daughter is some big deal real estate agent in Tampa and has, you know, the husband and the four kids and the business card with her face on it. But basically I'd kill myself if that was my life."

"Why? That doesn't sound so bad—couple of kids, house near the beach."

"But it's so insignificant. It's just, like, eighty years of driving to the grocery store and back. Can't we aim for something higher?"

"No offense, but why is it any better to be a writer?"

"Why is it better to make art?"

"Yeah. Why is that better than helping someone find a home? That's real."

"Art is real."

"I'd rather have a home than a story."

"Okay, but stop thinking like the consumer for a second. What about *your* life? Do you really think you'll be satisfied spending the majority of your time on earth touring people around houses? That's your purpose?"

"I mean, my purpose is just to, like, be a good person."

Florence looked at Nick's face to see if he was serious. He was.

"I guess that's important too," she muttered.

Nick shook his head. "Don't get me wrong, I'm not saying

that has to be everyone's purpose. I think it's awesome that you actually think about this stuff and you've found your passion. All I'm saying is that no one's path is intrinsically *better* or *worse* than anyone else's, you know?"

Florence raised a skeptical eyebrow, and Nick laughed. He glanced at the sliding glass door that led inside. "Okay," he said in a low voice, "don't repeat this, but there are some girls in there who just want to be, like, Instagram influencers, and yes, I'll admit that maybe that path is *slightly* less noble than, say, Gandhi's."

Florence laughed. "Well, I have like seven followers on Instagram, so don't worry, I'm in no danger of falling into that career."

Nick nodded enthusiastically. "See? That's what I mean. Fuck what everyone else thinks of you, right? Fuck the *likes* and the *comments* and the constant *posturing*."

"Exactly," Florence agreed, aware even as she said it that she spent most of her time worrying about what other people thought of her.

But Helen didn't.

Florence leaned forward and plucked Nick's lit cigarette from between his fingers. "So what brings you to Semat?" she asked, taking a long drag.

"The wind."

"You're one of the kiteboarders?"

"Yeah. You?"

Florence laughed. "No. Definitely not."

"I was serious before. You should try it. I can teach you if you want."

Florence tilted her head. "I'll think about it." She wondered whether Helen would accept his offer or think herself above it. The problem with trying to predict what Helen would do in any given situation was that Florence had always found her highly unpredictable.

Well, she could be unpredictable too. She put a hand on Nick's thigh. "Come here," she said.

Fifteen minutes later, Florence was straddling him on a bare mattress, a filthy sleeping bag bunched at their feet. She unbuttoned his shirt roughly. He sat up and held her face in his hands. "You're beautiful," he told her. She pushed him back down.

"Say my name," she said.

"Helen," he gasped.

"Again."

"Helen."

33.

Florence dipped the last nub of her croissant into a small pot of jam and popped it in her mouth. She poured what remained of the coffee from the French press into her cup. Then she lit a cigarette from the pack she'd brought downstairs from Helen's room. She tapped it on the edge of her plate. She smiled when she saw the red lipstick mark on the filter. Watching the gesture she'd seen Helen make countless times, she had the sensation that she was actually looking at Helen's hand. It was unnerving. She took another drag. She thought she could feel the smoke charring her lungs, transforming her into Helen from the inside out. Then she was overwhelmed by light-headedness and stubbed the cigarette out in the jam.

Last night had been exhilarating. Not the sex—Nick had been altogether too stoned and too floppy. But the entire evening had been a revelation. She'd been Helen. She'd actually been her.

What had at first disappointed Florence about the scene—the shabbiness of the surroundings, the charmlessness of the company—had turned out to be the perfect environment in which to incubate her new self. Disdain, after all, has always been a useful stepping-stone to confidence, and that was what was required of her now. Something verging on hubris, not her usual muck of insecurity and self-doubt. Among the Helen Wilcoxes and Amanda Lincolns of the world, Florence was used to feeling small and inadequate. But last night, she'd had the sense that Meg and Nick and that girl who'd asked her for writing advice had actually been impressed by her. The power had been in *her* hands for once.

Helen had loved power. Not physical power; that was irrelevant. Emotional power, psychological power—that was her currency. She'd enjoyed exercising it just as a musician or a dancer takes simple, sheer pleasure in his craft. In conversation, Helen had dictated the direction and the tone. She constantly withheld information for no good reason, and she'd loved to throw Florence off guard with outlandish assertions. Even *Mississippi Foxtrot* was, at its heart, an exploration of power—first the power that lecherous Frank wields over Ruby, and then Maud's, after she wrests it away from him in a single act of violence.

Florence's own attempts to master interpersonal power dynamics had often floundered. Her friendships in middle and high school had been based on little more than a shared fear of absolute alienation. In college, she'd made friends in her English classes but none that she developed any particular closeness with. She'd always needed to retreat into solitude after spending a few hours in anyone else's company.

This, then, was someplace she could practice a new way of being in the world; a way of relating to people not as a supplicant but as the object of supplication herself.

Just calling herself by a different name, a name that was for her associated with such magnetism and strength, had retuned the whole tenor of her being. She'd felt...transfigured. Even among people who didn't matter, who didn't know that Helen was a world-famous writer; even alone in the back of the taxi on the way home. Putting on the guise of Helen, she really had felt more commanding, more interesting, more worthy in every possible way. Oddly, she felt more like *herself*—more like the woman she had always suspected was somewhere inside her.

She'd even seduced Nick, just to see if she could. She, who'd only ever been the mark, if rarely that.

Florence took a sip of orange juice and swished it around her mouth to get rid of the nicotine taste. She moved from the breakfast table to the desk inside where the laptop was set up. There was another email from Greta, this time to her own account:

Hi Florence,

How's Maud doing today? Think she can get on the phone? I don't want to bother her while she's ill, but I just found out that TPR would want to publish the interview in the Fall issue so we're working with a bit of a time crunch here.

It dawned on Florence: TPR was *The Paris Review,* the quarterly literary journal known for its in-depth interviews with famous authors.

In her earlier email Greta had said she wanted to discuss TPR "in further detail." Did that mean Helen had agreed to do an interview? Florence frowned. That didn't make any sense. Helen had no need to justify herself or her work. She wasn't that type of person. Was she going to use her real name, reveal her identity? *The Paris Review* had published an anonymous interview before—using just the writer's pen name—but only once.

She did a quick search of Helen's inbox; there were no other emails that mentioned *The Paris Review.* She went upstairs and rooted around Helen's room for her personal laptop; she'd caught a glimpse of it in Helen's carry-on at the airport. She found it fairly quickly, in the drawer of the bedside table, but when she opened it, she was thwarted by the same password request that had stopped her when she'd been snooping in Cairo. Florence typed in a few feeble attempts: *MississippiFoxtrot, Jenny, Ruby.* None of them worked.

Back at the computer downstairs, Florence wrote to Greta:

Maud's still sick, unfortunately. But she did say that she's having second thoughts about the interview.

There was no way *she* could do the interview.

A few seconds later, an email pinged back. She looked at her watch. It was five in the morning in New York. On a Sunday.

Florence, can you give me a call?

Florence clenched her jaw. She hated talking on the phone. There was no time to plan and refine what you were going to say. Maybe that's what other people liked about it; Greta didn't seem like a person who self-edited. Florence trudged reluctantly into the kitchen where the house phone was and dialed the number Greta had included in her email.

"Hi, Florence," said the familiar husky voice.

"Hi, Greta. It's early there."

"Oh, I never sleep past five. One of the hazards of getting older. So what's going on with Helen?"

"She ate some bad octopus."

"And she can't even come to the phone?"

"She basically hasn't moved from the bathroom floor in twenty-four hours."

"That doesn't sound good. Have you called a doctor?"

"Yes, of course. He just said to keep her hydrated."

"Twenty-four hours is a long time to be that ill. I think you should consider going back to Marrakesh. I can call the hospital there and tell them to expect you. I can't imagine the one where you are is much better than a Civil War tent."

"It's not that bad."

"You've been?"

"Oh. Yeah. I took Helen yesterday."

"And?"

"That was when they told us to keep her hydrated."

"Hm." There was a long pause. "You said something about Helen having second thoughts about the *Paris Review* interview."

"Yes. She said she changed her mind. She doesn't want to do it anymore."

"Interesting." She paused again. "You know, she hadn't even agreed to it yet. I was still trying to convince her that it was a good idea. So her mind, it seems, is *un*changed. If I have my facts straight."

Fuck. "Oh, really?"

"Really."

"That's weird. Maybe she misspoke. She's really out of it. Kind of delirious."

"Hmm."

Another pause.

"Florence, I'll admit it, you have me worried. You say that Helen is delirious, she can't come to the phone, she hasn't moved from the bathroom floor. None of this sounds good. I really urge you to go back to Marrakesh to get some treatment. Lauren would be happy to make arrangements for you. I could have a car come pick you up today."

"No...She'll be okay, I think. I'll ask her, but she's been pretty adamant about staying here and finishing the research."

"From the way you've described it, it sounds like perhaps Helen is not in the right frame of mind to be making these decisions for herself. Listen, Florence, you're young, and Helen can be intimidating, I know that. But making sure Helen is taken care of and gets healthy is more important than being on her bad side for a few hours."

"No, I know. I'll think about it, okay?"

"Okay. I'll call back this afternoon to see how the situation is progressing. Oh, that reminds me—I've tried both of your cells and I can't get through."

"Yeah, the service is really bad here."

"So this is the number I should use?"

"Yes, this is the house line."

"Great. Talk soon."

Florence slammed the phone into the cradle. *Shit.* What was she going to say to Greta in a few hours, or days, when she still couldn't produce Helen?

"Hi, Greta, actually I *killed* Helen—whoops!—so can I be Maud Dixon now or what?"

Perfect.

34.

Florence sat on the beach and buried her toes in the sand. The wind that had pounded everything ceaselessly since her arrival had disappeared without explanation. The air sat still and heavy around her. There was no relief from the sun's relentless onslaught.

She tried to put the phone call with Greta out of her mind. She wanted to regain that rush she'd woken up with; the electrifying pleasure of being Helen. She hadn't liked going back to being Florence while dealing with Greta. It left a residue. Something sticky and uncomfortable that she wished she could scrub off. She wanted the lightness back, the confidence, the strength.

She picked up a handful of sand and let it stream through her fingers. Her skin was pink from the sun. Underneath, her bruises were changing from purple to yellow and green. She poured sand on her legs, covering them up.

After the call, she'd looked up the article in *Le Matin* and done her best to translate. It was only a few lines long. A tourist from New York named Helen Wilcox had driven her rental car off Rue Badr at ten o'clock on Saturday night. By chance, engine trouble had kept a local fisherman out late, and he heard the splash. He made it to the car while it was still floating, and pulled Ms. Wilcox from the open window. She arrived at the hospital with minor injuries and was expected to make a full recovery. It was already the fifth crash on Rue Badr this year. Two people had died in an accident there the year before.

Florence had shut the computer in frustration. She hadn't learned anything that she hadn't already been told. Her memory was still a black hole, and she was terrified that Officer Idrissi was going to fill in the blanks before she did. Then not only would her new life as Helen Wilcox be ruined, but her old one would be too.

She stood up and brushed the sand off her body. She noticed a scraggly group of kiteboarders assembled a ways down the beach. She gathered her things into her bag and began walking in their direction. As she got closer, a few of the boarders turned to look at her, but none of their gazes lingered for long. Her looks weren't suited to the beach; the sunlight reflected harshly off her pale skin, and she barely filled out Helen's bikini top.

She spotted Nick sitting on a towel the size of a place mat. His wet suit was unzipped halfway, and the top half of it sprawled out behind him like a shadow. He was lapping furiously at a melting red popsicle. "Hi," she said, standing over him.

Nick looked up and smiled happily. "Hi, you!" He'd paused just long enough for the dripping popsicle to make inroads onto his forearm. "Shit," he said, and craned his head to drag his tongue from his elbow to his wrist.

Florence finally realized who Nick reminded her of; it was Bentley, the golden retriever that belonged to Helen's neighbor.

"What are you up to?" she asked.

"Not much. It's total mush out there." He gestured at the nearly flat water.

Florence looked at it and nodded thoughtfully.

Nick threw the rest of the popsicle into the sand. "Jesus, that thing was eating me alive." He wiped his hands roughly on the thighs of his wet suit and smiled up at Florence. "What are you up to?"

"Not much. I was just reading but it's too hot to stay on the beach. I was maybe going to go walk around town." She paused. "Do you want to come?"

Nick was unguardedly delighted. "Yeah. Let's do it." He immediately stripped off his wet suit and dug around in a small backpack for a wadded-up T-shirt. When he pulled it out, a book came with it. Florence picked it up and looked at the cover: *The Sheltering Sky*, by Paul Bowles.

"Are you reading this?"

"I just finished it. You can borrow it if you want. It's awesome."

Florence tried to hide her surprise. She hadn't thought of Nick as the type of guy to be reading a book by a writer Helen had spoken highly of. She'd almost bought a Paul Bowles book before their trip, but Helen had inundated her with so much research that she hadn't gotten around to it. She flipped it over and read the description on the back. It was about a trio of Americans traveling through the North African desert in the 1940s. It had been Bowles's first book and enormously successful. She read the first few sentences. He was right; they were good.

"Ready?" Nick asked.

Florence nodded and handed the book back to him.

"Later," he called over his shoulder as they walked away from the group.

They ambled slowly up the beach. Nick was explaining something about kiteboarding, but Florence wasn't listening. She let her mind wander.

They trudged up the hill, through Place Hassan II, toward the center of the town. When they reached the busy road surrounding the walls of the medina, Nick reached his tanned, blond-tufted arm across her torso to block her from walking into a stream of motorbikes. She looked up at him and smiled.

As they crossed the street, a familiar face suddenly snagged her attention. There, standing ramrod straight in front of an ornate building, was Idrissi, the policeman from the hospital.

Her breath quickened. She told herself that there was no reason to be afraid. As far as he knew, she was just a stupid tourist who'd gotten away with driving drunk and crashing her rental car because she happened to have American dollars to spend. But she remembered the way he'd looked at her in the car, when he'd asked about her friend from the restaurant. He suspected something.

And why shouldn't he? She *was* keeping a secret. The thought of Greta's phone call returned on a gust of apprehension. She pushed it away. Idrissi's head rotated slowly as he surveyed the crowd. Florence instinctively flattened herself against a wall.

"What's up?" Nick asked.

"Nothing. I thought I saw a rat."

"You're adorable," he said, drawing her close and giving her a sloppy kiss. He tasted like Coppertone and artificial strawberry flavoring.

"Let's look in here," she said, drawing him into the souk.

It was cooler and darker inside the marketplace. Dust glistened in the shafts of sunlight that managed to slip through the cracks of the slapdash ceiling.

"What do you think?"

Florence turned around. Nick was standing in front of a stall hung with colorful fabric, holding a long blue tunic against his body.

Florence laughed. "No."

The shopkeeper approached them. "It's a kaftan," he said. "For women." He pulled a black tunic from a stack. "This, for men. Try." He started to pull it over Nick's head. Nick waved his hands and said, "No thanks, man," but it was no use. It was already halfway on. The man ran his hands over the fabric to smooth out the wrinkles. "And this," he said, rolling some gray fabric into a twist and wrapping it around Nick's head. A turban. Nick stood awkwardly, his arms held away from his body. He looked at Florence. "Well?"

Florence laughed and shook her head. "Really, *really* no."

"Here, I take picture," the man said, holding out his hands for a phone. Florence opened her hands uselessly. "I don't have one." The man turned to Nick.

"It's in my pocket," he said. The man reached his hands into the pockets of the tunic—they were just slits, designed so that you could reach through to the pocket of your pants.

"Oh, cool!" Nick exclaimed to Florence, "they're slits!" Florence began laughing again.

The shopkeeper took a dark, blurry picture of them, looking at each other in a fit of hilarity. Afterward, once Nick had struggled out of the tunic, and unwrapped the turban, he held up the blue kaftan he'd picked out first and asked the shopkeeper, "How much?"

"For the beautiful lady? I do 200 dirhams."

"No, that's okay," Florence said to Nick. "You don't have to buy that for me."

"We have to buy *something*."

"No we don't, I'm sure he does this fifty times a day." But Nick was already pulling out the money. He offered the salesman 150 dirhams, which was accepted with a nod, then handed her the wrinkled plastic shopping bag containing her new kaftan.

"Thank you," she said, embarrassed.

"Don't be too grateful. I only bought it for you so I can borrow it."

Florence rolled her eyes, trying not to show how pleased she was. But Nick was already wrist deep in a basket of beans at the stall next door.

Florence wandered over to a fishmonger and watched him skin and debone a silver fish with quick, expert flicks of his knife. It reminded her of Helen hacking away at the chicken during her cooking lesson. The man tossed the cleaned fish, no longer a fish but simply fish, into a pile. A fly pounced on it and began to knead the flesh with its furry, thread-like arms and delicate elbows.

Florence wandered deeper into the souk. The wares here were similar to the ones she'd seen in Marrakesh, a mix of the picturesque and the practical.

Suddenly she felt a hand on her arm, and she spun around. A small, wrinkled man was pulling at her shirt toward a stall of silver jewelry. "Amethyst," he whispered. "Very good quality. Very beautiful." She pulled her arm back.

"No, thank you."

He took another step toward her. "Only fake that way. Here, is real."

"No," she said more harshly. She walked quickly away from him, turning down a small alley leading off the main artery, where it was even darker. A few men sat huddled on small stools, drinking from steaming cups. They glanced up at her, then away, disinterested. She ran her hand along a row of bright leather slippers. They emitted a warm, dank smell like a wet animal. Her heart was beating quickly, though she couldn't say why.

Suddenly she felt his hand on her again, spinning her around. She jerked away violently and turned to face him.

"Florence!"

She took a step backward and stumbled on the uneven ground. She regarded the face in front of her, the oversize teeth, the bright pink polo shirt, the dry, flat-ironed hair.

"Whitney?"

It was her old friend from Florida, staring at her in wide-eyed amazement. They paused awkwardly before leaning in to hug one another. Whitney had been five-eleven since seventh grade, and Florence had to stand on tiptoes to wrap her arms around her. She hadn't seen Whitney since high school graduation and they'd probably exchanged only a couple dozen messages since. After Florence had moved to New York, she'd stopped responding altogether. Whitney's smile didn't seem to be hiding a grudge, but perhaps it had just been momentarily set aside in the serendipity of this encounter.

"Oh my gosh!" Whitney exclaimed. "How crazy is this!?"

"What are you doing here?"

Whitney suddenly gasped. "What happened?" she asked, gesturing to Florence's cast and face, which was still discolored from the bruising. "Are you okay?"

"I was in a fender bender. It's not as bad as it looks."

"I'm so sorry to hear that."

"What are you doing here?" Florence asked again with a slight edge to her voice. She had felt so threatened by her recent encounters with Idrissi and Greta, even the man selling amethyst, that she was now primed for alarm. She had to remind herself that Whitney was just Whitney. The same girl who'd belted out the theme song from *High School Musical* at the talent show four years in a row. From the sudden vantage point of someone who'd known her as a child, Florence saw her current self with a brief flash of horror. But it passed as quickly as it had come.

"I'm on vacation with a college friend," Whitney said. "We just got to Semat this morning. We've been in the Atlas Mountains for a few days."

Whitney had worked hard in high school, but she had never been as good a student as Florence, and it still stuck in her craw that Whitney's father—Florence's dentist—had paid full tuition at Emory while Florence had been shunted off to UF like everyone else.

"What are *you* doing here?" Whitney asked.

"Working, sort of."

"Really? What do you do?"

"I'm—well, it's a long story. I'm doing research."

"How cool! Are you still in publishing?"

"Yes, pretty much."

"That's so great. I'm really happy for you. You always loved books."

Florence had noticed that people who didn't feel the way she did about literature—that it was, as much as biology or physics, one of life's organizing principles—regarded it as little more than a collection of physical objects: *books*. Did they think the power of music could be whittled down to the look and feel of a violin string? In fact, Florence did love books—the smell of the binding, the roughness of the pages—but they were nothing compared to the magnitude of what was inside them.

"What about you?" Florence asked. "What are you up to these days?"

"I'm a project manager at Verizon in Tampa. I tried Atlanta for a while, but I missed the beach and my family. And Verizon is just, like, the best place to work."

Florence remembered that Whitney's great social failing in high school had been her unchecked enthusiasm at a time of life when most people they knew would have gnawed an arm off before expressing any form of eagerness, about anything.

Whitney suddenly closed her eyes and took a deep breath through her nose. She reached out and took Florence's hands. She had always been a toucher. "Actually, Florence, can I just say? I feel like this is fate, running into you here, because there's something I've been meaning to tell you for months."

Florence couldn't imagine what Whitney could possibly have to say to her after six years of little to no contact.

"Trevor and I are seeing each other," she said all in a rush.

Florence struggled to keep a smile from her face. "That's great, Whitney. I don't mind. Really. We dated a long time ago. It feels like another lifetime, back when we were very different people."

Whitney exhaled loudly. "Oh my gosh, I'm so relieved. We've both been feeling wracked by guilt." Florence could believe it of

Whitney, but she doubted that Trevor, whose two great passions when she'd known him had been Minecraft and Ayn Rand, felt much remorse.

"Hey, babe." They both turned. There was Nick, clutching a sack of bright orange turmeric in his big, paw-like hand.

"Hi," Florence said tightly, realizing all of a sudden the predicament she was in.

"Hey, I'm Nick," he said to Whitney when Florence failed to introduce them.

"I'm Whitney. I grew up with—"

"Whitney and I grew up together!" Florence interjected loudly.

"Oh, wow," said Nick. "Small world."

"Whitney's traveling around Morocco with a friend of hers from college."

"Awesome."

"It's been *super* awesome," Whitney said.

Florence glanced around. "Is she here?"

"Amy? No, she's passed out at the hotel. We had a *very* late night last night."

"Niiice," said Nick.

A silence settled on the three of them.

"Well you should totally come hang out with us tonight," Nick said, turning toward Florence. "Right, babe?"

Florence frowned. This "babe" business had come on fast and strong. "Oh, it sounds like Whitney could use a quiet night," she said.

"I'd love to, actually," Whitney said. "It'd be fun to catch up. I just need to check with Amy when she wakes up." She pulled out her phone. "Do you still have your same number?"

Florence shook her head. Getting a New York area code had been one of the first things she'd done after moving. She recited her 917 number as Whitney punched it in.

"Wait, you don't have your phone," Nick interjected.

"Oh. Right." She turned to Whitney. "I lost it in the accident."

"Here, take mine," Nick said, rattling off his number for Whitney.

"Amazing. I'll call you when I know our plans. I think Amy already made us dinner reservations, but if she's up for it, we'll come meet you after." She took Florence's hands again and looked her in the eye. "I can't tell you how glad I am that I ran into you."

"Okay," Florence said lamely.

When she had gone, Nick turned and asked, "What's up? You don't like her?"

"No, I do, I just—I don't know. I was surprised to see her, that's all."

Nick took his hand in hers as they walked out into the bright noonday light. Suddenly, Florence heard a now-familiar voice behind her: "Madame Weel-cock."

She spun around.

Idrissi was planted just next to the entrance to the souk. Had he seen her go in? Had he been waiting for her? "I'm glad you're feeling better," he said.

"Thanks," she managed. She was still off-kilter from her run-in with Whitney. This was the last thing she needed.

Nick looked back and forth from Florence to the police-man. "Hey man, I'm Nick," he said to Idrissi, sticking out his hand.

Idrissi glanced at it dismissively before turning back to Florence. "So have you heard from your friend?"

Florence shielded her face from the sun. What was the smart move here? Saying yes was riskier—one more lie to build up and defend—but saying no would only heighten his suspicions about this mysterious, missing woman.

She finally nodded. "Yes. She's in Marrakesh. As I thought."

Idrissi stared at her for a beat. "Good," he said crisply. "You know, it's interesting: I've been having trouble finding the taxi that picked her up at Dar Amal that night."

"Does it matter?" Florence asked. "She's back in Marrakesh. She's fine."

"Just tying up loose ends. Policework isn't all car chases and shootouts," he said with an unpracticed smile. "Do you have her phone number? It would be helpful if I could speak with her."

"Her phone number? Um, not on me. It was in my phone, which was lost."

"Perhaps it is at the house, then? If you've spoken."

"Oh, maybe. But actually she called me. On the landline."

"Well, that makes it easier. I'll check the phone records."

Florence paled. "Right." She felt the sun scorching the top of her head. "I'm actually still not feeling a hundred percent," she said abruptly. "I was just going home to rest." She turned away from Idrissi and walked directly into the busy road, forcing a moped to veer around her while the driver shouted something unintelligible.

Nick took her arm and guided her safely across the street. "What was that all about?" he asked when they reached the other side. "Who's your friend?"

"He's not my friend!" Florence exclaimed.

"No, the friend he was talking about."

"Oh. I was traveling with someone for a while but she went back to Marrakesh. Now this policeman investigating the car accident is totally fixated on her. I don't know why. It was just an accident, but he won't stop hounding me about it." Her voice took on a hysterical edge. "I don't know what else to tell him. I don't remember anything!"

Nick put his hand on her arm to slow her down. "Hey, hey, relax. Listen, the cops here are all notoriously corrupt. He's probably just pissed you haven't tried to bribe him yet."

Florence stopped walking. "Really? Is that true?"

"Yeah. Liam slipped like forty bucks to the one who caught him with a dime bag and the whole thing went away."

"Oh."

She looked back at where Idrissi was standing, watching her. Was this whole thing a misunderstanding? Could she make it go away right now?

Florence checked her purse. She still had close to fifteen hundred dirhams of Helen's. She took out two bills and crumpled them in her hand. Recrossing the street, she felt Idrissi scrutinizing her and smiled uncomfortably.

"Hi, again," she said when she reached him.

He nodded at her.

"I just wanted to say that I really appreciate all your help after the accident—driving me home and returning my scarf and everything. And all the work you've put into the investigation. Thank you." She awkwardly held out the money, now crumpled in a soft, soggy ball in her palm. This must be how Helen's lover felt, she thought, trying to tip the staff at the hotel under her judgmental gaze.

Idrissi's eyes traveled down to her hand then back up to her face. He didn't move.

"This is for you," she said, thrusting her palm forward. "To say thank you."

"My English is still not as good as I'd like," he said after a beat. "Is this what is called a bribe?" He smiled mirthlessly. "Is that the right word?"

"No, not at all! It's just a gift. Or...whatever you want it to be."

"So you must often give *gifts* like this to the police in America then?"

"Sure. Sometimes." Florence felt the blood rushing to her face.

"Do you? I thought it was illegal there. As it is here, of course."

"Is it? I didn't realize." Florence shoved the money back into her bag. "Sorry. I just wanted..."

"To say thank you?" Idrissi finished for her with a smirk.

She nodded.

"Or maybe you want me to stop investigating the accident."

"No, not at all. I mean, is there really anything else to investigate? It all seems pretty clear to me." This was patently false. Nothing about that night made any sense to her.

"Does it, Madame Weel-cock? Because it's not clear *to me* why you and your friend left the restaurant separately; it's not clear why I can't find the taxi that took her back to the villa; it's not clear why she disappeared the day after the accident; and it's not clear why you can't simply put me in touch with her, to clear up all these questions."

"I'm sorry. I didn't mean to offend you," Florence said quietly as she turned away.

She hurried back to where Nick stood smiling encouragingly.

"All good?" he asked.

She forced herself to smile. "All good."

35.

A few hours later, Florence lay in the bath, her cast resting on the lip of the tub. She slipped under the water briefly and let her hair float weightless around her before coming back up for air. She'd half-hoped that being submerged in water would trigger more memories from the crash. The few flashes she'd recovered—the hand grabbing her arm, the rush of cold water—were becoming less crisp, not more.

Meanwhile, her problems continued to mount.

The most immediate challenge would come to a head in just a few hours, when Whitney arrived at Nick's apartment. Whitney hadn't given her number to Nick or mentioned the name of her hotel, so Florence had no way of getting in touch with her to cancel. She'd thought about asking Nick to tell Whitney that she wasn't feeling well, but that would still require them to have a conversation about her, each using a different name. Nick would find out her real name was Florence Darrow, and Whitney would discover that she was calling herself Helen Wilcox.

Florence had spent the afternoon considering the consequences of this. Would it really be the end of the world? She could come up with some plausible-enough explanation. Maybe she traveled under a made-up name to "leave everything behind." It sounded pretty lame, but neither Nick nor Whitney had any reason to suspect anything more nefarious.

The problem was that there were other people who did. Or who were at least starting to.

Idrissi was slowly chipping away at her lies, and Greta was getting more and more impatient to speak with Helen. As long as she was facing threats on those two fronts, she couldn't risk anyone—even someone as insignificant as Nick or Whitney—knowing that Florence Darrow and Helen Wilcox were now the same person.

She wished she could fast-forward through the next few weeks, or months—however long it took—to when everything was all worked out. When she was settled in Helen's house, writing and gardening and cooking, and Florence Darrow was part of the past. But she had to figure out how to get from here to there.

She dried off and wrapped herself in Helen's robe. It never would have occurred to Florence to own—much less travel with—a silk robe. She stood in front of the closet and ran her fingers over the clothes hanging neatly in a row. She pulled out a cream-colored dress with red embroidery and held it up to her body. The red matched the color of Helen's lipstick perfectly.

She dressed and applied her makeup in the bathroom mirror with precision. While she was lacing up her sandals, the phone rang. A few moments later, Amina knocked on her bedroom door.

"Yes?" Florence said warily.

Amina poked her head around the door. "It is a Madame Greta Frost. On the telephone."

"Can you tell her I'm not home, please?" One problem at a time.

"Yes, of course, Madame." She closed the door gently and Florence listened to her shuffle down the stairs.

Nick arrived to pick her up shortly afterward.

Stepping into the villa's foyer, his face registered for the first time the realization that he and Florence were traveling on very different budgets.

"You're staying here all by yourself? It's massive."

Florence shrugged. "It wasn't that much more than a hotel room. Look, there's mold everywhere."

"Still. This is way nicer than our place."

Florence couldn't argue with that. He asked for a tour, and she obliged, skipping only the bedroom she'd occupied before the accident. She'd gone back in there just once, to retrieve her toothbrush.

"This place is *sick*," Nick pronounced at the end of it.

A thought occurred to Florence. "Do you want to just hang out here instead?"

"Seriously? Yeah, totally. Should I text the others?"

Florence shrugged. "Sure. Whatever you want."

"Oh and we should tell Whitney. She texted by the way. She and her friend are going to stop by around ten."

Florence smiled stiffly. "Great. Let's just stick to the plan then. We can hang out here tomorrow night if you want."

Nick nodded. "Okay, cool. Yeah, Liam's already ordered pizza anyway."

———

The pizza was dry and inedible. Florence poked at her slice distractedly. Every time the intercom buzzed she whipped her head around to hear who it was. So far, no Whitney. She took a sip of her beer—it was warm and flat and at this point tasted more like the can than what it contained. She'd been nursing it for over an hour. Tonight, she needed to be sharp.

Not just tonight. She'd need to be sharp for the rest of her life. As sharp as Helen. She couldn't permit weakness or indecision anymore. Her slip-ups with Greta and Idrissi over the past few days had been a wakeup call. She could *never* let her guard down.

Getting a new identity was like getting a new organ; she would have to take anti-rejection drugs for the rest of her life.

At ten thirty, the intercom buzzed for what felt like the dozenth time, and Florence heard Whitney's cheerful voice announce itself through the speaker. She jumped up and bee-lined for the kitchen. She poured vodka into two empty cups and topped them both off with Sprite. Then she took a piece of paper from her pocket and unfolded it carefully. Inside was a pile of white powder—three hydrocodones that she'd ground up earlier that evening at the villa, using the top of Helen's face cream as a pestle.

She hoped that drugging Whitney would cut the evening short and, in the meantime, make her entirely unreliable, so that any references to "Florence Darrow" would be disregarded as the confused babbling of a drunk. She knew she was being overly cautious, but she wanted to keep her new identity entirely uncontaminated. She was Helen Wilcox; there could be no confusion about that.

She tapped the powder gently into one of the cups, then stirred it violently with a knife. She threw out the paper, tossed the knife in the sink, and carried the drinks out to the door. Nick was ushering Whitney and her friend into the apartment.

"Chin-chin," Florence called out loudly by way of greeting. She handed the cups to the two women. They both looked slightly startled, but took them anyway.

"Alright," Whitney said with a laugh. "I guess we're not screwing around tonight."

"We're on vacation!" Florence yelled, again too loudly.

"Amen to that! This is my friend Amy, by the way." Whitney gestured at the athletic-looking brunette next to her. Then she turned to Amy and said, holding out her arm toward Florence, "And this—"

"Oh, let's skip all the small talk!" Florence interrupted. "It's dull. Call me Cleopatra! Call me Queen Elizabeth!"

Nick, Whitney, and Amy all looked at her with unconcealed concern. No one said anything. At last Nick broke the silence.

"You okay, babe?" he asked, leaning in close.

"I'm fine, babe! It's a party! Drink up!" She gestured at their drinks with her beer can and took another sip of warm beer. The rest of them dutifully raised their cups.

Whitney grimaced. Florence hoped it was vodka, not the taste of the pills. But Whitney just said, "Florence, I've never seen you like this!"

"It's been a long time, Whit. I'm a whole new woman."

"Apparently."

Florence lowered her voice and leaned in. "Actually, do you think I can talk to you in private for a sec?"

"Um...sure." Whitney glanced at Amy. "Are you going to be okay?"

"Don't worry, Whit, I like vodka waaay more than I like you."

"Oh, thanks."

"Don't mention it."

Florence pulled Whitney into Nick's bedroom and closed the door. She eyed the mattress that she and Nick had shared the night before. It looked even more gruesome with the lights on. She sat on it anyway and patted the space next to her. Whitney crouched down awkwardly.

Florence was dreading this conversation, but she had decided she had no choice. She'd determined that she would need to keep Whitney away from the group for at least ten minutes to let the painkillers kick in. She wanted Whitney to be fairly incapacitated by the time she left the room.

"So, I know I said earlier that I didn't care that you were dating Trevor, but I couldn't stop thinking about it all afternoon. And actually I'm really upset."

Whitney covered her face and shook her head. "I knew it."

Florence bit the inside of her cheek and fought the dueling impulses to laugh in Whitney's face or to slap it. Trevor had always smelled like Totino's pizza rolls. He had cried when he took her virginity; not a tear or two, but great, big, heaving sobs. He'd told her that majoring in English would be a "a total waste." No, she had not spent the last eight years pining for Trevor Gilpin.

"Can you tell me how it happened?" Florence prodded.

Whitney took a sip of her drink. "Well, he works at Verizon too, did you know that?"

"I think my mother mentioned it."

"He's a systems engineer." Whitney looked up to see how that had landed.

"Okay." Florence didn't know what a systems engineer was and she didn't particularly want to find out.

"It's a super competitive field."

"I'm sure."

Whitney nodded and took another sip. She proceeded to recount the story of their relationship: The run-in at the on-site fitness center. How much they had in common. How they were thinking of adopting a cat together.

Florence hated cats.

"I'm so sorry," Whitney concluded. "I broke the number one rule of friendship."

Florence suspected that she was the one who'd broken the number one rule of friendship, by unilaterally ending said friendship, but she stayed silent. She rubbed at her eyes and wrinkled her forehead and looked out the window.

"Oh my god, I'm the worst," Whitney said. "What can I do to fix this?" She was chewing on the rim of her cup. Florence peeked inside—half-empty.

"Are you going to marry him?" Florence asked, for lack of any other ideas for continuing the conversation.

Whitney's large mouth twitched. She was trying not to smile, Florence realized. "I don't know," she said. "I hope so? I'm sorry, is that awful to say?"

Florence didn't know how much longer she could stand this.

"You know what? I'm happy for you guys. Truly. Let's toast to you and Trevor."

"Really?"

"Of course, we're all adults now."

Florence raised her beer and tapped it to Whitney's cup. Whitney took another sip. Florence waved her hand to tell Whitney to keep drinking. "Now this is a celebration! Drink, drink!"

Whitney took a giant gulp, then laughed and spluttered. She wiped her mouth with the back of her hand.

"You're a good friend, Florence." Whitney's speech had taken on a sludge-like quality. *Florence* came out sounding like *Florsch*.

"Speaking of friends," Florence said brightly, "Amy must be wondering what I've done with you. Let's go back out there."

Whitney stumbled a little when she got to her feet. Florence steadied her and asked, "You good?"

"Fiiiine, fiiiiiine."

Florence pried the drink from Whitney's fingers. "Here, let me take that. I think we're done with this." She poured the rest of the drink out the window, then looked in the empty cup. Some of the powder had congealed into a white sludge at the bottom. She chucked the whole thing out the window. She led Whitney back into the living room, holding her by the hand. Nick and Amy weren't there. She found them in the kitchen laughing by the sink.

"Hey," Amy said brightly, then her smile fell when she saw Whitney's slack-eyed expression. "Whoa, you okay, Whit?"

"Oh, fiiiiine."

Amy turned a questioning gaze at Florence.

"She downed her drink in like one gulp," Florence said. "I'm sorry, I shouldn't have made them so strong."

Amy took Whitney's hand and looked her closely in the eyes. "Whit?"

Whitney's eyes struggled to focus on her friend. She smiled, but couldn't maintain the tension in her lips, and they collapsed into a limp gape.

"Okay," Amy said. "Apparently we're going to call it a night after what has apparently been a very wild ten minutes. Quick work, Whit." She turned to Nick and said, "Sorry, do you mind calling us a taxi? I don't have an international phone plan."

Nick took out his phone. "Of course."

"We're staying at Riad Lotus." She turned to Florence. "I'm so sorry, she's not usually like this."

"Oh, we're all allowed to lose ourselves on vacation," said Florence.

"Five minutes," Nick said, putting his phone back in his pocket.

All three of them helped corral Whitney down the stairs and into the back of the car. She lay her head on Amy's lap. Amy stroked her hair gently and apologized again to Florence.

"It's totally fine. It happens to the best of us."

"You're so sweet, both of you. Thank you again."

As they drove off, Nick put his arm around Florence's shoulder and pulled her close.

———

Later that night, Florence lay nestled in the crook of Nick's arm as he rubbed her back slowly up and down.

"Can I ask you something?" he said quietly.

"Mmm."

"Amy kept calling you Florence."

She opened her eyes.

"And she seemed kind of confused when I referred to you as Helen."

Neither of them spoke for a few moments. She noticed that Nick had stopped rubbing her back.

Finally, she said, "I was known as Florence growing up. I started going by Helen in college. It's my middle name."

Nick didn't say anything. It was too dark to see his face.

Then he said, "Oh. Okay. I like the name Florence, though."

She breathed a sigh of relief. One of Nick's greatest assets—for her purposes at least—was his total lack of mistrust. He tended to see the best in people, and to believe whatever he was told.

"No, it's so stodgy."

"It's not. It's pretty."

"Well, thank you, but I prefer Helen now. Okay?"

"If that's what you want, sure. I don't care what your name is. I just like *you*." He pulled her closer, and Florence smiled bright-eyed into the darkness.

36.

The next morning, she woke before Nick. Her chest felt tight with anxiety. And then its bedfellow, regret. Why had she let Nick be alone with Amy? She should have drugged Amy too, of course. That was obvious now. She had shrunk from leaving them both incapacitated, trying to find their way home like two injured lambs. But that was silly. They were adults. It was one drunken night. She was sure they had both had plenty of them in the past.

Her plan had been too limited; she saw that now. She needed to loosen the restraints. Boldness, audacity—that was what was required of her. No more half measures. How many times did she have to remind herself?

She wanted to roll over, to curl up onto Nick's chest again, return to where she'd spent last night—a place of comfort and warmth. But that, she knew, was a trap. She forced herself to sit up. She pulled on her clothes and went into the kitchen, where she scooped handful after handful of cold water into her mouth. Then she patted her cheeks with her wet hands. Onward. The plan was still in effect. She wasn't tossing away this opportunity just because of an ill-timed encounter with an old friend.

She paused for a moment. She'd made the same mistake with Greta, she now realized. She'd been too cautious. That story about food poisoning had been too small, too tame, too short-sighted. Not Helen's style at all.

She went back to Nick's room and woke him up.

"Hey," she whispered, "can I borrow your laptop?"

He sat up and rubbed his eyes blearily. "Yeah, it's over there." He gestured at a pile of dirty clothes. She dug underneath it and found an old, cracked Dell.

She signed into the Maud Dixon Gmail account. Then she opened a new message and started typing. When she was finished, she read it over.

Dear Greta,

I haven't been honest with you. I'm not sick, and it isn't fair of me to ask Florence to keep lying for me. The truth is, I wanted a few days off the grid to consider some things. I've done that now, and I've reached an important decision.

I'm going to change representation. I appreciate everything you've done for me over the last few years, but I need an agent who supports my literary ambitions wholeheartedly. I understand why you keep pushing me to write a sequel to *Mississippi Foxtrot,* but I want to write a different type of book, and it will take the time it takes. Since you can't give me the space to do that, I'll find someone who can.

Maud

Florence thought it hit the right note: direct, considered. She hovered the mouse over the Send button, then forced herself to click it. She logged out of the account, then abruptly shut the laptop and tossed it back onto the pile of clothes.

Done.

Nick had gone back to sleep. There was a stack of tattered secondhand paperbacks in the corner of his room. She started picking through it, and saw another book by Paul Bowles. She pulled it from the pile. It was called *Let It Come Down.* According to the back cover, it was his second novel. It was about a bank teller who moves to Tangier and falls into moral dissolution. She flipped through it. A page heading caught her eye: "The Age of Monsters." She frowned. Where had she heard that phrase recently? She read a few pages:

> When she heard the word "forceful" being used in connection with herself, even though she knew it was perfectly true and not intended as derogation, she immediately felt like some rather ungraceful predatory animal, and the sensation did not please her.

It hit her when she saw the word *predatory*. It was the same passage that she had transcribed for Helen back in Cairo. Helen had handwritten it, word for word, on a notepad and presented it as a draft of her own second novel. Why? Was it some sort of statement on the male-dominated literary canon? No. That was ridiculous. It was flat-out plagiarism.

This must have been why Helen was withholding the manuscript from Greta. But what was her endgame? It didn't make any sense. She would have known she'd never get away with it. Someone was bound to catch her before the book was even printed. Was she deliberately trying to torch the Maud Dixon name?

"Whitney just texted," Nick said behind her.

Florence looked at him in confusion. She'd forgotten where she was for a moment. "What?"

He was sitting up cross-legged on the mattress, naked. He repeated himself and held out his phone to her. She looked at the screen: "Hi Nick, please tell Florence I'm sorry about last night. I don't know what got into me. Can I make it up to you guys tonight?"

Florence felt a wave of relief that she was okay.

She wrote back: "Hey, it's Florence. No worries at all, but I think we're just going to lay low tonight." After she sent it, she deleted the entire message chain and blocked Whitney's number. She handed the phone back to Nick, who tossed it onto the mattress without looking at it and reached out his arms toward her.

"Breakfast?" he asked. She nodded. She felt better. She was finally getting things under control.

They went to a nearby café run by a couple from New Zealand. Over coffee and avocado toast, they watched the sky change from light blue to purple.

"Whoa," said Florence, pointing. Dark clouds were gathering forces on the horizon. Discarded napkins and cigarette butts started to swirl at their feet.

"Look at that wind," said Nick. The leaves on the trees began struggling violently for release from their branches. It was as if the wind had been storing up its strength throughout the long, limpid day before for this. "I've gotta get my board."

"You're not going to go out on the water in this weather, are you?"

"Fuck yeah, that's why I'm here."

"Is it safe?"

Nick smiled at her. "You're so sweet. It's totally fine. I promise."

Florence watched a man across the street struggle to attach a makeshift awning above a table laid with small, carved animals. The wind kept ripping the fabric out of his grasp.

"Have you gone out when it's this stormy before?"

"Yeah, tons of times. Actually, the first week we were here, it was insane. Thirty knots, side-on shore wind, epic waves. A fucking *shark* washed up. A legit shark."

Florence froze.

Nick laughed. "Don't worry, I'm not going to get eaten by a shark."

Florence said nothing.

"Babe? You okay?"

All of a sudden, Florence recognized the gaping hole in her

plan: Helen's body was going to wash up. Bodies always washed up. It was simple luck that it hadn't already. She looked out at the gathering storm with a new sense of dread. How could she have been so careless?

She turned back to Nick. "I have to go," she said robotically.

"What, right now?"

"I feel sick all of a sudden. Anyway, you should go kiteboard-ing if you want to."

"Alright, let's go. I'll drive you back."

She nodded.

On the way to Villa des Grenades, she kept her eyes on the sky. It was a dark granite color, and the clouds churned around each other ominously. She wanted to leave Semat as soon as she could. She had to pack. And book a rental car. And maybe even move up her flight out of Morocco. She had to test out Helen's passport sooner or later.

Would they put it together if a body washed up? Would Idrissi figure out what had happened?

Of course he would. It was the missing puzzle piece he'd been waiting for. Forensics would show how long the body had been in the water, and perhaps even where it had gone in, based on the tides and where it landed.

Then he'd come knocking on her door.

Nick slowed to a stop in the driveway. She climbed off his bike and stood for a moment looking at him. This was the last time she would see him, she supposed. She wanted to say something to mark the moment, but she didn't know what.

"See you tonight?" he asked.

She nodded.

And with that unceremonious goodbye, he kicked the gear shift and drove off, raising a hand in salute.

"Be careful," she called out after he'd already disappeared.

She turned back to the house. The leaves were shivering in

the wind, showing their pale, vulnerable undersides. The birds had all disappeared. A few fat drops fell on the stone. She ran inside as the darker spots began to accumulate and the ground turned shiny and black.

She went right to the laptop and checked Helen's email. Still no response from Greta. Fine. Good. She found a car rental agency in Semat and booked the only SUV they had, something called a Dacia Duster. It could handle bad weather, and it was available immediately. She looked out the window. The rain was thrashing the glass, and thunder shuddered in the distance. A few seconds later, the room was lit up by a flash of lightning. Could she even drive in this? With a cast on her wrist? Well, she'd find out.

She went into the kitchen to call Delta to see if she could change her flight, but when she picked up the phone to dial, she heard a tinny voice shouting from the receiver: "Hello? Is anyone there?"

She put the phone to her ear. "Hello?"

"Who is this?"

"Who is *this?*" Florence realized that she must have picked up before the phone had even begun to ring.

"This is Greta Frost calling for Helen Wilcox."

"Oh. Hi."

"Helen?"

Florence paused. "Yes."

"Helen, I got your email. Could we please talk about this?"

"Okay."

"Helen?" she asked again.

"Mm–hmm."

"Or Florence?"

Shit. "Yeah?"

"It's Florence?"

"Yep."

"Why did you say you were Helen?"

"What? Sorry, this connection is terrible. There's an insane storm going on here right now."

Florence ran her shirt over the phone, trying to create the sound of static.

"Could you please put Helen on the phone?" Greta asked curtly.

"Pardon?"

"I'd like to speak to Helen. Now."

"I'm sorry, she's not here."

"Where is she?"

"I don't know, actually. She left this morning."

"Where did she go?"

"I'm not sure." And then, an idea: "She fired me."

"She fired you?"

"Yeah."

"Oh." Greta paused. "She fired me too."

"Really?"

"Yes."

"That's insane."

"Yes, that was my reaction too." Then she asked, "Did she say why?"

"It was sort of convoluted. She kept saying I was on your side, whatever that means. She suspected I was passing information to you." Florence paused. "Actually, she said that *I* should just write the sequel to *Foxtrot;* then you and I would both be happy."

"What?"

"I mean, she was joking."

"Obviously."

Neither of them spoke for a moment.

"Did she say where she was going?" Greta asked.

"No . . . just that she needed to go on this journey alone."

"What journey?"

"It was like an artistic journey, I think? That's the impression I got. A . . . creative walkabout, of sorts."

"Helen said she was going on a creative walkabout?" Greta asked doubtfully.

"Mm-hmm."

"And did she say where this walkabout was going to take her?"

"I think that's sort of the thing about walkabouts? They don't have a destination?"

"Did she seem, I don't know, in her right mind? This doesn't sound like the Helen I know."

"She sounded pretty sure."

Neither of them said anything for a moment. Then Greta said, "Where are you, exactly?"

"What?"

"Remind me of the name of the town you're in?"

"Why?"

"I'm going to come."

"Come *here*? To Morocco?"

"I think I have to. Helen is one of my biggest clients, and frankly I'm worried about her. She hasn't been herself recently."

"Greta, I don't even know where she is."

"We'll find her."

Florence said nothing.

"Florence—don't worry, we're going to get everything all sorted out. Helen is volatile, but she always settles down."

"Uh-huh."

"Listen, I'm going to get Lauren to book me a flight. You flew into Marrakesh, right?"

"Yeah."

"Then where?"

Florence paused. Then she slowly replaced the phone into its cradle.

It started ringing less than a minute later. Florence just stood there with her hand still on it, not moving, while Amina watched.

"This is why I don't like talking on the fucking phone!!!" she

wanted to scream. A creative walkabout? What the fuck was that? And Greta was coming *here*? No. No.

She released her frustration in a low, grumbly growl. As she did, the lights flickered and went out. Amina looked at her in alarm as if she'd done it.

37.

As Florence climbed the stairs she realized she was gnawing on her knuckle and abruptly stopped. Helen was right: Panic is a waste of energy.

She had a plan. She was leaving Semat today. She was leaving Morocco as soon as possible. And she was taking over Helen Wilcox's life. No one was going to stand in her way. Not Officer Idrissi. Not Greta Frost. Not anyone.

Florence started packing. She would have liked to leave all of her old belongings behind, but that would raise questions. It shouldn't look like two people had arrived at the house and only one had left. Especially if a body washed up. So she packed two bags, one filled with Helen's things and one with her own. She dragged them one by one down the stairs, ignoring the pain in her wrist.

The rain had stopped while she was upstairs. She left the bags by the front door and walked out onto the back terrace. Everything was dripping. A few brave birds were hopping around, seeing what items of interest the storm had turned up. They were rewarded: Dozens of drowned worms, their bodies swollen with rainwater, clung to the top of blades of grass. Florence took a deep breath. The heat had broken.

She turned to go inside and tell Amina she was leaving. She'd need her to call a taxi to the car rental agency. She'd be back in Marrakesh by nightfall. She'd have to make a reservation at a different hotel, because tonight she was checking in as Helen Wilcox.

Suddenly she froze. She could hear voices coming from inside the house. She poked her head in.

From the foyer, a man's voice said, "There she is."

Officer Idrissi stood in the doorway, along with a man in his thirties—American, by the look of him—in khaki pants and a light blue button-down.

Amina was holding the door for them, looking uncomfortable. They both strode toward Florence with wide, confident steps. Their shoes tracked mud on the floor, and she saw Amina eye the marks with dismay.

The man she didn't know stuck out his hand and introduced himself. "Dan Massey. US State Department. I work at the embassy in Rabat."

Florence looked back and forth between the two men. "What's going on?" *They found Helen's body.*

"Please, let's sit," Massey said, extending an arm toward the living room. As they walked past the foot of the stairs, Massey glanced at her luggage.

"Going somewhere?"

"Yes," she answered without elaborating.

All three of them sat down. Massey placed his briefcase on the table in front of him and opened it. "So, Ms. Wilcox"—he glanced up—"you are Helen Adelaide Wilcox, of Cairo, New York, correct?" He pronounced it the wrong way.

Florence nodded. "*Cay-ro,* yes."

"Alright, well, the Cairo Police Department has been trying to get in touch with you for a few days now."

"I was in an accident." She held up her cast. "I lost my phone."

"Do you know what this might concern?"

"Not a clue."

"A body has been discovered on your property."

For a brief, dizzying moment Florence thought—*Helen*? But no, that didn't make any sense.

"A body," she said dumbly.

Massey nodded. "It was found in your compost pile"—he pulled a file from his briefcase and checked it—"nearly a week ago now." He cleared his throat. "Apparently the corpse was quite far along in the decomposition process. Your neighbor's dog found it."

"Bentley?"

"What?"

"Is Bentley the name of the dog who found it?"

Massey frowned. "I don't know the name of the dog, Ms. Wilcox."

"Well, it's not important, I guess." She paused. "Whose body?"

"See, now *that* is the first question I'd have thought someone who's just been told there's a dead body on their property would ask. Not the name of the dog who found it." He consulted his notes again. "It has been identified as the body of Jeanette Byrd." He glanced up, watching her reaction. "That name mean anything to you?"

"No."

"No?" He raised his eyebrows. His face was hard and bony, the pale, freckled skin stretched taut across it. There was hardly enough skin on his forehead to fold into wrinkles. It was not a face that would express mercy easily, she thought.

"No."

Massey nodded his head. "According to Leslie Blackford of Jackson, Mississippi, the two of you had a conversation about Jeanette Byrd earlier this year." He flipped through some papers on his lap. "On March first, to be precise. Does that ring a bell?"

Florence shook her head. She had no idea who Leslie Blackford was.

"You are also listed as the emergency contact on Jeanette

WHO IS MAUD DIXON?

Byrd's release paperwork. Pretty odd to list someone you don't know, isn't it?"

"Release from what?"

"Ms. Byrd was granted parole from the Central Mississippi Correctional Facility on February twenty-fourth of this year."

Amina chose that moment to carry in a tray with three cups of steaming tea on it. As if by agreement, nobody said anything while she placed them carefully down on the table one by one. The last one clattered lightly and she left the room with small, quick steps.

Massey continued: "Leslie Blackford is Ms. Byrd's parole officer. Ms. Byrd apparently missed her first meeting with her. A few days later, Ms. Blackford received a phone message from Ms. Byrd from the landline in your house."

Florence had been trying to hold an unperturbed smile on her face since Massey's arrival, but here it began to falter.

Massey went on. "Ms. Blackford called you the next day. Yet you claimed you hadn't seen or heard from Ms. Byrd.

"Mississippi issued an arrest warrant for Jeanette Byrd on March twenty-seventh, on the grounds that she had violated her parole agreement. She'd missed three meetings with Ms. Blackford by that point. It says here that Detective Michael Ledowski of the Cairo Police Department then met with you at your home to inquire about Ms. Byrd's whereabouts. You claimed you hadn't seen her." He looked directly at Florence. "But you're telling me you don't remember your conversation with Leslie Blackford. And you don't know Jeanette Byrd. The woman whose body was found decomposing on your property."

Florence shook her head slowly. "I don't know what to tell you," she said. That, at least, was true.

Idrissi leaned forward onto his knees and spoke for the first time since they'd sat down. "It's strange, this. So much bad luck in such a short period of time."

Florence said nothing.

"I apologize for my English; is that the right word, Madame Weel-cock? The car accident. This...dead woman at your house. It's called bad *luck*?"

Florence paled. "Bad luck, yes," she whispered.

Idrissi continued staring at her. He obviously suspected her of *something*, but she could tell that he couldn't quite put it all together. After all, how does one connect a car accident in Morocco with a dead body thousands of miles away? She certainly couldn't.

She stared back at Idrissi, trying her best to appear unfazed.

Massey cut the tension. "Alright, listen," he said, relaxing his posture. "I'm not here to interrogate you. I'm not a police officer. But obviously the police in both Mississippi and New York are very eager to speak with you. I've come to urge you to return home as soon as you can. Today, if possible. I can help you make arrangements."

"Can't I talk to them over the phone?"

"No, Ms. Wilcox. You need to go back."

"I *need* to go back? Am I under arrest?"

"I don't have the authority to arrest you, Ms. Wilcox. I am simply offering a very strong suggestion."

"There is no extradition treaty between the United States and this country," Idrissi interjected. "We are not required to send you back."

"He's right," Massey said. "That said, it is not a good idea to stay. Ms. Wilcox, you are an official suspect in a homicide investigation. If you refuse to return home and cooperate, the United States can and will invalidate your passport. You will not be able to travel outside of Morocco for the rest of your life. If you break any laws here, and from what I hear from my friend"—he gestured at Idrissi—"it sounds like you already have, then the Moroccan police can prosecute you at any time, and the US embassy won't be able to intervene. And let me assure you,

Ms. Wilcox, American prisons are much more comfortable than Moroccan prisons."

Idrissi smiled. "I'd say Moroccan prisons are more comfortable than the electric chair your country is so fond of," he said.

Massey rolled his eyes.

"Okay, wait, this is crazy," said Florence. "I didn't kill anyone." As soon as she said it, she realized that wasn't true. But they weren't talking about the car crash. "I wasn't even living in Cairo in February, or whenever you say this happened."

Massey said, "According to your tax returns, you purchased the property at 174 Crestbill Road two years ago, and you've listed it as your primary residence ever since."

Florence stood up and walked to the window. It had started drizzling again.

Fuck.

Fuck, fuck, fuck.

It was all slipping away from her. Of course this was how it would happen. Everything had been handed to her, everything she'd ever wanted, and now it was getting yanked away. A joke. The universe's proffered handshake pulled back at the last minute.

She'd done everything she was supposed to do: She'd worked hard in school; she'd gotten a scholarship; she'd spent all her free time writing, with little to no encouragement; she'd put in long hours at a pointless job. All for nothing. And then someone like Amanda Lincoln got everything she wanted—everything they both wanted—with none of the struggle. Had it been so absurd for Florence to think that her reward had *finally* come due, after all this time?

Apparently it had.

She sighed. "Here's the thing." She turned around. "I'm not Helen Wilcox."

Idrissi and Massey exchanged a look.

"Pardon?" Massey asked.

"I'm not Helen Wilcox," she repeated, gesturing to his file.

Massey neatened the papers on his lap and placed them gently on the table. "Ms. Wilcox, I'm sure you have a perfectly reasonable explanation for all of this. You just need to tell the police what it is, and then you can go on with your life. You can even return to Morocco if you like."

"No, I'm serious. I'm Florence Darrow. I was born in Daytona Beach, Florida, in 1993. You can look it up. Helen was my boss. But she—she's gone. And I was just pretending to be her for a little while. It was just kind of a joke."

"A joke," said Massey flatly.

Idrissi cut in: "At the hospital five days ago, you told me your name was Helen Wilcox."

"Well, not exactly. You just started calling me that and I didn't correct you."

Idrissi sighed. "Your credit cards, your driver's license, and your passport say Helen Wilcox. The rental contract for the car in the accident was in the name of Helen Wilcox. This house"—he gestured around him—"is in the name of Helen Wilcox." He paused. "You have friends, here, I think. What do they call you?"

Florence looked up sharply. "Have you been watching me?"

"What name?"

Florence threw up her hands. "Helen! Okay? Helen Wilcox! I know, I *know* how this looks. But I swear, I was just pretending."

Massey said, "Consider things from our point of view, Ms. Wilcox. Which is more likely—that you lied about your name while you were injured in a hospital bed *and* among friends *and* on legally binding documents, or that you're lying now, when it appears that you might be in a spot of trouble?"

"I don't care how it sounds. I'm Florence Darrow. I just am."

"Alright," Massey said. "Can you show me some identification then?"

"I don't have any." Florence shrugged and emitted a shrill laugh. "I know it sounds crazy, but I don't. It was all in the car when we crashed. It's probably in the middle of the Atlantic ocean by now."

"Right," said Massey, drawing out the word.

"Can't you check my fingerprints?"

"Have you ever been arrested?"

"No."

"Then they're not on file."

Florence exhaled loudly but didn't respond. They sat quietly for another moment.

"Wait!" Florence suddenly said. "Wait right here." She ran upstairs and grabbed Helen's passport from the top of the dresser in her room. Downstairs, she handed it to Massey triumphantly. "Look, it's not me. Look closely." He opened it warily and looked at the picture. He passed it to Idrissi. They both inspected the photo, glancing up at Florence to compare.

"I don't know," said Massey, shaking his head.

"It is not clear," Idrissi agreed.

"Look at her nose."

"Noses can be changed," Massey said.

Florence snatched the passport back. She looked at the photo.

"It's clearly not me," she said, with dwindling conviction.

Massey held out his hand. She gave it back to him. "It doesn't look a thing like me," she said.

"Well, for one thing," he said, "I can't think of any good reason why you would have Helen Wilcox's passport if you're not Helen Wilcox, but listen, it's not up to me to determine whether this is you or not. As I said before, this is a matter for the police." He slipped the passport into his inside jacket pocket.

"Wait—you can't have that," Florence said. "Give that back."

"Ms. Wilcox, given that you are wanted for questioning in a homicide case in the state of New York, I must inform you that I do in fact have the authority to confiscate your passport. I can, however, issue you temporary paperwork that will authorize you to fly to the United States and the United States only. There you will be met by a uniformed officer and brought to the Cairo police department for questioning. Let me ask you again: Is that something you might be interested in?"

Florence didn't answer. She stared at the table in front of her.

Massey nodded as if she had answered. "Alright, please call me at my office if you change your mind." He placed a business card on the table. "If not, well, like I said, I can't compel you. But the United States will not issue you a new passport until this crime is sorted out."

Massey stood up and started packing his files back into his briefcase.

"What now?" asked Florence, looking up helplessly.

"It's out of my hands," said Massey. "You should go home, back to New York. That is my advice. I hope you'll take it." Then he pointed at her bags at the foot of the stairs. "And if you plan to leave Semat, I would advise you to keep me apprised of your whereabouts. It will make things easier for you in the long run."

Florence ignored him. "And you?" she asked Idrissi. She felt a sudden reluctance for him to leave even though his presence in her life had done nothing but unsettle her.

Idrissi shrugged. "I do not know, Madame." He seemed genuinely at a loss for the first time since she'd met him.

38.

The first thing Florence did after the men left was Google Jeanette Byrd. She found an article from 2005 in the Mississippi *Clarion-Ledger*. A local seventeen-year-old girl with that name had been found guilty of killing a man named Ellis Weymouth in a motel room in Hindsville, Mississippi. The paper said that she had always maintained her innocence, but the alibi she'd given—that she'd been with a friend all night—had fallen apart when the friend changed her story. They didn't mention the name of the friend because she was a minor, but Florence could guess it: Helen Wilcox.

Jeanette Byrd was Jenny. Ruby, from the book.

So she'd been paroled in February. Then what? After fifteen years in prison, she'd gone to find her old friend Helen? That was plausible, but it didn't explain how she ended up in the compost pile. Helen was selfish and a narcissist but she certainly wasn't a murderer.

Florence stopped herself.

Certainly? She wasn't sure she could describe Helen, whose moods were as variable as the weather, who even Greta had called volatile, as "certainly" anything.

According to Massey, the corpse had been in the compost pile on Crestbill Road since February. That meant that the entire time Florence had been living there, Jenny's body had been decomposing just yards from where she slept. She'd thrown banana peels on top of it.

245

What else had he said? That Helen had lied to both Jenny's parole officer in Mississippi and a local Cairo police officer. Florence's mind flashed to the overweight officer hitching up his pants in Helen's driveway and Helen staring him down from the bottom step. She'd watched the whole conversation.

There were two possible explanations, as far as Florence could tell. Either Helen had been covering for Jenny, or else she had, in fact, killed Jenny—and Florence had been living with a murderer for weeks.

She shut the laptop, but didn't otherwise move. She felt weighed down by a crushing lethargy. The need to leave Semat that she'd felt so urgently earlier in the day had dissipated. Now she wanted nothing so much as to sleep. She craved oblivion.

She couldn't leave anyhow. She had no passport. The only identification she had in her possession was Helen's driver's license, and she obviously couldn't be Helen anymore—Helen was wanted for murder. But she had nothing proving she was Florence. She was no one. She was nothing.

She pushed herself up and retrieved the whiskey bottle from the dining room. She poured a splash in her empty teacup and sipped it slowly. Outside, the leaves continued to drip.

Eventually, she knew, she would be able to convince whoever needed convincing that she was Florence Darrow. There were people she could call. There were documents they could dig up. But she felt no relief at this idea. Instead, she felt bereft. She hadn't grieved after Helen's death, but now she felt the loss of Helen's identity keenly.

Besides, she would still have to explain Helen's disappearance and all of the lies she'd told since the crash. She may not have murdered someone and shoved them in a compost pile, but she had killed someone, even if it was by accident. She was a criminal too. And somebody, somewhere, either in New York or Morocco, would make her pay. She was sure of it. That was the thing about being Florence Darrow: She always paid.

She wondered briefly whether she could transfer all of Helen's money to Florence Darrow before she took up her old identity again. Or even a numbered account. How did one do that? But then they'd charge her with theft. Not identity theft, just plain old theft.

At some point, Amina came in and asked if she wanted dinner. Florence shook her head. When Amina turned to leave Florence called out, "Wait—Amina, do you know my name?"

"Your name, Madame?"

"Yes, my name."

"Madame Wilcox, *n'est-ce pas?* It is on the paper."

"You're right. That is what's on the paper," Florence said with a resigned sigh. "Amina, do you ever feel like ... like you've made so many mistakes you'll never find your way back? And you're not even sure if you *want* to go back?"

"Back to ... the United States?"

"No. Never mind. I'm not making any sense. I'm sorry, Amina."

"Amira," the older woman said, patting herself on the chest. "My name is Amira."

"Amira? I thought it was Amina."

Amira shrugged.

"I'm sorry," Florence said as Amira walked back to the kitchen.

She sighed. What had she thought Amira was going to offer her? A solution? Redemption? If she wanted either of those, she'd have to find them herself.

She poured another splash of whiskey in her teacup.

———

Florence's eyes shot open. Someone was pounding on the door. She sat up and looked around. It was dark. She'd fallen asleep on the couch in the living room, the nearly empty whiskey bottle on the table next to her. She looked at her watch. Almost ten o'clock.

"Amina?" she called out. "Amira?"

There was no answer. She must have gone home.

Florence walked on shaky legs to the door and called out, "Who is it?"

"Me!"

Florence frowned. "Who?"

"Meg!"

It came back to her now. That morning, before breakfast, Florence had invited everyone over after dinner. That seemed like ages ago. She opened the door a few inches. Meg's moon-like face filled the crack, first one eye, then the other.

"Did you forget?" Meg asked cheerfully.

Florence nodded, rubbing her eyes.

"Do you want us to go?"

"No, that's okay. Come in." She opened the door all the way. Nick was standing behind Meg, smiling. He came in and draped an arm around her shoulders. The others trundled in after.

Florence led them out to the back terrace. Now that the storm had passed, the stars gleamed as if freshly washed. Meg was carrying a six-pack and held out a beer in Florence's direction. She nodded and took it.

They settled around the table on the terrace. Someday soon, Florence realized, this group might hear about a murder suspect named Helen Wilcox who'd fled to Morocco. What would they think? Would Nick be horrified by the thought that he'd slept with a murderer? Or would he know by then that the woman he'd been sleeping with had lied about who she was?

Nick caught her staring at him and smiled. "You okay?"

She nodded. "Just tired."

Meg wanted to play a game called "Never Have I Ever." Everyone took turns saying something they had never done before; if anyone else in the group had done it, they had to take a drink. Florence hadn't done any of the things that elicited jeers and feigned embarrassment among the others. She'd never had a threesome. She'd never done mushrooms. She'd never joined the mile-high club.

For the first time, she felt keenly the age difference between herself and this ragtag group. She was only two years older than Nick, but somewhere along the way she had started to feel closer to Helen's age than her own. Who cared about threesomes and plane sex? Those were their thrills? That was glory?

Even if she had to go back to being Florence Darrow, she would never allow herself to sink to such triviality. She would refuse an average life. She would send it back like undercooked chicken. She would—

"Babe, your turn." Nick nudged her elbow gently.

"Oh, sorry. Um. Never have I ever..." The group looked at her expectantly. "Never have I ever..." *Thrown bananas on a corpse? Drugged a friend? Stolen my boss's identity?*

She abruptly stood up. "Just skip me. I'm going to get another drink."

The group fell silent. She had ruined their fun.

39.

Florence was hungover. She rolled over in bed. Nick had left hours before to go kiteboarding. She looked around the empty room. All her belongings—and Helen's—were still in suitcases in the front hallway. She stood up and trudged downstairs to drag up Helen's so she could get dressed.

She peeked into the living room. It was immaculate. Amira had already cleaned up the mess they'd left last night.

As she passed through the front hall, she suddenly froze, certain she'd just seen Helen. She turned her head. It had been her own reflection in a mirror on the wall. She peered closely at it. Her hair had gotten blonder in the sun, and the storm had broken the humidity so that her curls now hung in loose waves. If she squinted, she might really have been looking at Helen.

She could have easily used Helen's passport at the airport, she realized. If her new life hadn't been snatched away from her.

"Florence," she said into the mirror in a loud, dull voice.

Just then she noticed another presence in the room. It was Amira, watching her from the kitchen doorway. She forced herself to smile.

"Good morning," she said as brightly as she could.

"Good morning, Madame. Coffee?"

"That would be great. Thank you."

Once she was dressed, she tried to regain some of the momentum she'd felt yesterday. Helen's body could still wash up, she reminded herself. But that thought no longer inspired the same sense of urgency. Once she'd decided to stop being Helen, she'd felt absolved of all her sins—as if without the reward there could be no misdeed. Besides, if Helen's body washed up, at least they'd know Florence hadn't murdered Jenny.

No, she reminded herself. *No.* If Helen's body washed up they'd ask how she ended up in the ocean and why Florence had never reported her missing. If they could prove that Florence had been drinking—maybe even if they couldn't—she'd go to prison for manslaughter.

She was fucked. That was the long and short of it. Florence Darrow was fucked and Helen Wilcox was fucked. At least Helen was lucky enough to be dead.

She toppled over on the couch, planted her face into a pile of pillows, and screamed as loudly as she could. She wished she'd never come to Morocco. No, farther back. She wished she'd never met Helen Wilcox.

When she sat up, her hair in disarray, Amira was setting a cup and saucer gently on the table in front of her.

"Thank you," she said, as if all were normal, as if this woman were not witnessing the disintegration of her self.

"Je vous en prie."

Florence sipped the strong, hot coffee and felt her wits begin to sharpen.

The first step was getting out of Morocco. If she had to explain what had happened to Helen, it would be better to do that in America. After all, extradition treaties go both ways. Morocco couldn't compel the United States to send her back to stand trial for manslaughter.

She Googled how to replace a lost passport in a foreign country. It appeared that she would need to go either to the embassy in Rabat or to the consulate in Casablanca. She'd also need a new passport photo, a photocopy of her old passport, and her driver's license.

Well, fantastic. She didn't have any of those. She noticed she was gnawing on her knuckle again. She removed it from her mouth, and picked up Dan Massey's card from where it still sat on the table. She tapped it against the glass a few times.

Finally she stood up.

It was time to embark on the long, unpleasant process of becoming Florence Darrow again.

She went into the kitchen and dialed the number.

"Massey here."

"Hi, Mr. Massey. This is Florence Darrow."

There was silence on the other end of the line.

"The woman from yesterday?" she prodded. "You were at my house?"

"I certainly remember visiting *Helen Wilcox's* house. What can I do for you, Ms. Wilcox?"

"It's Ms. *Darrow*," Florence said emphatically. "I want to go back to the United States. But I don't have a passport. Or any photo ID."

"I have your passport."

"No, you have Helen Wilcox's passport."

Another silence. When he spoke again, it was in a tone eager to show off how very reasonable he was being. "Alright, we'll do this your way. Remind me of your name again."

"Florence. Florence Margaret Darrow. I was born in Daytona Beach, Florida, on October ninth, 1993."

"And you have nothing with your name on it? Nothing at all?"

"No. But I can give you my mother's phone number—she'll tell you. Or wait, actually, there's someone here in Semat right now—an old friend, she's known me since I was six—she can tell you who I am."

"Uh-huh. But you see how I can't issue a legal government document using the assurance from a *friend* as proof of identity, right? You understand that?"

"I know, but..."

"Do you have access to your birth certificate or your social security card?"

"No." Both of them were in a shoebox in her closet in Helen's house. "But I can tell you where to find them."

He sighed. "Alright. Listen. I'm going to talk to a few people in the office and see what our options are. Maybe your friend could sign an affidavit. I'm not sure. To be honest, I've never encountered a situation quite like this before. What's the best number to reach you at?"

Florence rattled off the phone number from the yellowed piece of paper taped to the wall next to the phone.

"Okay, sit tight. I'll get back to you as soon as I can."

"When?"

"Hopefully later today. Goodbye, Ms.—" he stopped himself. "Goodbye."

Florence hung up and immediately retrieved the laptop from the living room. She had no plans to sit tight.

She Googled the number for Riad Lotus—that was where Amy had said she and Whitney were staying—and asked to speak to Whitney Carlson. It was nine thirty in the morning; she hoped they were still in the room. She hoped they were still in Semat.

"Hello?"

She breathed a sigh of relief. "Whitney? It's Florence."

"Florence, I'm so glad you called! I feel absolutely horrible about the other night. I don't know what happened."

"It's fine—don't worry about it. Listen, we didn't really get a chance to catch up, so I was wondering how long you were staying in Semat."

"Just until tomorrow."

"You're leaving tomorrow?"

"Yeah, we're taking the bus to Marrakesh in the morning then flying back to the States around eight."

"Okay. Listen, I'm going to call you in a little bit, okay? I might need your help with something."

"Of course. Anything."

"Great, thanks, Whitney."

"Is everything okay, Florence?"

"It's fine. Or at least it will be fine." She paused. "I'm really glad I ran into you." She considered how unlikely she'd have been to say that just forty-eight hours earlier.

"Me too."

"One more thing—I'm sorry I never responded to any of your calls or emails after I moved to New York. I should have, and I'm sorry."

"That's okay. People drift apart. I understand."

They hung up, but Florence stayed by the phone and leaned her head against the wall. She was dreading her next call. Finally, she picked up the handset and dialed the only number she knew by heart.

Vera sounded bleary when she picked up. Florence looked at her watch. It was the middle of the night in Florida.

"Sorry to wake you, Mom."

"Florence? What's going on? Where are you?"

"I'm traveling."

"Hang on."

Florence heard the bed covers rustle then the click of her mother's bedside lamp turning on. She could picture the room perfectly: the pink bedspread, the faded Monet posters on the wall. When Vera spoke again, she sounded more like herself.

"Florence? Is everything alright? Are you hurt?"

"I'm fine."

"Then why are you calling me in the middle of the night?" Florence heard the chill settle into her mother's voice from all the way across the Atlantic. It took her off guard. She had assumed Vera would fall on her knees in gratitude when Florence finally got in touch.

"What?"

"First you tell me you never want to see me again, now

you're waking me up at three in the morning. Make up your mind, honey."

"I didn't say I never wanted to see you again; I said I'd be out of the country for a few weeks. You always exaggerate."

"You absolutely did say *never*. I have the text message to prove it."

Florence felt a wave of rage surge up from her gut. She'd never asked her mother for anything, then the one time she needed help, Vera couldn't set aside her petty recriminations for even one minute. Florence slammed the phone down.

She went to the sink and held both hands under scalding-hot water. It seeped under the bottom of her cast, and the damp gauze began to itch. She clawed at it savagely, stopping only when the burning pain kicked in.

Afterward, Florence sat at the kitchen table and stared at the phone. What was there to do but wait for Massey to call back? Until then, she was caught in a bizarre limbo. She wasn't Florence and she wasn't Helen. She was no one.

There was a certain freedom in it, actually. Without a self, she couldn't be held accountable.

She picked up the phone again and called Nick. He answered almost immediately.

"What's up?"

"Are you still at the beach?"

"Yeah, but I could be done."

"Come over."

Oblivion beckoned.

40.

Florence lay on the couch with her head in Nick's lap. Her frame of vision was occupied by a corner of the coffee table with a baggie of weed and a dented can of pizza-flavored Pringles on it. It was ten o'clock. Amira had laid out a dinner of roasted vegetables and grilled lamb a few hours ago, and they had attacked it like animals. They were now draped around the living room, stuffed and listless. Nick hummed tunelessly. A girl she'd never met was straddling Liam on the couch opposite them. Meg tapped at her phone.

Florence forced herself to sit up. Nick used the opportunity to lean forward and start rolling a cigarette on the table. Florence walked outside to the back terrace. She shivered. The air had been cooler ever since the storm. She lay down on one of the lounge chairs and looked up at the sky.

Massey hadn't called back that afternoon, but Greta had, more than once. Florence had asked Amira to say she was out. She didn't know what to tell Greta. Even if she had been sober enough to make sense, she wasn't prepared to explain Helen's death or her own thwarted attempt to steal Helen's identity or the dead body that had just been found at the house on Crestbill Road. She hoped Greta would never find out about her week as Maud Dixon; it seemed horribly embarrassing now, and she still wanted Greta to help her get published one day.

She went into the kitchen and grabbed a water bottle from

the fridge. She drank half of it in a single gulp. The effects of everything she'd drunk and smoked were finally wearing off.

She walked back through the foyer, where Meg was holding open the front door.

"Hey, Helen, let me introduce you to someone," Meg said when she noticed Florence. "This is Florence. She just got here."

Meg pulled the door open another few inches. From behind it, a blond woman stepped into the light. She was wearing a cherry-red dress and smiling broadly. She stuck out her hand in Florence's direction. "Hello," she said. "You must be Helen."

Florence stood stock-still. There are some emotions, like rage and lust, that seem to speed up time. But shock creates a moment of stasis, a pocket of time outside the passing seconds, during which the mind has to veer off the neural pathway it has just been traveling down in order to start hacking away at a new one. She said nothing. She could only stare.

Standing in front of her was Helen Wilcox, who had died in a car crash a week ago.

41.

"lorence and I just met this afternoon," Meg said to Florence. Then she went into her familiar routine, saying to Helen, while gesturing toward Florence, "Helen is a *writer.*"

"Oh, are you?" said Helen, raising her eyebrows. "How fascinating!"

Florence found herself nodding dumbly.

"I always wanted to be a writer but I don't have the imagination. You just make up characters from nothing? A whole life? It seems impossible!" Helen laughed lightly.

Florence finally found her voice. "What are you doing here?"

Helen wrinkled her forehead in concern. "Oh, I'm so sorry. Meg said it would be okay if I came by, but the last thing I'd want to do is impose."

Meg gave Florence a bewildered look. "Of course you can stay," she said emphatically to Helen. "The more the merrier."

"Come with me to the kitchen," Florence said. "I'll make you a drink."

"That's alright. I don't drink."

"Then I'll get you a water." She put her hand on Helen's upper arm as if to pull her.

Helen shot Meg a questioning look. Meg, in turn, asked Florence, "Are you alright?"

"I'm fine."

Helen was enjoying this, she realized.

"Let's all just go into the living room, okay?" Meg said, leading Helen by the arm. Florence trailed behind them like a dog on a leash.

Meg introduced Helen—as Florence—to the group grandly. It was the same way she'd introduced Florence just days before. Florence looked over at Nick to see if he'd notice the name and remember that it was the same one Amy had called her by, but he just nodded and said, "Sup."

Florence sat down stiffly on the couch. Helen ensconced herself in an armchair and lit a cigarette. She looked entirely at ease. She was tanner than she had been the last time Florence saw her, but other than that she looked just the same. No bruises, no cuts, no broken bones.

Florence felt herself reluctantly pulled back into her old role, that of the supplicant, being careful, trying to accommodate Helen's sharp angles. If Helen wanted to play this game, she thought, fine, she'd play.

"So where are you from?" she asked Helen.

"Florida," Helen said with a smile.

"Whereabouts?"

"Port Orange."

"Never heard of it."

"I'm not surprised. It's neither here nor there."

"That's okay. Here and there are overrated."

Helen smiled with something like delight. Florence thought she saw something else in her eyes—surprise, maybe. She reluctantly felt herself flush with pleasure.

"Have you been traveling for long?" Florence went on.

"Oh, a week or so."

"Where? Here in Morocco?"

"A bit. I was in Rabat most recently."

"What brought you there?"

"I was taking care of some business."

"What line of work are you in?"

"Manufacturing."

"What do you manufacture?"

"Cogs, mainly."

Florence started laughing. "Cogs." She couldn't help it. "For boats, I presume?"

"Oh, for all seagoing vessels, really."

The rest of the group was following their banter with new attention, turning their heads from one to the other like spectators at a tennis match.

"Do you guys know each other or something?" Meg asked slowly.

"Heavens, no," said Helen.

Florence just shook her head, a smile still on her face.

For the next few hours, the evening proceeded as these evenings do. Helen and Florence relinquished the group's attention. Everyone continued to get drunker and drunker. But Florence didn't let another drop of alcohol pass her lips, and Helen didn't partake of anything besides cigarettes. It was as if they were slowly moving toward the foreground of a picture, getting sharper and sharper, while everyone else receded into blurriness.

Finally, at around midnight, after the rest of the group had shared a joint and fallen into a collective daze, Helen stood up and held her hand out to Florence. "Shall we?" she asked, as if it were the most natural thing in the world.

Florence nodded and took Helen's hand. She was surprised to feel herself shudder violently. It was like touching a ghost.

42.

Helen steered her into the first room at the top of the stairs—the one that used to be hers but now bore the traces of Florence's occupancy.

"Making yourself at home, I see?" Helen asked, looking around.

Florence blushed. She felt like she'd been caught trying on Helen's underwear. She was, in fact, wearing Helen's underwear. "I thought you were dead," she said by way of excuse.

In the pocket of silence a burst of laughter wafted up from downstairs.

"Clearly you were quite broken up about it."

"Helen—what's going on?"

"Sit," Helen commanded, pointing at the bed.

Florence obeyed.

"I had to go to Rabat," Helen said.

"But you just disappeared. I thought you were dead. Why didn't you tell me?"

"I couldn't tell you—for your own benefit."

Florence blew out her breath in exasperation. She didn't want to wait for Helen to mete out information at whatever pace she saw fit. She didn't like playing the fool anymore. "Is this about Jeanette Byrd?" she asked.

Helen narrowed her eyes. "Where did you hear that name?"

"A man from the embassy was here yesterday. Jeanette Byrd is dead. She's buried in your compost pile. It's pretty clear that they think you murdered her. No, correction, they think *I* murdered her. They think I'm Helen Wilcox."

"And why would they think that?" Helen asked, gesturing around the room.

"Yes, obviously you know that I've been pretending to be you. Is that what you want to hear? Because that transgression seems rather meager compared to whatever you've been up to."

Helen raised an eyebrow but said nothing.

"Did you kill Jeanette Byrd? Jenny?"

"It's complicated, Florence."

"Either you're a murderer or not."

Helen sat down on the bed next to Florence. "I'll tell you what happened, okay? Just...give me a moment." She took a pack of cigarettes out of her pocket and lit one. Her hand was trembling slightly, Florence noticed.

"Jenny got out of prison earlier this year. We hadn't kept in touch so I had no idea until she showed up on my doorstep. It was in the middle of a vicious snowstorm, around seven or eight at night. I was reading downstairs by the fire when I saw headlights in my driveway. You've lived there—you know that no one ever visits, and it's pretty much impossible to end up there on a wrong turn. So I went upstairs to get my gun—"

"You have a *gun*?"

"Of course I have a gun. Only a supremely naive or stupid woman would live all alone in the woods without one. So anyway, I came back downstairs and I saw that it was a taxi pulling in. I figured most murderers and rapists don't take taxis to their victims' houses, so I put the gun down and went to the door.

"And there she was. My god. I didn't even recognize her at first. She used to be beautiful, Florence. *Beautiful.* All the boys in Hindsville were obsessed with her. The men too. There was one teacher who used to stalk her like a wounded animal. But there was nothing beautiful about that person. She looked like a meth addict. Her hair was long and dirty and it had gone entirely gray. Several of her teeth were missing. She's my age, but she looked like she was sixty years old." She stopped herself. "*Was* my age," she corrected.

"She grabbed me and hugged me. And I can't even describe how terrible she smelled. Like . . . cat sweat. Fermented cat sweat. But what could I do? I hugged her back. I invited her in. She was my oldest friend.

"I brought her back to the kitchen and poured us some coffee. And then we just sat there. It was uncomfortable. The last time I'd seen her we were seventeen years old. At this point, we had nothing in common anymore. Nothing. And she had this nervous tic of picking at her hands. The skin around her fingernails was totally worn away, like someone went at it with a Brillo pad. I finally noticed her glancing at the bourbon above the fridge, so I offered her some. We both put a little in our coffee, and then it got a little easier. She started to talk. She told me that I was the only thing that got her through prison. *Me.* That she understood why I did what I did. That she forgave me. That we were sisters—we always had been and always would be."

"Forgave you for what?"

"What?"

"You said she said she forgave you."

"Oh. That. I took away her alibi. She had asked if she could say that she was with me the night of the murder, and I said yes. Then my father explained what a terrible idea that was. Thank god. I mean, I didn't know what perjury was. I thought lying to the police was basically the same thing as lying to a teacher. So I went back and told the truth—that we'd been together earlier in the night, but she'd gone off with Ellis at around eleven." Helen paused. "That's when her case fell apart."

Helen took another drag of her cigarette and went on: "The more she drank, the more wired she got. Manic almost. She was pacing around the kitchen. She started picking up glasses and vases and asking me how much they cost, opening cabinets and slamming them shut. She was getting angry. Then suddenly her version of events was that it was *my* fault she'd been in prison. And all that time I'd been getting rich off her story."

"She knew about the book?"

"Yes, it had made its way into the prison, and people were talking. As soon as she heard what it was about, she realized it was her life. She said I stole it." Helen rolled her eyes.

"Well, you did, didn't you?"

"All great writers steal. Dostoyevsky. Shakespeare. Everyone. Anyway, it was *our* story. It was always ours."

"So what happened?"

"She went crazy, that's what happened. She said she wanted the money I made from the book, that it was *her* money. This went on for hours: screaming, yelling, weeping. I finally got her to go to sleep in the carriage house at around four in the morning. The next day, we both slept late, and we actually had a nice time. We went for a walk, we talked, I made us lunch. But then I told her I thought she should go back to Mississippi. That it was a mistake to violate her parole. I even offered to help get her back on her feet. But she just... I don't know. She snapped. She came at me."

"What do you mean she came at you?"

"She grabbed a knife from that wooden block on the kitchen counter and she just rushed at me. I didn't know what to do. Instinct took over. I grabbed a pot and I hit her as hard as I could. Have you ever heard of anything so ridiculous? It's like something out of a Saturday morning cartoon. I thought she was going to sit up all dazed and cross-eyed, with a little halo of stars dancing around her head. But she didn't. She just lay there. Dead."

"Jesus."

Helen said nothing.

"So then what happened?"

"I panicked. You have to understand. I saw it all coming out. They'd find out who I was. That I wrote that book. God, can you imagine the publicity? It would have been so awful. So vulgar. I couldn't stand the idea of it."

"Helen." Florence looked at her in disbelief. "You killed Jenny to protect Maud Dixon's identity?"

"No," Helen said, eyes narrowed. "I killed her in self-defense. I *buried* her to protect Maud Dixon's identity. I mean, really, who cares what happens to a dead body? It didn't make any difference to her." Florence remembered that she had made the same argument to herself when she'd thought Helen was dead. As if reading her thoughts, Helen said, "Did you tell anyone about *my* dead body after you thought you'd killed me?"

"It's not the same thing," said Florence unconvincingly.

"Of course it is. Anyway, it all happened so fast. It wasn't like it was a rational decision. I was high on adrenaline and all I was thinking was that I couldn't let that body be found in my house. I couldn't bear the scrutiny. I didn't want the questions. I'm a very private person, Florence, you know that."

Florence found herself nodding, as if this were a good reason for burying a body.

"So you put her in the compost pile?"

"Well, it was February. In a snowstorm! Do you know how hard the ground was? Besides, a compost pile is actually the perfect place to dispose of a body. A whole cow will break down in under six months—teeth, bones, everything. I learned one useful thing growing up on a farm."

Florence remembered Helen telling her that she'd learned how to chop off a chicken's head when she was eight years old. Maybe she hadn't been lying.

Helen went on: "Of course the next morning I realized what a colossal mistake I had made. But I couldn't exactly call the police at that point. What, drag her out of the compost pile, brush her off, and lay her back on the kitchen floor? Seems a little harder to claim self-defense after you've *buried the fucking body.*"

Florence said nothing. She tried to imagine Helen shoveling kitchen scraps and dirt and wood chips on top of the body of her oldest friend. Somehow it seemed like it hadn't really happened. Like Helen was just telling a story.

"So that's when I started to think about running," Helen said.

"Running?"

"Just giving up on Helen Wilcox. Walking away from it all. I was ready for a change anyway. I hadn't been able to write anything worthwhile in ages. You've read the new book. You know it's not as good as *Mississippi Foxtrot.*"

Florence shrugged. She thought of telling Helen about her discovery in the Paul Bowles book, but she didn't want to interrupt the story.

"It was just a thought experiment at first, a game I played with myself—how would I disappear? Where would I go? How would I get a new identity? Could I continue to publish as Maud Dixon? How would I get paid? Should I tell Greta?

"I settled on Morocco because there's no extradition treaty. And it seemed like a nice place to live. Nicer than North Korea anyway. Good weather, good culture, good food, lots of expats, but also enough corruption that I could easily establish myself with a fake name. But it was all just speculation until I got that phone call."

"From Jenny's parole officer?"

Helen nodded. "She called in early March. She said Jenny had missed their first meeting and asked me if I'd heard from her. I said I hadn't. And then she said, 'Well, isn't that interesting' because she'd received a voicemail from Jenny and the call had come from my house." Helen shook her head. "My god, what an idiot. Only Jenny would call her parole officer from an out-of-state landline."

"And the parole officer sent the local cop?"

"You know about that too, do you? Well, of course you do, you were there. Yes, he showed up after they finally issued an arrest warrant for Jenny. She'd missed a few appointments by then. This cop clearly thought I was harboring a fugitive. But he didn't have a warrant, so I told him to leave. That was a mistake. I realized it afterward. If he came back with a warrant, he could tear the place apart. Maybe even the backyard. Maybe even the compost pile. I should have just cooperated and given him a nice little tour. But I didn't. That's when I realized I was actually going to have to start laying the groundwork for running. Remember? I suggested we go to Morocco the very next day. If and when he came back, I wanted to be out of the country, with a new identity ready to go. And if they found the body, I'd put the plan in motion. I'd leave Helen Wilcox behind and become someone else."

Florence shook her head. Something wasn't clicking. "But why did you bring me?"

"Honestly? Because I was scared. I didn't know if I could go through with it alone." Florence watched Helen's face. She felt a pool of warmth welling up inside of her. She pushed it back down. "Bullshit, Helen."

Helen let out a small laugh. "Okay, fine. I needed you to report me missing. I couldn't just disappear without a trace. I knew they'd assume I'd run and come looking for me. But if you reported an accident, that would at least allay their suspicion. I needed you to truly believe I'd died. Really, it was for your own protection. I didn't want you to be an accessory to a crime. Your ignorance was your alibi."

Florence abruptly stood up from the bed. The missing piece had finally clicked into place.

"You *planned* that accident? Helen, I almost died!"

"Florence, no, of course I didn't plan the car accident! I would never do that to you. My plan was to hire a boat and go for a swim out past the waves, and then I was going to disappear from there. The car accident was just that—an accident. I promise. But I saw the opportunity, and I took it."

"What do you mean you took it? Were you even in the car? Where are *your* bruises? Where are *your* broken bones?" She thrust her cast in Helen's face.

"I don't know, Florence," Helen said calmly. "I was lucky. It all happened so fast. I swam out of the car and made it to the beach at the base of the cliff. We went over the edge pretty close to where the cliff started to rise. It was only a ten-foot drop into the water. On the shore, thank god, I saw that that fisherman had rescued you. I stayed on the beach until my clothes were dry. Then I hitched a ride to the bus station. I'd hidden a lot of cash at the riad we stayed in in Marrakesh. I retrieved it and went on to Rabat. That's where I'd arranged to get new papers."

Helen was explaining it all so dispassionately, like she was re-counting a recipe for lasagna. As if Florence would be a fool for not understanding. Maybe she was a fool, because she didn't understand. Not at all. The facts weren't cohering into a cogent narrative.

"So why did you even come back?"

"I was sitting at a café in Rabat a few days after the accident and I happened to glance over at my neighbor's paper, and there it was—my name, Helen Wilcox. I asked him to tell me what it said. And that's when I realized what had happened. I realized that you were pretending to be me. Or I don't know, maybe you'd hit your head and you thought you *were* me. And you had no idea what you were getting into. I knew the police would come after you. For Jenny. For this mess I'd left behind."

Florence felt like her legs were going to collapse. She sat back down next to Helen. They were silent for a moment.

"Listen," Helen finally said. "I know this is a lot to process. And I understand that you might be angry. You have every right to be angry. But I have tried at every turn to keep you as safe as possible. I came back to protect you. I have always had your best interests at heart."

There was an unfamiliar tone in Helen's voice: needy and pleading. Florence realized all of a sudden that she held all the power. She could turn Helen in if she wanted. She could call the police right now. She'd love to see the look on the faces of Officer Idrissi and Dan Massey when she produced the real Helen Wilcox.

But then what? Then Florence would have no choice but to fly back to the US with no home, no job, and no money. Knowing that she'd put Maud Dixon in prison.

Florence put her head in her hands.

"You're exhausted," Helen said. "Why don't you get some rest. We can talk more in the morning."

Florence nodded. "Here, let me get my stuff out of your room," she said halfheartedly.

"It's fine. You stay. I'll go down the hall."

"Are you sure?"

"Of course." At the door, Helen turned back to Florence with a sly smile. "Do you want to know what my first reaction to seeing that newspaper article in Rabat was?"

"What?"

"I thought, *Good for her.* I was impressed you'd pulled it off. I realize that might be an unorthodox response to learning that your assistant has stolen your identity, but as you know, the herd mentality has never held much appeal for me."

Florence smiled wearily. "I guess I learned from the best."

"I can't deny that. Though even I might have slipped up. There's really no one here who knows you're Florence Darrow?"

"Well...I sort of had to tell this guy I'm seeing."

"Does Helen Wilcox have a boyfriend?" Helen asked, amused.

"Kind of. That guy Nick? With the dreds?"

Helen grimaced. "I see I still need to teach you a thing or two about your taste in men."

Florence laughed. "He's sweet."

"Sweet is just a polite way of saying dull."

In a gentler tone, Helen added, "Listen, all joking aside, I know I've given you a lot to take in, and I understand if you're feeling overwhelmed. Just remember that we're on the same side here. My plan is still to disappear, but I'm going to do it in a way that leaves you safe. And very well compensated. Okay?" She caught Florence's eye.

Florence nodded. "Okay."

"Good girl." She slipped out the door and pulled it shut behind her with a crisp click.

———

Florence drifted in and out of fitful sleep. The music from downstairs kept waking her up, then she'd remember that Helen was back and a whir of questions would start up in her head. Things she wished she'd asked but hadn't.

At one point she felt a presence in the room. She sat up. It was Helen, standing a few feet away, watching her. A shaft of moonlight illuminated half her body.

"Helen? Are you okay?"

"I couldn't sleep. I thought maybe you'd be up too. But never mind. It's late."

"It's okay." She pushed herself further up. "Come sit."

"No, no. Go back to sleep." Helen left the room.

A few minutes later, Florence wasn't sure that it hadn't been a dream.

Then she woke up again. It was still dark. The air felt tense, like a shrill violin string had just been plucked.

She put her feet on the cold floor and walked out into the hallway. It was quiet except for the fountain gurgling in the courtyard below.

She went downstairs. The living room was a mess, but no one was there. Meg and the others must have left.

There was a shuffling sound from out on the terrace. She

opened the French doors at the back of the house and saw Helen silhouetted against the dark sky. She was standing by the pool.

"Helen?"

Helen jumped and spun around with her hand on her heart. "Florence, you scared me."

"What are you doing?"

"I couldn't sleep. It's so peaceful out here now that the heat has lifted."

"Are you okay?"

"It's been a long few days. Weeks. Months."

"Do you want company?"

"No, go back to sleep. I'll be in soon."

"Are you sure?"

"I'm sure. Good night."

Florence went back upstairs but she couldn't get back to sleep. She picked up her book. A half hour later she heard Helen's footsteps on the stairs. They paused briefly outside her room, then kept going down the hall. The door to Helen's room shut quietly.

43.

Florence went downstairs shortly after dawn. She hadn't been able to fall back asleep after finding Helen outside by the pool. She guessed that had been around four in the morning.

Amira started when Florence walked into the kitchen.

"It's early," she said.

Florence nodded. "Is there coffee yet?"

"I'm making it now."

Florence wondered what time Amira arrived in the morning. She was always already there.

A few minutes later, Florence settled outside on the terrace with a mug and a brioche. The sky was brightening at a drowsy pace, the palm trees still just outlines against the sky.

Florence considered the one question that had kept her awake far longer than any of the others: Should she turn Helen in?

After all, Helen had killed someone. It had been in self-defense, but that didn't change the fact that Jenny was dead. Was Florence really willing to risk being charged as an accessory after the fact?

On the other hand, Florence gained nothing by sending Helen to jail. Helen had said she wanted to disappear in a way that left Florence safe and "compensated." What, in practical terms, had she meant? Florence seemed to be in a position to name her price. Besides, she didn't like the thought of Helen in prison. It would be like keeping an exotic bird in captivity. A waste.

"You're sunburned."

Florence jumped. Helen was standing in the doorway.

Florence drew her hands up to her face.

"You're all red. I didn't notice last night. You should take better care of yourself. There's SPF in my toiletries kit." Helen sat. "Did you end up getting any sleep?"

"Not really. You?"

"Some. I'm okay, though. Nothing a little coffee won't cure."

As if on cue, Amira stepped out onto the terrace with the pot. She greeted Helen placidly, as if she'd always expected her to return. Maybe she had.

When she'd gone back into the house, Helen asked, "What did you tell Amina?"

"Nothing, really. I said you were in Marrakesh." She realized how odd it was that she'd never explained her injuries or why she was driven back to the villa barefoot by a policeman. "Her name is *Amira,*" she added, for lack of any other explanation.

"Is it?" Helen asked, uninterested, as she pulled apart a croissant and spread honey on it. "Listen, I have to run into town this morning. When I get back, let's talk about next steps."

"What are you doing in town?"

"It's better that you don't know."

"We don't have a car anymore."

"I have one." Helen took a sip of coffee. "By the way, what was the name of the guy from the embassy?"

"Dan something. His card is on the table in the living room. Why?"

"I have a plan. I'm going to take care of a few details, then I'll tell you everything." She drank the rest of her coffee in a single gulp and stood up.

"You're leaving *now?*" It wasn't even seven yet.

"The early bird etcetera, etcetera."

Helen disappeared into the house to get ready.

Half an hour later, she was gone, and Florence was alone again.

She was still sitting there when she heard the phone ring. Amira stuck her head out onto the terrace. "It is Madame Greta again, Madame."

"Can you tell her I'm not home, please?"

Amira nodded, but reappeared a moment later. "She says if no one talks to her she will call the police."

Florence knew that if Helen came back to Villa des Grenades and found the police there, she'd never forgive her. And the truth was, Florence wasn't ready to choose sides yet.

She pushed herself up from the table and followed Amira into the house.

"Hi, Greta," she said tentatively into the phone.

"Florence? What's going on? I've been trying to get in touch with you for over twenty-four hours."

Florence looked at her watch. "What time is it there?"

"Florence, I'm *here*. I'm in Marrakesh."

"What?"

"I've been here since yesterday afternoon."

"Where?"

"At La Mamounia." Florence recognized the name of the hotel from the research she'd done before booking their trip. It cost over five hundred dollars a night. "Listen, where are *you*? I don't know where to come meet you."

"I'm leaving. I'll come to you."

"But what about Helen?"

"I told you—Helen left. She's not here anymore." As soon as she told the lie, she realized that she was never going to turn Helen in. Her loyalty would never belong to rule-bound functionaries like Officer Idrissi and Dan Massey. Nor, even, to Greta Frost.

"Do you think she came back here, to Marrakesh?"

"Yes," Florence said decisively. "Our return flight is on Wednesday. I have no reason to believe that she won't be on it."

"Alright. Let's meet here then. You're leaving today?"

"As soon as I take care of one or two things."

"Fine. Let's plan on getting a drink at my hotel this evening. There's a nice bar just behind the lobby. I'll be there at six."

"Okay. I'll see you then."

"Call my cell if anything comes up."

Florence hung up and wondered whether she would actually go through with the meeting. What would she tell her?

She'd ask Helen. Helen would have a plan. She always did.

44.

Half an hour later, the high-pitched whine of a scooter grew in volume, then abruptly cut off. Florence looked out the window. Meg was climbing off her motorbike in the driveway. Florence went to open the front door.

"Is Nick here?" Meg asked without preamble.

"No, why?"

"Have you heard from him?"

"No. What's going on?"

"He was supposed to meet Liam and Jay to surf this morning, like two hours ago, but no one can get in touch with him. He's not at their place either."

"Didn't he go back with them last night?"

"No, they said he stayed behind." Meg looked uncomfortable. "He was talking with Florence? I mean, totally platonically or whatever."

Florence smiled. "That's okay. He's allowed to talk to other women."

"Well, if you hear from him will you let one of us know?"

Florence nodded.

After Meg had left, Florence sat down in the living room. There was an uneasy churning in her gut she could no longer ignore. The coffee had kicked in, and all the questions that she hadn't been able to formulate the night before bombarded her with insistent clarity.

How had Helen emerged unscathed from the accident? How, exactly, had she swum out of a sinking car? Had she even *tried* to save Florence? Why couldn't Florence remember anything from that night? And, while she was at it, why had Helen hired her to transcribe pages from an already published novel?

There had been something off about Helen's confession. It had been too forthright. Helen was brilliant and engaging and thrilling, but transparent? Sincere? Never.

Unless it wasn't a confession at all.

And if it was something else, then what was Helen still hiding? If she'd admit to killing her best friend, what deeds were too dark to name?

Florence suddenly had an idea of where to look.

Helen had left her laptop behind at Villa des Grenades after faking her death because nothing could be missing. But why had she brought it to Morocco at all? They already had a computer—the one Florence had been using to type up Helen's drafts and send her emails.

Florence used it now to Google: "Forgot my mac password." Why hadn't she thought of this before? The process for resetting a computer password couldn't have been simpler.

She ran up to her bedroom, taking the stairs two at a time, and took out Helen's computer from the drawer she'd found it in three days ago. It was dead. She plugged it in and hit the Power button while holding down the Command and R keys. She consulted the instructions again on her own screen. Now Helen's laptop was in recovery mode; all she had to do was type "resetpassword" into the terminal.

Suddenly she froze; there was a noise coming from downstairs. She listened closer. It was Amira singing softly to herself. It was nothing.

She turned back to the computer and reset Helen's password to "zoodles." Now there was no turning back. The next time

Helen tried to use her laptop, she'd know that Florence had been tampering with it.

Florence watched as Helen's desktop filled the dark screen. Her excitement deflated quickly. There were no files or folders on the desktop. She clicked through the documents folder and the trash. They were both empty. She opened the Internet browser. The search history had been wiped.

Florence tapped her fingers lightly on the keyboard. Then she Googled "recover deleted files on mac." The top hits were ads for software that claimed to do just that. She downloaded the first one for $1.99, and watched as it searched the hard drive. A neon green status bar showed its progress; it hit 50 percent, then 80, and still nothing.

Finally, at 87 percent, the computer emitted a bright ping. The program had found something: a folder called "Book2." Florence opened it. Inside were several documents labeled "Draft1" through "Draft4." She clicked on the most recent. It was not the Paul Bowles novel that she had been typing up for weeks. She had never read these words before.

A cover page read:

The Morocco Exchange

A novel

by Maud Dixon

Florence picked a page at random and started reading.

> Lillian glanced over at Iris, who had gone pale in the heat as she watched the fisherman pound the limp octopus to death. Lillian knew that Iris's usefulness lay precisely there, in her naivete, but still she found it abhorrent. Weakness disgusted her in the same way she imagined cruelty or bad manners appalled others.

Florence stopped. She realized she'd been holding her breath and released it all at once. She scrolled to the end of the document.

> Lillian slipped six clonazepam into the pocket of her dress. The doctor had told her to take half a pill for the flight.
>
> She rechecked the route to the restaurant on her phone. Rue Badr was the only way to get there—or back.
>
> Suddenly she heard a soft tapping at her door. Even Iris's knocks were tentative.

Florence shut the laptop violently. She forced herself to take several deep breaths, then stood up and walked to the bathroom on unsteady feet. She braced herself over the toilet for a moment, but nothing came up. She moved to the sink and ran the hot water for several seconds. As soon as she felt the burning sensation on her skin, her breathing slowed. She watched herself in the mirror. When she felt steadier, she turned off the tap and went back to the laptop. She closed the document without reading any more of it and Googled the number for the Cairo, New York, police department.

Downstairs, in the kitchen, she listened to the phone ring several times before someone picked up.

"Cairo PD."

"Hi, can I speak to Detective Ledowski, please?"

She was put on hold and then another voice came on the line. "Yeah?"

"Detective Ledowski?"

"Who's asking?"

"This is Florence Darrow. I'm Helen Wilcox's assistant."

A brief pause. "I hope you're calling to tell me what flight she's on."

"She wants to know first if she's a suspect in the Jeanette Byrd case."

"She wants to know if she's a suspect?" He snorted. "She's not *a* suspect. She's *the* suspect. She's it."

"And Jeanette Byrd was definitely murdered? It couldn't have been self-defense?"

"Two bullet wounds to the back of the head? Yeah, I'd say that's a murder. An *execution* is what it is."

Florence hung up the phone. She reached out for the nearest chair and pulled it toward her.

She heard Helen saying, "So I ran upstairs to get my gun. . . ."

Florence tried to recall everything Helen had said the night before. What else was a lie? All of it? That seemed safe to assume.

Suddenly she remembered finding Helen standing over the pool in the middle of the night. No, she thought. No. She shook her head violently to dislodge the ugly thought that had settled there.

But still she stood up.

She hurried out back, toward the edge of the scummed-over pool. She stared into its black-green depths. She could see nothing. She picked up a rock from the flowerbed and threw it in. Its path ripped a small hole in the surface that quickly healed itself. There was no trace of the stone.

Florence glanced back at the house then started rolling up her pajama pants. They kept falling down so finally she just took them off.

"You are swimming?"

Florence jumped and spun around. Amira was standing on the terrace holding a watering can.

Florence nodded. "I think I will," she said with forced gaiety.

"I'll bring a towel."

"Thank you."

She stepped gingerly onto the first step of the pool with a

grimace. It was colder than she'd expected. The algae on the surface was stringy and slippery. Dozens of long-legged bugs jumped across it.

She climbed down the rest of the stairs with her teeth clenched, then waded around the shallow end in waist-deep water. Nothing.

She trod deeper into the water, kicking out her legs in wide arcs. She'd covered almost the entire pool. She was starting to feel ridiculous.

And then all of a sudden she felt something. *There*. What was that?

She moved her foot around. It was difficult to stay rooted in one place with the water up to her armpits. There! She felt it again.

She took a deep breath and plunged under the surface. She opened her eyes, but she couldn't see a thing. No light penetrated the scum overhead. She held out her hands in front of her. They landed on something soft—fabric. She moved her hands. Teeth. A nose. She moved her hands again. She felt a thick plait of dreadlocked hair.

Florence struggled toward the shallow end, spluttering violently. "Fuck," she said over and over.

She climbed out of the pool and grabbed the towel Amira had left for her.

"Fuck."

She wrapped the towel around herself and ran into the living room. Her wet feet slipped on the tiled floor; she had to grab a wall to steady herself. Where was it? Where was Dan Massey's card? It wasn't on the table. She checked under the table, under the chairs. It was gone.

"Fuck."

She grabbed the laptop from the dining table and Googled the number for the embassy in Rabat. She carried it into the kitchen, startling Amira again. She dialed and shrieked "Dan

Massey!" at the chipper voice that answered. A moment later, he was on the line.

"Massey here."

"She killed him," Florence said, her voice shrill and panicked. "She killed him."

"What? Who is this?"

"It's Florence Darrow."

"Ah. I was about to call you."

"Helen came back. The real Helen. She was here. She killed a friend of mine. She killed Nick. Please, you have to help me."

"Slow down, slow down. Start again."

Florence took a breath. "Helen came back last night. My boss, Helen Wilcox, the one whose passport you have. And she killed someone. She killed Nick." Florence's voice broke. She remembered him in the kaftan and turban in the souk, smiling and blushing. He was only twenty-four. What had she done? Florence didn't even know whether she meant Helen or herself.

"Nick who?"

"Nick. *Nick.*" She didn't even know his last name. "He's in the pool."

"Ms. Wilcox, I want you to listen very closely, okay? I'm going to come back to your house, but it's going to take me a few hours to get there. I'm also going to call Officer Idrissi and see if he can get there sooner. But I want you to know that I spoke to Florence earlier today."

"What?"

"She told me a little bit about what's been going on."

"What do you mean?"

"She said you've been floating some crazy ideas. Suicide. Fleeing from the law. She said you've been drinking a lot, that you'd gotten your hands on some illegal narcotics. She even said you offered her ten thousand dollars for her passport."

"No, that was *Helen*. She took your card. She took it."

"We're all here to help you, okay. We're all on your side. Let's just calm down for a moment. I'm going to leave my office now. It'll take me about five hours. I'll call Idrissi as soon as I hang up. If I can reach him, he should be able to be there in twenty, twenty-five minutes, okay? I'll be there soon too. Just sit tight and don't do anything rash."

"Okay," Florence said. "But hurry."

When she hung up, her adrenaline receded like the ebbing of the tide. The world slowed down. She saw herself as Amira saw her. Standing in a puddle of dirty water. No pants on. Clutching a laptop to her chest, the charging cord trailing loosely on the ground.

"I'm sorry," she said to Amira. "I'm sorry."

Florence walked upstairs. She was wet and shivering. There was algae hanging from her hair and eyelashes.

Idrissi would be here soon, she repeated like a mantra in her head. She never thought she'd be so grateful for his presence.

She went into her own bathroom for the first time since the accident and locked the door behind her. She let the shower run until it was scalding, then stepped into the stream. She didn't bother to hold her cast outside of it this time. It was already soaked.

Idrissi would come. Massey would come. Eventually she would get them to see the truth. Whitney could sign an affidavit. She could fly her mother over. There was no way they'd actually put her in jail as Helen Wilcox. She just needed to be patient. Calm and patient.

She stepped out of the shower and was toweling off when she heard someone rap gently on the door.

"Florence?" Helen said lightly.

Florence froze. "Just a second!"

"Everything okay in there?"

"Yes, everything's fine."

"Amina put out lunch. Get dressed and come eat."

"Okay. Just give me a second."

Florence listened to Helen walk away. She rubbed the towel on her face vigorously. She pulled on some clothes and looked out the bedroom window, which faced the driveway. There was no sign of Idrissi yet. But she couldn't hide in the bathroom all day. Her one advantage was that Helen didn't suspect that *she* suspected anything.

Downstairs, she heard Helen talking to Amira on the terrace. Helen's purse was sitting on the table by the front door. Florence glanced out the door to the terrace and moved quickly toward the table. Inside was a US passport. She pulled it out and opened it.

It was her passport. Of course it was. There was her full name, Florence Margaret Darrow and her date of birth as she'd seen it listed officially countless times in her life. But next to it was a photograph of Helen Wilcox.

She slipped the passport into her back pocket.

How had Helen done that? Is that what she had been doing in Rabat? Florence knew from her own research that all Helen would have needed was a photocopy of Florence's passport and her driver's license. That and new photos.

Outside, Helen sat at the table in the shade where Amira had set up lunch. She pulled a grape off the stem and popped it into her mouth jauntily.

"Nice shower?"

"Yes. Thanks. How was town?"

"It was fine. I ran into some of your friends. Meg and that guy Nick, I think?"

"Oh. That's nice."

Florence sat and raised the glass of juice at her place to her mouth before realizing it had been sitting on the table alone with Helen before she arrived. She faked a sip then put it back down. She felt nauseous. She couldn't eat. She noticed that her hand was shaking. She shoved it under the table. Where was Idrissi?

She didn't even know if Massey had reached him yet.

"You look pale," Helen said.

"I'm a little hungover."

Florence watched Helen butter and eat a piece of bread. She pulled back her lips into a grimace with each bite to avoid smudging her lipstick. A murderer. She was eating lunch with a murderer. She'd killed two people: Jenny and Nick. Ellis Weymouth too, probably—the man Jenny had served fifteen years in prison for murdering. What was more likely: that two young girls, best friends, both grow up to be homicidal, or that one of them is a psychopath, sadistic enough to frame the other for her own crime? Certainly someone who had no reservations about taking a life would have no compunction about sending someone to prison. Even her closest friend.

And now she'd stolen Florence's passport. In order for Helen to use it, of course, the real Florence Darrow needed to be out of the way—for good.

But what could she do besides sit across from Helen and eat lunch as if everything were normal? She couldn't confront her. Who knew what Helen was capable of? After all, she'd had a gun in Cairo without Florence ever knowing. No, Florence just needed to wait for help to arrive.

Amira came out carrying a platter of chicken salad. She set it down on the table and turned to Florence.

"You had a nice swim?" she asked.

Florence froze. She looked at Helen, who had narrowed her eyes and was staring at her darkly. Neither of them moved. Amira, receiving no answer, returned to the kitchen. Then Helen flexed her right hand and Florence jumped up, kicking her chair to the floor with a loud clatter. She ran inside and raced up the stairs, Helen's steps pounding behind her.

Florence darted back into her old room, into the bathroom, then spun around and locked the door. She sat down against the door, panting.

A second later, Helen rapped gently against the door.

"Florence," she sang. She rapped again. "Florence, are you alright?"

Florence jumped up and moved into the bathtub. She pulled up her knees and hugged her legs to her chest.

Helen jiggled the doorknob, tentatively at first, then harder. Finally she heaved her entire body against the door. It was old but the wood was thick and strong. It would hold, Florence thought. The lock—a clunky brass contraption—looked solid too.

The door stopped shaking. She could hear Helen panting on the other side. The sound of their two bodies taking in air was all that could be heard for a few moments.

"Why did you have to kill him?" Florence finally asked. "He was just a sweet, simple boy."

Getting Helen to talk was the best way to buy time until Idrissi's arrival, but more than that, Florence simply wanted an explanation.

"Kill who?" Helen asked innocently.

"You know who. Nick. Why did you kill Nick?"

Helen's tone changed. "If you're pointing fingers you might want to look in the mirror, Florence. *You* killed him. The moment you told him your name was Florence Darrow. You ruined the whole thing. You should have just kept up the ruse. It was a good one. You wanted to be Helen Wilcox? *Great!* By all means, take her. But you can't have both. You can't have Helen *and* Florence. That's just greedy. *I'm* Florence Darrow now."

"I didn't even tell him my name was Florence Darrow!" Florence cried. "I told him that my real name was Florence but now I go by my middle name, Helen. I *never* said my real last name. I'm not stupid."

"Florence, you told me that he knew your real name. I had to assume you meant your full name. I couldn't take any chances. You should have been clearer. It's a shame, but again, that's on you, not me."

"He was just a sweet boy," Florence said again, more softly.

"Oh, bullshit," Helen spat. "He was an overgrown stoner who acted like a boy to get women into bed."

Florence didn't respond.

After a beat, Helen said, "Hang on—I'll be right back." She added with a manic, trilling laugh, "Don't run off!"

Florence heard Helen's footsteps recede quickly. She waited a few seconds and cracked open the door to peer out. Helen wasn't in the room. Florence hurried to the window and looked down into the driveway. Still no sign of Idrissi. She turned around. Where should she go? She could already hear Helen coming back up the stairs. She retreated back into the bathroom and locked the door again.

"Now, where were we?" Helen asked.

"Helen, please just tell me what's going on. The truth this time."

There was silence for a moment. Then Helen said, "Here, take a look at this." A folded piece of paper was slipped under the door. "This will explain everything."

Florence eyed the paper warily. What could it possibly say? She put her hands on the rim of the bathtub and pushed herself up to standing. And then there was a dull crack and the door splintered at hip level. The sound was unmistakable. Helen had fired a gun at the door, and the bullet had lodged midway.

"Helen!" shouted Florence. "Are you insane?" She heard the sound of muffled laughter on the other side of the door.

"Worth a shot."

From inside the tub, Florence reached for the plunger beside the toilet and used it to draw the paper toward her. She unfolded it. It was blank.

There was an interlude in which both women were silent. Helen tapped what Florence assumed was the gun lightly against the door, as if bored. Florence pulled down a towel from the heavy brass rack on the wall and folded it underneath her in the tub.

"Amira must have heard that," Florence said. "She's probably calling the police right now."

"I sent her home."

Fuck.

It was time to show her cards. "Well, *I* called the police," Florence said. "Before lunch. They're on their way as we speak."

Helen paused. "Bullshit."

"It's true. Call Dan Massey at the embassy. Ask him."

"No, you're lying. I can tell when you're lying. I'm going to stay right here, Florence, and wait for you to come out. You *will* have to come out eventually, you know."

Florence shut her eyes tightly. Idrissi would be here soon. Then he'd find her being held hostage with a gun. Everything would be clear.

"You staged the crash," Florence finally said. "So I would die and you could steal my identity."

"Oh, bravo," said Helen.

Florence realized, absurdly, that her feelings were hurt. All she'd wanted these past few weeks was for Helen to like her. And instead Helen had tried to *kill* her. That was not generally something people do to people they like.

"How?"

"Jesus, Florence, haven't you ever seen a movie? I drugged you; I put the car in neutral; I pushed. *Fin.* Well, no, not *fin.* That was the problem, wasn't it? That fucking fisherman. What was he even doing out at ten at night?"

"But why didn't you just let me be Helen Wilcox?" Florence asked. "If you knew that that was what I was doing anyway? Why'd you come back at all?"

"The money, of course."

"What money?"

"My money. I made you the beneficiary of my estate. Helen Wilcox has to die for Florence Darrow—that's me now, remember—to get the money."

Florence begrudgingly admired the elegance of the plan. Helen could live as Florence Darrow and still get her money through standard legal channels.

"But why did you involve me at all? Couldn't you have just bought a fake passport or something?"

"Where do you do that, Florence? At the fake passport store? Do they sell social security numbers too? And credit histories? I haven't a clue where people get false papers."

"You were really just going to kill me?" Florence asked in a quiet voice. "No qualms whatsoever?"

A sigh. "Florence, I thought I'd been clear with you. We're all in this alone. We just do what we can to survive."

Florence said nothing. It was true; Helen had been clear.

Helen's voice softened somewhat. "In the beginning I wasn't *necessarily* going to kill you. If six months had passed and Jenny's body had decomposed, I would have just fired you and gone on with my life. But after that visit from Detective Ledowski, I had to presume it was all going to come out. We had to get out of the country. And then I watched them find the body on my Nest cam, and I knew I needed to put the plan in motion."

"Your what?"

"My security system. There are cameras all over the property. The police discovered the corpse the day after we got to Semat."

"Why are we even in Semat, by the way? It's obviously not to research your new book, which is just a Paul Bowles rip-off."

"You caught that, did you? Well, you couldn't expect me to write a whole new novel just for you to have something to type up. Anyway, we came to Semat for Rue Badr. Google 'most dangerous roads in Morocco.' It's the first one listed."

Florence remembered the manuscript she'd recovered from Helen's computer. Iris had checked and rechecked the route to Dar Amal—via Rue Badr—on her phone. "I found your new novel," she said. "The real one. *The Morocco Exchange*."

"It's good, isn't it?" The pride in Helen's voice was unmistakable.

Florence ignored the question. "I finally understand. You don't write fiction. You probably *can't* write fiction. Every word of *Mississippi Foxtrot* was true—you killed that man and let Jenny go to jail for it even though she'd done nothing."

"She hadn't done *nothing*. She was there. Her job was to get him drunk, which she did. We were just going to fuck with him a little...but I couldn't stop. I just couldn't stop. It was the best feeling I'd ever had."

"And to write another book, you need another story."

"I'll admit it, yes, I needed new material. But killing you also happened to be the most efficient way to clean up the mess Jenny had dropped at my doorstep. Besides, I was ready to leave that life behind. I was bored." Helen's voice dropped an octave. "And I think you understand, Florence—that desire to become someone new. Life is so varied. There are so many ways to experience it. What a shame to taste only one—especially the lives you and I were born into. I could sense that wandering soul in you the first time I saw you. It's part of the reason I chose you. I knew you could cast off your old life like you were shrugging off a coat."

"Chose me?"

"Chose you as my new coat."

In that moment, Florence saw it all. It hadn't been sheer luck that Helen had hired her as her assistant; Helen had sought her out. There's no way Florence could have been the most qualified candidate—she'd just been fired for stalking her boss's family. What Helen needed wasn't a talented assistant; it was a new identity.

Florence remembered seeing her own LinkedIn, Instagram, and Facebook accounts in Helen's search history. She'd done her research: She'd found someone who looked enough like her and whom nobody would miss. You couldn't ask for a better coat than Florence Darrow. Helen had been planning Florence's murder before they'd even met.

Florence knew, then, that she was not going to be able to talk her way out of this. Her only options were to keep stalling or to fight. She looked around for something she could use as a weapon.

"So, now what?" Florence asked. "You shoot me? Throw me in the pool too?"

"Well, the plan *was* to give you a fatal dose of heroin—I already told Massey that you, aka Helen, were using—but I guess you're not going to come stick out your arm for me, even if I ask very nicely."

"Fuck you, Helen."

"It's not *such* an absurd idea, Florence. Not to be unnecessarily cruel, but what do you have to live for? Your life is empty. I could tell that just from your writing."

"I guess I should kill someone, too, so I have something to write about? Is writer's block a valid defense on a murder charge these days?"

Helen laughed. "See—you can't even come up with your own idea; you have to steal mine. But how about this: I'll wire a hundred grand to your mother, for her trouble, if you come out and cooperate. Think about it."

Florence couldn't help but laugh back at her. "Helen, I don't give a shit about my mother, and I'm not going to let you stab me with a heroin needle."

Helen sighed. "Fine."

Neither of them spoke. Then a loud metallic ring echoed

through the bathroom. Florence ducked below the lip of the bathtub. When the reverb faded, she peeked out. Helen had shot the lock. It was slightly askew but still in place. She wondered how many bullets Helen had.

Another shot rang out. The lock rattled in the door. Helen started pounding on it. Florence jumped up. The lock was almost entirely off. One more blow and she'd be in.

"Wait," Florence said uselessly. "Wait."

Helen kicked the door in.

45.

Florence had flattened herself against the wall next to the doorway and was clutching the brass towel rack she'd unscrewed from the wall. As soon as Helen stepped inside, Florence swung her makeshift weapon at Helen's head as hard as she could. She felt the crunch as it connected with bone.

Then she ran.

She was halfway to the stairs, still gripping the towel rack, when she heard something clatter to the bathroom's tiled floor.

The gun.

She made a split-second decision, stopped, and turned back.

Helen was on her knees in the bathroom, holding her head in both hands. Blood gushed from between her fingers. Florence grabbed the gun from the floor near the toilet and pointed it at her.

Helen looked up but didn't move.

They stayed locked in that tableau for a moment. Then Florence picked up a towel that had fallen to the floor and tossed it at Helen. Helen wadded it up behind her head and leaned against the doorframe.

Florence stepped over her and walked back to the window in the bedroom, keeping her eye, and the gun, trained on Helen. She quickly glanced out. Still no Idrissi.

Florence turned back to Helen. "I thought it was an act," she said. "The callousness. The whole I-don't-owe-anyone-anything schtick."

"I don't have to pretend to be someone I'm not," Helen said hoarsely. "Unlike you."

"I'm not pretending," Florence said defensively.

Helen snorted. "Of course you are. You started pantomiming me the day you arrived. Don't you think I noticed? Your new-found interest in opera and wine and cooking? 'It's hot as blue blazes?' I mean, Florence, you're literally wearing my clothes."

Florence looked down at the dress she was wearing. "Well, so what?" she exclaimed. "I hated my life! I wanted something better; is that so terrible!?"

"So then you *make* a better life," Helen said. "You don't *steal* it."

Florence said nothing, but she could feel her face burning brightly. That was bullshit. Everyone steals, including Helen. She'd stolen from Jenny. She'd stolen from whoever had intro-duced her to Verdi and Châteauneuf-du-Pape.

No, Florence wasn't going to apologize for how she'd gotten here. She was done apologizing. She could be whoever she wanted to be and she would get there however she had to. She had dropped the gun to her side, but now she lifted it again and pointed it at Helen. A cruel smile parted her lips.

"Listen," Helen said with more apprehension in her tone than before, "we'll split the money." Blood was dripping from her right earlobe.

Florence shook her head, still smiling.

"You can have all of it, then. You can even have Maud Dixon. I'll start over."

Florence shook her head again.

Helen paused. Then one of her familiar toothless smiles appeared on her bloodstained face, and her eyes shone brightly. She laughed mirthlessly. "You won't do it, Florence. I know you. You don't have the nerve."

Helen stood up shakily, leaning against the doorframe for support.

"Stop," Florence said. "Sit back down."

Helen started walking unsteadily through the bedroom, toward the hallway. "Didn't you learn anything from my story, Florence?" she asked over her shoulder. "You can't shoot someone in the back and then claim self-defense."

Florence watched helplessly as the distance between Helen and herself widened. "Stop," she said again.

Helen paused just beyond the doorway, still facing away from Florence so that a bullet could only enter her body from behind. "What a waste," she said quietly. "I would have made Florence Darrow great. But you? You're no one. *No one.*"

Florence took a deep breath.

No more half measures.

She strode across the room in three long, quick paces. Helen stood just a foot from the railing above the drop down to the courtyard. Florence put her hands on Helen's back and pushed. Hard.

Helen teetered, windmilling her arms wildly, trying to regain her balance. Then her whole body tumbled over the railing.

A dull thud sounded from below. Florence peered over the edge. Helen lay face-up on the tiled floor, her eyes open and unseeing.

Suddenly, Helen let out a low moan.

Florence hurried downstairs. A circle of blood was growing around Helen's head like a halo. Her eyes caught Florence's. There was real fear in them.

"Help," she said wetly, licking her lips. "Help me."

Florence stepped briefly into the living room. When she returned, she told Helen, "Everything's going to be okay."

"Doctor?"

"No. Sorry. I meant everything's going to be okay for *me*."

Florence lifted the pillow she'd taken from the living room couch and held it over Helen's face. Helen tried to struggle, but she was too broken. She was like a beetle trying to get off its back. Florence stayed in that position for what felt like a long time, growing nervous and stiff. This would be an inopportune moment for Idrissi to arrive. Finally, Helen's spasmic clutching quieted and she was still.

Florence pulled back the cushion. Helen's eyes were open and glassy.

Just then she heard car tires crunching on the gravel outside.

46.

Ramzi's broad silhouette appeared in the doorway, and Florence threw herself into his arms. The policeman accepted her embrace with obvious discomfort.

"Thank god you're here," she cried.

Florence felt his muscles tense as his eyes fell on Helen's inert form on the ground behind her. He gently but firmly pushed Florence away from him and approached the body. Kneeling, he put two fingers on her neck. He stayed like that for a full minute, occasionally moving his hand a millimeter or two. Then he slowly looked back over his shoulder at Florence. She saw sadness, and horror, in his eyes.

Idrissi stood up and made a short phone call. Putting his phone back in his pocket, he said to Florence, "This is your friend. The one who went back to Marrakesh." She couldn't tell whether he was asserting this fact or asking her.

"This is Helen Wilcox," she responded.

He looked again at the body, then back at Florence.

"And who does that make you?"

"Florence Darrow," she said in a whisper. And then louder: "I'm Florence Darrow."

———

Half a dozen officials traipsed in and out of Villa des Grenades that afternoon. Dan Massey arrived from the embassy a couple hours after Idrissi. He'd brought Helen Wilcox's passport with him, the one he'd confiscated from Florence two days earlier.

His knee cracked loudly as he knelt down to compare the photograph to the dead woman. From the way he snapped it shut and clenched his jaw, Florence could tell that he realized he'd been wrong about Florence. She wasn't Helen Wilcox after all.

Florence sat with Massey and Idrissi in the living room for close to an hour, explaining what had happened. Helen had tried to kill her to steal her identity, because she knew the body on her property in New York would be discovered. First she'd staged a car crash, then she'd come back to finish the job. And nearly succeeded.

They made her go through the story several times, but Florence knew her facts stayed consistent because she was, incredibly, telling the truth. She made only one omission and one alteration. She never mentioned the name Maud Dixon, and she said Helen had fallen over the railing as they grappled for the gun.

"So you thought your boss had died in that car accident, but you said nothing?" Idrissi asked at one point. "To anyone?"

Florence shrugged.

"What if she had survived? What if she could have been saved?"

"But she wasn't even in the car," Florence responded, allowing herself a small, serene smile.

Idrissi just stared at her.

"Tell me again what happened in the corridor upstairs, during the argument," he demanded.

She went through it all again. "She was pointing the gun at me. I lunged at her. We struggled. In the process, Helen fell over." Her voice cracked. She rubbed her eyes until they were red and raw.

Idrissi continued to glare at her.

"Listen," Florence said more forcefully. "She'd already tried to kill me once, in the car accident. She'd already killed her best friend. I wasn't about to underestimate her again."

Massey cut in. "We were all pawns in her game," he murmured.

Idrissi and Florence both turned toward him in surprise.

He'd been mostly silent as he listened to Florence's story, asking few questions and nodding his head often. The case was an embarrassment for him, Florence knew. He hadn't believed her. He'd fallen for Helen's invented narrative.

And that was when Florence told them about the body in the pool.

This set off a new flurry of activity as Nick's body was found, dredged, photographed and—finally—removed. Florence averted her eyes through all of it.

Instead, she watched Massey's face register the realization that if he'd just believed Florence, Nick would still be alive. It was then she knew that he wanted the case closed as badly as she did.

Idrissi was the only one left sputtering in anger and disbelief. But what could he do? He had suspicions that her story was off, but no proof that she'd actually done anything illegal.

Finally, they gave her permission to return to Marrakesh in the morning. After all, there could be no trial. The murderer was dead.

47.

Twenty-four hours later, Florence arrived at a dramatically arched entrance on Avenue Hommane Al Fatouaki in Marrakesh. The name of the hotel was spelled out grandly across the top: La Mamounia. She stepped through it and entered a courtyard lush with olive and palm trees. At the far end, a building with an intricately carved facade emerged from the foliage.

The walk from her hotel, a few blocks from the one she'd stayed in with Helen, had taken only ten minutes. This time, she'd navigated the warren of narrow streets with surprising ease and turned onto the bustling avenue feeling invigorated by the chaos rather than overwhelmed.

She wore sunglasses and a wide-brimmed straw hat she'd bought in the souk that afternoon, even though dusk had just started to fall.

Two men in red capes and white fezzes heaved open a pair of wooden doors as she approached. A brightly lit lantern swung dizzily above.

The lobby had the air of a high-end mall, with an Yves Saint Laurent boutique and a famous Parisian macaron shop. It was just another marble-clad temple of luxury commerce. Helen was right, she thought: Solitude and freedom were far more precious forms of opulence.

Florence had called Greta the night before, after Idrissi and Massey had finally left Villa des Grenades, to push back their meeting until the following day, but she hadn't explained why. Now Florence found her tucked away in a dark corner of the Churchill bar behind the lobby. Her face was lit by the unearthly glow of her phone, and a pair of reading glasses balanced on the tip of her nose.

She jumped when Florence said hello.

"Florence, you surprised me." She took off her glasses and snapped them shut. "Please, sit."

Florence settled into the plush velvet chair opposite Greta's.

"Here's the man," Greta said, beckoning a server in a burgundy vest. "Tell him what you'd like."

"Whatever you're having," Florence said, gesturing at the nearly empty wineglass on the table.

"Two more of the same," Greta told him. "The Pinot Noir." The man nodded and retreated as unobtrusively as he'd arrived.

"What happened to you?" Greta asked Florence, frowning at her injuries.

"Well that's one chapter in the story I have to tell you. And I should warn you: It doesn't have a happy ending."

Greta raised her eyebrows. "Okay, you have my attention."

The waiter arrived with their drinks, and they both sat in silence as he carefully arranged the glasses on white doilies. When he left, Florence took a sip of her wine and began.

"What would you say if I told you that *Mississippi Foxtrot* was a work of *non*fiction? That the murder was real, and Helen Wilcox is the one who committed it."

Florence watched Greta's face carefully. She saw both concern and disbelief flash across Greta's features, as if she couldn't quite decide whether to take Florence seriously. But there was no doubt in Florence's mind that she was taken aback. Florence had half-wondered whether Greta might have known Helen's secret this whole time.

"Let me start at the beginning," Florence said.

She then proceeded to explain what had happened between Jenny and Helen when they were teenagers, how Helen had killed a man and let her friend go to prison for it. How Jenny had gone to visit Helen after she was paroled in February; how Helen had killed her.

Greta listened mostly in silence, but when Florence got to the part about the compost pile, she interrupted: "Florence, these are incredibly serious allegations. How sure are you about all this?"

"Look it up," Florence said. "Google 'Helen Wilcox Cairo New York.'" Some of the local papers had already picked up the story; the discovery of a dead body in a compost pile was big news in a small town like Cairo.

Greta hesitated, then started typing into her phone. Florence watched as the blood slowly drained from her face.

"Good god," Greta whispered.

Florence went on. She explained why Helen had hired her: so that she could fake her own death and assume Florence's identity, even changing her will so she could keep her money.

Greta shook her head. "I knew something was off when she told me she wanted an assistant. It made no sense. Privacy had always been her principal concern."

Florence described the car accident. "That's how I got this," she said, holding up her cast. As she recounted Helen's return to Villa des Grenades to complete the job she'd botched, tears welled up in her eyes.

"She had a gun, Greta. I didn't know what to do."

"Where would Helen even get a gun?" Greta asked in wonderment.

"Rabat, I think. Where she got the passport. The police are looking into it."

She doubted this last part was true. Massey certainly wasn't; perhaps Idrissi would. Either way, Florence wasn't too concerned. Anything the police found in Rabat would corroborate Florence's story. Helen was the criminal. *She* was the victim.

"The police..." Greta said. "So Helen is in custody?"

Florence shook her head and a tear dripped down her cheek. "I've never had a gun pointed at me before," she whispered.

Greta's voice dropped an octave. "Florence, what's happened?"

"It was pure instinct. I lunged at her before she could pull the trigger. And in the struggle, Helen went over the railing. She fell down into the courtyard. According to the police, she was killed instantly."

Greta's eyes grew wide. "Helen's dead?"

Florence nodded.

"My god."

Florence sat silently while Greta absorbed the news.

"My god," she said again, shaking her head.

"I'm so sorry."

After a moment, Greta placed her hand on top of Florence's cast. "I'm sorry too. It must have been a terrible experience, watching Helen die like that."

"It was awful. I keep asking myself what I could have done differently."

"Don't do that. Don't blame yourself. If she was pointing a gun at you, what choice did you have?"

"I don't know. Maybe I should have tried harder to reason with her."

"Reason with Helen Wilcox? That's a tall order in the best of circumstances."

Florence smiled sadly. "True."

Greta shook her head again. "I just can't believe it."

"I know. I'm still in shock." Florence paused. "And I don't even have as much of a stake in all this as you do."

Greta glanced up sharply at Florence. "What do you mean?"

"Well, Maud Dixon is dead too, of course."

"Florence, I assure you, that's not my primary concern

right now," Greta said, but her tone lacked its usual confidence.

"Of course not. It's awful that Helen is dead, I just meant that it's *also* a tragedy that the world will never get another book by Maud Dixon. She was so talented."

Greta nodded, rotating her wineglass in one hand. "She was."

They both sat quietly for a minute. Florence looked around the room, which was filling up quickly, and took another sip of the wine. She quite liked it. It wasn't as heavy and oppressive as the Châteauneuf-du-Pape that Helen had favored.

Greta had gone back to staring blankly at the tabletop. Florence wondered what she was thinking; her expression was inscrutable.

After a beat or two more, Florence cleared her throat. "Unless..."

Greta looked up. "Unless what?"

"No, you're right, this isn't the time to be thinking of things like this."

"Unless *what*?" Greta said impatiently.

"I just thought I should mention that I have Helen's manuscript—for her second novel. It wasn't what I was typing up in Cairo at all; she was working on something entirely different. *The Morocco Exchange.* The story was based on the plan she was carrying out while she wrote it; the plan to kill me and steal my identity."

Greta put down her glass. "Helen finished her second book?"

"It's not finished. I mean, it's certainly too early to be calling it a *book*. But I can already tell that it's the same caliber as *Mississippi Foxtrot*."

The color started to come back to Greta's cheeks. "You have it here? With you?" She glanced at Florence's bag on the floor.

"No, I didn't think that was prudent. It's in the safe in my hotel room."

"Florence. I need to see that manuscript."

"Well, like I said, it still needs a *lot* of work."

"That's okay. We can find someone to help with that. Fitzgerald died before he finished *The Last Tycoon*." She let out a small laugh. "Come to think of it, that was a *roman à clef* too."

Florence smiled with her. "Actually, Greta, I was thinking *I* could do it."

Greta frowned. "Do what?"

"Finish it. I've worked with Helen more closely than anyone else, other than you of course. I know her voice. I know how she thinks. Besides, you said I had talent. You even said I reminded you of her."

Greta nodded slowly. "I did. I did say that." She took a sip of her drink and glanced at the table next to them, where two young women were staging a photo of their cocktails. "And I stand by it; you *do* have a lot of potential. But this would be a delicate undertaking, Florence. I think for a project like this, given...everything.... Well, why don't we just see what we have before we make any decisions about how to move forward."

Florence stared back at Greta without speaking. The camera at the table next to them flashed. Greta flinched. Florence did not.

"Greta," Florence said calmly. "I have a broken wrist and two fractured ribs. I have no job and no place to live. And not to put too fine a point on it, but you're the one who got me into this predicament. You were Helen's accomplice, witting or not."

Greta had grown pale again. But Florence couldn't let up now.

"You can denounce Helen's crimes all you want, but you also profited from them. How much did you make off of *Mississippi Foxtrot*? What other opportunities did it attract? You're a party to her crimes—*both* of them. I'm the victim."

Greta stared back at Florence without saying anything.

"I'm not asking for a million dollars here, Greta. I'm just asking for a chance. That's all. A foot in the door. I don't think that's out of bounds, all things considered." She took a sip of her wine. "Do you?"

"Florence," Greta finally said. "I understand where you're coming from, and you're right—I am partly complicit in some of this. I certainly don't take that lightly. But I cannot in good conscience let you write Maud Dixon's next book simply because you were victimized by her. You probably *do* deserve some form of compensation, but I can't tell you right now that this is it. I'm sorry."

Florence sat very still. Then she shook her head and smiled. "You're right, Greta, of course you are. I don't know what I was thinking. It's been a very long few days." Underneath the table she gripped the strap of her bag with white knuckles.

"I'm sure. This has been a lot to take in for me too. Let's just digest all this for a moment. Do you want another drink? I'd say we both deserve one under the circumstances."

She looked around for the waiter, even though both of their glasses were still half full.

Florence nodded and reached for hers, but she missed and knocked the entire glass over. The dark red wine splashed onto Greta's silk blouse and pooled in her lap. Greta and Florence both jumped up.

"I'm so sorry," Florence exclaimed, patting at Greta's chest in-effectually with the paper doily. Greta pushed her hands away.

"It's alright. Just leave it. *Leave* it. I'll go clean up in the ladies' room. Excuse me a moment."

Greta walked quickly out of the room, holding her wet shirt away from her body.

Florence sat back down. A man in a tuxedo started playing a grand piano in the corner. The table next to her erupted in laughter at some shared joke.

Greta returned a few minutes later. If anything, the stain looked worse.

"I'm so sorry," Florence repeated.

"It's alright. Really. My dry cleaner in Manhattan is something of a miracle worker. Let's move on. Did you order more?" She finished the rest of her own wine in a single gulp, grimacing slightly.

"No, I thought you might want to go change. And to be honest, I'm not feeling that great. The pain medication I'm on makes me feel a little woozy. I mean, *clearly*. Maybe we could just get room service in your room or something? Eating usually helps."

"Oh. Um...sure. We could do that. Let me just tell the waiter to put this on my bill."

48.

"'m sorry it's such a mess," Greta said as she opened the door to her suite.

The room was large and bright with a mosaic of tiles running along the walls and a giant king bed. It was immaculate but for a sweater tossed over the back of a chair in the corner.

Florence walked over to the window and looked out. Below lay a vast garden planted with rows of orange trees. The moon was just visible in the darkening sky.

Greta handed the room service menu to Florence. "Order anything you want. And take a water from the minibar."

Florence sat in the chair and perused the menu while Greta changed clothes in the bathroom. When she emerged, she sat down on the bed and rubbed her face. "God, I'm exhausted," she said.

Florence nodded. "I'm not surprised."

Greta closed her eyes, and for a moment Florence thought she'd fallen asleep sitting up. Then she opened them and struggled to speak. "What were we..."

Florence sat down next to Greta and eased her back onto the bed so that she was lying down. "I know how you feel. You've had a shock."

Greta looked up at her, her blue eyes wide with plaintive confusion.

"It's hydrocodone," Florence explained. "That's the pain

medication they gave me at the hospital after the accident. I stopped taking it because I don't like the way it makes me feel. So foggy, right?"

Greta nodded. "Foggy . . . Yes . . . But you . . . "

"Why don't you just close your eyes for a bit?"

Like a child, Greta obeyed. Florence sat watching her for a moment. She was surprised that the pills had worked as quickly as they had. She'd ground up four of them—one more than she'd given Whitney—at the hotel and put the powder into Greta's drink while she'd been trying to salvage her shirt.

When Florence was sure that Greta was unconscious, she retrieved a pair of plastic gloves from her purse. She snapped them on, then pulled out a crumpled paper bag. Inside was a brand-new syringe, a baggie of grayish powder, and an elastic band. She had found these on Helen's corpse in the seconds before Idrissi's arrival: all the tools necessary for the heroin overdose Helen had planned for Florence.

She'd had to improvise in Semat, but now, in Greta's hotel room, Florence worked slowly and methodically. She checked her watch. She had plenty of time.

She went into the bathroom and poured the powder into a glass on the counter. Then, from her purse, she took the box of rat poison she'd bought on her way to the hotel. She sprinkled that into the cup too. She'd learned through her research online that rodenticide was one of the most common—and deadly—substances with which street heroin was cut.

No more half measures.

She added a splash of water and swirled the cloudy mixture around in the glass.

She peeked inside a marble canister on the counter and found a wad of cotton balls. She took one out and held it over a second glass while she filtered the gritty liquid through it.

That afternoon, she'd watched a YouTube video containing step-by-step instructions on shooting up, which had been uploaded by a needle exchange program in Columbus, Ohio.

She dipped the tip of the syringe into the cloudy mixture and pulled up the plunger. With the needle still in the glass, she tapped the syringe to draw any air bubbles to the top.

She went back into the bedroom. Greta's mouth was slack and her breathing sounded thick and phlegmy.

Florence tentatively picked up Greta's right arm and dropped it. No reaction. Florence tied the elastic tightly around Greta's bicep until a purple vein popped out. Florence pushed the needle into it, but the vein scooted coquettishly to the side. She took a breath to steady her hand and tried again.

This time the needle found its mark. Greta moaned and fluttered her eyes. Florence pushed the plunger down slowly, watching the liquid descend. She stopped when the syringe was half empty and pulled the needle out. Then Florence moved to the other arm and repeated the process. She did this several times, refilling the syringe again and again, until there were nearly a dozen puncture wounds all over Greta's body. She wanted them to tell a story of habitual drug use, though she hoped the investigation wouldn't even get that far. She was counting on the hotel and the police sharing an interest in hushing up the incident. Tourism, after all, was important.

When Florence had the syringe between two toes, Greta's body suddenly seized up. It started jerking wildly and a yellowish liquid oozed from her mouth. Greta's eyes shot open and sought feverishly for something to gain purchase on. Florence instinctively ducked.

When Florence stood up, feeling sheepish, Greta's eyes were still open, but her body was still.

Florence held two fingers to Greta's wrist. She didn't feel anything. Just in case, she brought the vanity mirror from the bathroom and held it in front of Greta's mouth. It was an old-fashioned method, but Florence had to be sure. She couldn't have Greta waking up and telling tales.

When she was confident that Greta was dead, she placed the mirror back in the bathroom. Then she pressed Greta's fingertips onto the syringe and the glass of liquid. She found Greta's phone and entered a phone number into the contacts list.

Finally, Florence inspected the room until she was confident that it looked just as it had when she'd entered it. Except for the dead body on the bed.

She hung the Do Not Disturb sign on the doorknob and slipped out. In the hallway, she peeled off the plastic gloves and shoved them in her back pocket.

It was done.

As she waited for the elevator, she looked at her watch. Ten minutes to seven. The dealer that Liam had connected her with would be arriving soon. She'd told him to ask for Greta Frost at the front desk. He'd wanted the room number, but Florence had been firm. He was an integral part of the story. His phone number would be found in Greta's phone, but Florence also needed a hotel employee to register his arrival.

Florence passed quickly through the busy lobby into the dark, warm evening. On the street, the plastic gloves landed soundlessly in an overflowing trash can.

49.

L adies and gentlemen, we've reached our cruising altitude of thirty thousand feet. It's a beautiful evening, so just sit back, relax, and don't hesitate to let us know if there's anything we can do to make your journey more comfortable."

Florence took another sip of Champagne and stretched out her legs.

"May I get you anything, Ms. Darrow?" A flight attendant with impeccable eyeliner smiled down at her.

Florence smiled back. "Another blanket, please." Then she pressed a button and her seat reclined to a completely flat position. She pulled down the complimentary eye mask.

Now *this* was the way to travel. It didn't even rankle her, being called Ms. Darrow. She'd had to take up her old name again, but the three million dollars she'd inherited—along with the house—did offer some consolation. Quite a bit, actually.

Technically, the money and the property wouldn't be transferred into Florence's name for a couple more months, but she'd leave the small print to small minds. Besides, she hadn't even had to pay for the upgrade; she'd just switched Helen Wilcox's and Florence Darrow's seats when she got to the airport.

The flight attendant returned with a blanket and laid it gently over Florence's body.

As she lay there listening to the drone of the engines, Florence prodded her conscience for any tender spots. She found none.

She knew she could have let Helen live. She'd only have had to wait another five minutes for Idrissi to arrive. But Florence suspected that Helen would prefer death to the indignities of prison. Plus, there was no point in her fortune going to waste.

And she certainly could have let Greta live—if she'd been willing to give up Maud Dixon's name. She'd genuinely hoped that Greta would agree to her proposal and let her finish Helen's manuscript. Killing Greta had been her plan B: unfortunate but necessary.

No, she had no regrets. She had been offered what she most wanted in life. Even if she came by it in the most bizarre, inscrutable way possible. To let it slip away would have been foolish.

She did feel badly about Nick. But that wasn't *her* fault. Helen was the one who'd killed him. Besides, when it came down to it, she barely knew him. If their relationship had ended naturally, as most vacation flings eventually do, he would have already faded from memory.

The nasal-voiced man across from Florence cut into her thoughts as he called loudly down the aisle for another Pinot Noir.

Florence pushed off her eye mask and sat up abruptly. Her heart was pounding. The flight attendant scurried up the aisle with a bottle of wine.

Florence shook her head. It was nothing.

She lay back down, but when she closed her eyes she saw Greta looking at her with those startlingly blue eyes. "Foggy . . . Yes . . ."

Florence maneuvered her seat back into an upright position. She patted her cheeks lightly. Then she dug out a notebook and a pen from her bag.

She'd decided to leave the first half of Helen's manuscript as she'd found it. Then, in the middle, the narrative would suddenly switch to Iris's point of view.

She started writing.

Lillian was wrong: Iris wasn't weak. She'd been hardened by a lifetime of disappointment, and by underestimating this uglier, scrappier version of fortitude, Lillian had made a crucial mistake. She'd used herself as bait, not realizing that Iris was too famished to be sated by mere proximity to greatness.

50.

The old house on Crestbill Road was cool inside, even though an early May heat wave was pressing on it from all sides. Florence shut the door behind her and took a deep breath. She walked through the silent rooms slowly, seeing them as if for the first time. Because this time they were hers. Everything here was hers.

Florence scooped coffee into the coffeemaker and turned it on. As it spluttered to life, she looked out into the backyard. The compost pile had been entirely dug up. Yellow caution tape flapped in the wind where it had come loose from its stakes. She had been assured by the Cairo Police Department that Helen's death had effectively closed the investigation into the murder of Jeanette Byrd.

When the coffee was ready, Florence brought a mug back to the living room along with the portable phone and dialed her mother's number.

Florence knew Vera would be sitting in her small yellow kitchenette, drinking a cup of overly sweet coffee, before heading to work.

"Hello?" Vera trilled into the phone. She always answered unknown numbers, confident that the universe would bring only good things into her life.

"Mom, it's Florence."

Silence.

"Listen, I know you're angry with me, but I need you to do something for me. Can you read me the text message you were talking about before—the one where I said I never wanted to see you again? And tell me when it was sent."

Vera sighed. "Hang on, I've got to search for it."

When she came back on the line, she said, "It was sent on Sunday, April twenty-first. I remember because I'd just left church when I got it, and I was so excited to see your number pop up. Then I actually read it. 'Mom, I'm sorry, but this is the last time you'll ever hear from me.'" Vera's voice cracked, but she continued. "'You have done nothing throughout my entire life but belittle me and hold me back. I'm done. I never want to speak to you again. If you try to contact me, I'll simply change my number.'"

Florence felt the blood rush to her face. Even though she hadn't written those words, she'd certainly thought them, and hearing them on Vera's tongue made her feel guiltier than any of the things she'd actually done in the past two weeks.

April twenty-first. That was the day after the car crash. Helen must have been tying up loose ends before assuming the mantle of Florence Darrow.

For all the lip service Helen had paid to momentum and action, she had actually been incredibly careful about every contingency. Florence had appreciated that lesson while plotting Greta's murder. It was, perhaps, just as important an inheritance as the house and the money.

"Mom," she said, "I'm so sorry you had to read that, but you have to believe me—I didn't write that message."

Vera took a loud sip of coffee. "It came from your phone."

"I know. It's a long story." Florence took a breath. "Let me start at the beginning..."

By the time they hung up forty-five minutes later, Vera knew the whole story—or at least the version of it that Florence had repeated over and over for the authorities: the murder plot against Florence; the desperate act of self-defense.

As with Idrissi and Massey, Florence did not mention that Helen Wilcox was actually Maud Dixon; she wasn't sure her mother would even know who that was. Nor did she mention the name Greta Frost, whose death was just starting to cause ripples in publishing circles. There was no reason that Florence would have any connection to that.

Vera had lapped it up, desperate for confirmation that Florence hadn't actually turned her back on her. "I knew you weren't acting like yourself," she insisted. "I said as much to Gloria. She agreed. You're a good girl, Florence. The best."

Florence smiled grimly. "Thanks."

"Who loves you?"

"You do."

She and her mother agreed to speak again in a week. Florence would never allow Vera the closeness she wanted, but she would keep her in her life. Her brush with death in Morocco had taught her that total isolation was its own form of vulnerability. It was dangerous to have nobody. Somebody needed to notice if you went missing.

Florence poured herself another coffee.

She had one more call to make, and then it was time to get to work. She'd finally gotten what she wanted—Helen Wilcox's life and Maud Dixon's audience—and she wasn't going to squander them.

She'd started writing the second half of *The Morocco Exchange* the night Helen had died. When she sat down with a yellow legal pad on her lap, she'd been amazed by what she'd encountered: a torrent.

Under the cover of the Maud Dixon pseudonym, she'd found the freedom and confidence to just *write*.

And she finally had a story to tell.

She'd once read a biography of the artist René Magritte that

Agatha had edited. It claimed that during his early years, when critics had scoffed at his odd, unconventional paintings, he'd supported himself by forging works by Picasso and Braque.

Perhaps it was a type of apprenticeship, Florence thought. Just like *The Morocco Exchange* would be for her. Helen had said it herself: If you pretend for long enough, anything can become natural. Truly natural.

Magritte did, after all, find success on his own.

Someday, she might be able to tell the world that Maud Dixon was none other than Florence Darrow. She would have been twenty-three when *Mississippi Foxtrot* came out. That was a plausible enough age. Mary Shelley wrote *Frankenstein* when she was nineteen. And the timing worked out so that she would have been composing it toward the end of college and while living in Gainesville afterward, working at the bookstore. She thought how surprised Anne, the store's cheerful owner, would be to discover that her employee had been writing a modern classic the entire time she'd known her. She imagined Simon's face when he found out. And Amanda's. What restraint, what *dignity,* they'd think—keeping it secret for all that time.

She looked at her watch. She'd waited long enough. She dialed another number.

A young woman answered in a chipper falsetto: "Hello, HMK."

Harper Maston Khan was the biggest talent agency in New York. It represented not just writers, but actors, athletes, and musicians. Real celebrities.

"Hello," Florence said, "I'd like to speak with Denise Maston, please."

"May I ask who's calling?"

Florence paused. "Tell her it's Maud Dixon."

ACKNOWLEDGMENTS

My first debt of gratitude belongs to Jenn Joel—a brilliant editor masquerading as a brilliant agent. August 4th, 2019, will go down as one of the major turning points of my life. Many thanks also to the wonderful Tia Ikemoto and everyone else at ICM.

Thank you to Judy Clain for her early and continued enthusiasm for this book, along with the incredible team at Little, Brown: Miya Kumangai, Heather Boaz, Lena Little, Ashley Marudas, Gabrielle Leporati, and many others.

Thank you to my lovely UK editor, Imogen Taylor, along with Felicity Blunt, Jake Smith-Bosanquet, and Savanna Wicks at Curtis Brown.

Thank you to Halsey Anderson and Evonne Gambrell for always keeping a seat warm for me, despite my middling work ethic and frankly appalling attitude. I wouldn't have been able to write this book without it.

Thank you to Joan Truya in Paris and Koloina Andriatsimamao in New York for allowing me to take a break from caring for (and worrying about) Olive for long enough to write this book.

Thank you to Liz Campbell, Martha Campbell, Kathryn Doyle, Natalie Pica Friend, Molly Lundgren, Elizabeth Rhodes, Haven Thompson, Nell Van Amerongen, and Julia Vaughn for far too much to list here. I am beyond lucky to count you as my friends.

ACKNOWLEDGMENTS

Thank you to my family, both the one I was born into and the people I've gathered along the way: Henry Piper Andrews; Lindsey Andrews Schilling; Palmer Ducommun; Bob Ducommun; Charlie Schilling; Jock Andrews; the Westcotts; the Laportes; Jim & Nancy Beha; Jim & Alyson Beha; and Len & Alice Teti. I love you all.

Thank you to my mother, Lynn Ducommun, who has certainly earned her own paragraph after thirty-seven years of endless love and support throughout my many, *many* zigs and zags. (And anyone who thinks Vera Darrow bears any relation to her is sorely mistaken.)

But above all, this book—and my heart—belongs to Christopher Beha. Maud Dixon would not exist without his constant encouragement and keen editor's eye. (Turns out marrying a world-class novelist was a pretty prescient career move.) There's no one else I'd rather spend my life with.

And lastly, Olive and Henry: You didn't do a thing to help, but I love you with all my heart. Just thinking about you makes me happier than I ever imagined I would be. I adore you, I adore you, I adore you.